A Holiday Affair

A Holiday Affair

Michele Paige
HOLMES

Mirror Press

Copyright © 2019 Michele Paige Holmes
Print edition
All rights reserved
No part of this book may be reproduced in any form whatsoever without prior written permission of the publisher, except in the case of brief passages embodied in critical reviews and articles. This novel is a work of fiction. The characters, names, incidents, places, and dialog are products of the author's imagination and are not to be construed as real.
Interior Design by Cora Johnson
Edited by Haley Swan and Lisa Shepherd
Cover design by Rachael Anderson
Cover Image Credit: Deposit Photos #11991838

Published by Mirror Press, LLC
ISBN: 978-1-947152-85-4

Holiday Harbor Series

A Holiday Affair
Home Sweet Holiday
The Heart of Holiday

One

Valentine's Day

"Bree? Hello?" Carson pounded on the broken screen door, then pulled it open and stepped over the threshold and onto the worn carpet in the Wagners' house as he had hundreds of other times over the years. Bree had said she needed to talk to him for only a minute and that she'd meet him on the front porch. Instead, he looked up to see her coming down the stairs, not bounding with her usual enthusiasm and not floating ethereally as she'd seemed to the night he'd taken her to their junior prom when Annabelle had become sick last minute. Anna had encouraged him to take Bree instead and had even lent Bree the dress she'd been planning to wear.

Best friends did things like that.

Anna's other best friend, and one who happened to also be her boyfriend, didn't kiss his girlfriend's bestie in her place, though. Carson hadn't that night. Though it had been close. He'd wanted to, and remembered that now, watching Bree coming down the stairs again.

That night something had changed for him—for them. It was the beginning of an awareness of each other that hadn't ever been there before. Or maybe it had, on Bree's part, anyway. He'd probably been the clueless one, oblivious to her beauty and when and how her girlish figure had turned to womanly curves. He'd never before considered the feminine aroma of her shampoo or perfume or whatever it was she always wore, or how soft and silky the strands of her hair felt, or how he loved her laugh. She'd always been just Bree. Fun and constant. A friend you could count on.

Seeing her that night as she practically floated down the stairs, fabric shimmering all around her, her hair done up in something other than her usual ponytail, and lipstick highlighting her smile, had been like a wake-up call. Breanna wasn't just the third member of their trio. She was on the verge of womanhood as well, and she was stunning. A potential complication, as Carson adored her as a person already.

It had been *wow* and *uh-oh* all in the same breath.

Fortunately, somehow at seventeen, he'd been able to keep his hands and lips where they belonged and keep her solidly in the friend camp all evening. Though slow dancing with her had been its own kind of hell, temptation at his fingertips with the promise of infinite burning if he succumbed.

Too bad he hadn't been as smart or controlled at twenty-five.

If only kissing was all they'd done that ill-fated weekend before Thanksgiving. Now, looking up at Bree's pale, tear-stained face as she descended the stairs, he had a sick feeling in the pit of his stomach, like maybe hell was just getting warmed up.

She reached the bottom landing and stopped. Fresh tears filled her eyes and slid down already-wet cheeks, but somehow she produced a trembling smile. "Hello, Carson."

"Bree?" Instinctively he reached a hand out. Hers

flinched on the rail in response, as if it wished for the contact but held back. Carson let his hand fall to his side.

Her stoic smile remained, and she took a shuddering breath.

"I'm afraid I won't be able to attend your wedding. If you could—if you could let Anna know I'm so sorry."

His eyes flew to Bree's. "Let her know—" *What?* Had she told Anna? What wass Bree sorry for? Had she sent Anna a letter? Had—

Bree gave a little shake of her head, as if to let him know their secret was still safe. "Tell her I had an opportunity I had to take, and it couldn't wait. Tell her I'm sorry I'm not there."

The relief he should have felt didn't come. He and Bree had both agreed—that awful morning nearly three months ago—that they would never speak of what had happened between them to anyone. That night before had been a mistake. It would only hurt people. It was never going to happen again. All good reasoning and true, but he guessed that Bree, like himself, had been eaten alive with guilt the past weeks, particularly as the wedding—his wedding to their best friend whom they both loved and had betrayed—grew closer.

Carson shifted uneasily from one foot to another. He'd assumed Bree's request for him to come over for a minute tonight was about decorating the car. As the maid of honor, Bree, along with the best man—his brother Charlie—was in charge of decorating the car during the reception. Carson had set limits to what they could do. He and Annabelle had to drive all the way to the airport in Atlanta, and he didn't want some tin can or shoe contraption flying off the back of the car on the interstate and causing an accident. He also didn't want Oreos in the shape of body parts all over the hood—Charlie's idea. Carson had made them both promise to show him exactly what they'd planned before anything was done.

But now his concerns about the car seemed irrelevant. *Bree, leaving?* "What opportunity? It couldn't wait one more day?" *Twelve hours?* It was after ten now, and the wedding was at ten tomorrow morning.

"I—I can't be there, Carson. Please don't ask me to." Bree's pretty brown eyes lifted to his in a plea.

"O—kay." He shoved his hands in his pockets and took a steadying breath of his own. Anna wasn't going to like this. She wasn't necessarily going to buy it either. She and Bree were practically sisters.

"Want to tell me why you can't come?" *It's one day.* If he could go through with this and move on, couldn't Bree handle one day? Then, if she didn't want to stick around to see him and Anna living as a married couple, he got that. In fact, Bree not being around for a while might be helpful. The very thing he needed to get his marriage off on the right foot—if that was even possible now.

It wasn't that he didn't love Anna. He did and had as long as he could remember—since first grade, at least. But they'd spent a lot of time apart the last few years, each completing bachelor's and then master's degrees at different universities. That, plus what he'd done and his complicated feelings regarding Bree, could make for a rocky start.

And he really wanted his marriage to succeed. He wanted to be a great husband to Anna, to give her everything she deserved and more. And he was already starting with a huge deficit.

The sick feeling in his gut flared to life again. *Dishonesty. Betrayal. Infidelity.* All before he even said, "I do."

"You have to ask why I don't want to be there?" Bree's voice held fresh hurt.

"No." Carson shook his head. "I get it. It's just that Anna won't."

"I know," Bree whispered. "But what other choice do we have?"

"You could wait to leave just a couple more hours." He shrugged. This was as close as they'd come to talking about what had happened, tiptoeing around the elephant in the room, the night of intimacy they'd shared, which, ironically, had been the first time for both. His strict religious upbringing as a minister's son, plus his own small-town, old-fashioned moral code and values had kept him chaste so long. Bree's values were similar, and no doubt her gun-toting father and brothers had only added to that influence.

Carson's head snapped up, and he glanced around uneasily, then took a few steps to peer into the living room and at Breanna's father's shotgun—one of many—displayed proudly over the stone fireplace.

"They're hunting," she said, as if she'd read his mind. "It's the last weekend for deer."

"Ah." This time Carson did feel relief. He pulled his eyes from the sofa and stepped back. Bree's father and brothers lived for the hunting seasons—all of them, no matter what was being hunted. No doubt they'd shoot him down and stuff and mount his head if they knew what he'd done to her.

Carson turned back to Bree. "How long will you be gone? Where will you be?" He had no right to ask these questions, yet he wanted to know and felt sad—in spite of it all—that she wouldn't be around. It would never be the three of them together again. Holiday, Alabama's ABC was as much a thing of the past as the Jackson 5, from whom they'd claimed their theme song.

Nothing would ever be as easy or carefree as their one, two, three again. It hadn't been for a while, since he and Anna had gone off to college, leaving Bree here alone to take care of her family while she took online classes—the only opportunity available to her.

Now that he and Anna were done with school, Carson hoped to move back here to Holiday. His dad and brother needed him, and Carson wanted his children to have the same rural upbringing he'd had. The pace of life moved a little slower here and felt a little more peaceful than the hectic world outside. Once away, he'd found that he missed the small-town life he'd spent high school complaining about.

But if he had imagined life was going to be similar to their school days, he'd ensured it would not the previous November, the second he'd crossed the line from seeking comfort in Bree's arms to sharing passion with her.

Quickly he shuttered the memory from his mind.

She still hadn't answered his questions. Maybe she wouldn't. Her eyes were downcast, her fingers curled around the banister as if it were a lifeline. "I just have to get away for a while," she finally said. "It will be too hard here. Holiday is small. People talk..."

About? His eyes flew to Bree's, flooded with tears now. They held fast to his for a long second, a quick-then-slow heartbeat as a horrifying possibility entered his mind.

"I'm sorry," she whispered, then turned to go back up the stairs.

"Sorry for what? Are you—"

"Yes." She didn't look back, and her footsteps sped up. "Now you know. Please just go away, Carson."

Sucker punched, his breath whooshed out, ripped painfully from lungs he thought might never expand again. He reached for the newel post, needing support more than she had. *I know?* She hadn't said it exactly, hadn't voiced the fear they'd both felt that morning. And he didn't want to hear the specific words from her lips. Heeding her request to go away sounded like the best idea he could think of.

Go away and pretend this conversation never happened.

Keep pretending that night never happened. Pretend you never knew Breanna at all.

Impossible. Too many years of friendship between them forbade him from leaving. He'd loved Bree since first grade, too, just in a different way. And he'd already hurt her so much. More than he'd realized—until now.

Still dazed, Carson ran up the stairs, caught Bree, and grabbed her arm. Along with shock he felt a surge of anger. "Are you pregnant? Are you carrying my child?"

"Yes." She tried pulling away. "I just sai—"

"And you're just *now* telling me? The night before my wedding?" He rarely shouted but felt his voice vibrate off the papered walls of the narrow hall.

"No need to tell the neighbors too."

Carson looked back to see Bree's great-grandma Fay's white head at the bottom of the stairs.

"She's only just found out herself. Yelling won't help anyone or anything. And it's not entirely her fault, you know. Takes two to tango."

"Grandma." Bree brought a hand to her forehead. She turned her attention to Carson. "I wasn't going to tell you. I thought it would be better if I left. But—"

"I said if she didn't tell you, *I* would." Grandma Fay folded her thin arms across her chest. "And in front of the whole church too."

"I'm sorry," Breanna said once more.

"Sorry?" Grandma Fay huffed. "Little late for that. And don't be sorry you've told him. No need to apologize for the truth. No doubt he'll thank me for it later."

"No doubt," Bree and Carson muttered at the exact same time. He would have smiled had the situation not been so grave. Instead his frown deepened as his mind spun through the pages of this disaster.

If only his mother hadn't died. If only Annabelle had been around when it happened. If only he hadn't driven to Bree's house that night. If only she hadn't been home alone, if her father or one of her brothers had been here with her. If only he hadn't kissed her.

He'd wanted to talk to someone who would understand. Bree knew what it was to lose a mother. She'd been the perfect person to seek comfort from. *If only being enfolded in her arms hadn't felt quite so good.* If only the security they'd offered hadn't caused him to let his guard down. If only he hadn't sought more than solace.

Carson loosened his grasp on her arm and slowly slid his hand down to cover hers, still in its death grip on the rickety banister. He asked once more, softer this time. "Where are you going?" *With our child.* Though he'd known less than five minutes, it seemed real to him already. Another evidence of his upbringing. *Life begins at conception.*

Bree believed that, too, didn't she?

"Mississippi. There's a place I can work and live until the baby is born."

"And then?" He held in his relief, glad to have kept his mouth shut. Bree would never abort a baby. He shouldn't have even thought it a possibility. She couldn't pass up a motherless bird in the yard, a stray dog at the park, or even a turtle on the side of the road. More than a few times in the past she'd insisted that they turn around and rescue some creature or other from certain demise. And a child they'd created was certainly more than a stray animal.

She looked past him, down the stairs toward her eavesdropping great-grandmother. "The family paying for my care will adopt the child." Her gaze shifted to his, pleading for understanding. "I can't bring a baby back here to raise on my own. My father would disown me. The whole town would talk.

I'd be shunned, and so would that child. And what if it was a boy and he looked like—"

Me. Carson imagined a little boy with his curly hair and blue eyes running around, unaware who his real father—or mother—was. "Have you signed papers or anything?"

Bree shook her head. "No. Not yet. And I suppose you'll have to as well now, since you know."

He looked down at his hand covering hers, wondering who was supporting whom. He felt sick enough that he could imagine himself sinking onto the stairs in despair.

Why hadn't he been more respectful of her as his parents had taught him? What had she been going through these past weeks, while he and Annabelle had been busy planning their wedding? *How alone Bree must have felt.* How alone he felt suddenly.

Carson lowered himself onto the closest stair and took his head in his hands. *What now?*

The easy thing to do was to let Bree go, to sign whatever papers he needed to, releasing his child six and a half months from now, to be raised by strangers. *My child. Ours.* How was he supposed to do that? To pretend this baby never existed?

I can't. But he couldn't acknowledge this child and marry Anna too. *And Bree . . .* She was the one he really needed to consider. It was his fault she was in this mess. Wouldn't the worst mistake be abandoning Bree to handle this on her own?

Yet if I don't . . .

I can't.

But Anna—

He felt like screaming and sobbing all at once. Neither was an option, nor was feeling sorry for himself.

Doing the right thing now, the *only* thing he could do, was going to mean pain for others. His father was going to be terribly hurt—and embarrassed. And his mother . . . For the first time, Carson had reason to feel gratitude at her passing. At least she wouldn't have to suffer publicly for his mistake. Anna would, though. And her family too.

This will break her heart. And maybe her mother's too. How can I do this to her? To them? Carson loved Anna's family almost as much as he loved Anna. But there was no going back from here.

You've made your bed, he imagined his father saying. Carson choked out a grunt, thinking of other things his father was going to say, and things Bree's father was likely to do.

If this unborn child did end up fatherless . . . *It will be because I'm dead.*

Carson raised his head slightly. "Your dad's going to kill me when he finds out."

"Probably," Grandma Fay chirped from below.

"He won't find out," Bree insisted. "That's one of the reasons I've got to leave tonight. Before they get home."

Carson had no intention of letting her go to Mississippi or anywhere else alone.

"You mean *we've* got to leave." He looked back at her. On legs that felt shaky, he rose from the step and faced her again. "I'm not letting you deal with this alone, Bree. And I don't think we should give our baby away."

Her disbelieving eyes met his, and he held his gaze steady until he thought he detected what might be a spark of hope.

"I'm not going to desert you, Bree. Your grandmother is right. I'm at least as responsible as you are."

"But Anna—"

"—is the innocent in this and she's going to be *really* hurt." His eyes stung, and his heart physically ached, imagining Anna's pain. He knew the expression that would cross her face when she found out and could practically hear her gasp of denial and the outbreak of tears. He could see her collapsing in her mother's arms. The image was nearly enough to break his resolve to do the right thing. It was the hope of *not* hurting her that had kept his deceit from her until now. *And I've made everything so much worse.*

"It'll break her heart," Bree whispered.

"I know." Carson blinked rapidly to clear his watering eyes. "That can't be helped now. The only thing to do is try not to make another, worse mistake. We should have told her when it happened, but we didn't. And now we have to." He would have had to anyway. He realized that, had known it in his gut for some time. You couldn't lie to someone and expect to have a loving, trustful relationship.

His wedding day wouldn't have been the happiest day of his life, but a sham, another knot in the noose of guilt tightening about his throat. And now . . .

Carson glanced at Bree, looking pale and shaken. *Her* wedding day wasn't going to be the happiest either. *If she'll even have me.*

"Go on and ask her," Grandma Fay said behind him, as if she'd read his mind.

"We should get married, Breanna." There was no emotion or sentiment in the suggestion. It was a matter a practicality. They were bringing a child into the world, and that child deserved a mother and a father. *A home. A family.* Much of America might have a different view, but here in the Deep South, in Holiday, Alabama, that was still the way things were done.

"Talk to him, child," Grandma Fay coaxed.

"I can't," Breanna said, then turned and fled up the stairs. A second later the bathroom door slammed, followed by the sound of retching.

Not the most promising beginning.

Carson slid the envelope beneath the corner of the cheery flowered welcome mat, then stepped back quickly before his shaking fingers snatched the letter away. This felt like cheating, like making an already-horrible situation worse. At the very least Anna deserved to hear news like this from them personally. But Bree—curled up with a bowl in her lap in the passenger seat of his car—was in no condition to talk. Even worse, he'd seen her dad's truck come around the corner just seconds after they'd left her house.

Her father wasn't usually one to come home from a hunt early, so something must be up—hopefully not a premonition about his daughter. Carson had no intention of waiting around to find out. Grandma Fay had not only agreed with his suggestion of marriage—she'd encouraged them to elope and marry quickly, before any other trouble came.

What could be worse? With a heavy heart, Carson trudged down the Lawrences' manicured walk lined with spring bulbs just beginning to emerge but which, a month from now, would be in full bloom. Never again would he sit on the porch swing with Anna, holding her hand while they drank in the fragrance of her mother's flower garden. Never again would he help in her parents' store or enjoy a barbecue in their backyard or watch a game with her dad and brother. Carson loved her family and had been looking forward to calling them his.

A few short hours from now and his name would fall from their lips like a curse. Anna's dad would see the envelope either on the way to or from his morning run. And that would change everything—for Anna and her whole family. Carson's world had already shifted drastically—two and a half months ago and especially in the past two hours. Anna was never going to be his wife, and it was all his fault.

At the car he paused and looked back, up to the gabled window of her room, half hoping, half dreading seeing a light on there or her familiar face parting the curtain. When would he even see her again? Would they ever talk again? Would she call him tomorrow and shout at him and cry and tell him what a horrible, faithless cheater he was? It would be worth it to hear her voice just once more. He missed it already. Anna had been a part of his life, his *entire* life, and imagining living without her felt like leaving a limb behind. How was he supposed to function?

Carson opened the car door and stepped inside without looking over at Bree. His car smelled like vomit, and he wanted nothing so much as to get out of it, but first they had to get out of Holiday.

While Grandma Fay had convinced Bree to this course of action and helped her get the last of her things together, he'd done some searching on his phone and found out that Tennessee was their best bet for a quick wedding. They could get a license tomorrow—no blood test required. There was also no waiting period between the time the license was issued and when a couple could be married. They would just have to find someone willing and able to do it on short notice. Surely something a little well-placed money could arrange, though tomorrow was Valentine's Day.

He had a little cash in his wallet but would need to stop at a bank and get more. He'd left most of his money, along with the plane tickets and all the vouchers for what was supposed to have been his and Anna's Caribbean honeymoon, in the envelope on her porch. It was a paltry offering and one he wasn't sure she'd even take. Who wanted to go on what was supposed to have been a romantic trip with a mother or sister instead of a spouse? He didn't think he would have, but he wanted Anna to know he wasn't going to be off having fun either. Yes, he was going to marry Bree, but that didn't mean he was happy about it, or that Bree was, either, for that matter. But they were going to do right by this child.

Somehow.

Carson held in a sigh as he left Anna's neighborhood, with its tree-lined streets and charming turn-of-the-century houses. He'd dreamed of owning one of those houses someday and living right here, of giving their children the kind of childhood he and Anna had enjoyed.

A few short miles later he drove onto the bridge, crossed the Magnolia River, and left Holiday behind. *Forever?* He hoped not. But how could they go back? Bree was right. People would talk. By this time tomorrow, he'd bet every single resident would know what had happened—what he had done.

I've hurt my two best friends. The two girls I loved the most. He wasn't sure how he could ever make this right, for anyone. But he had to try, especially with Bree. That was probably best done with everyone else out of the picture. Using Bree as his excuse, he turned his phone off, then tossed it in the back seat.

She was too fragile to deal with gossip and stares right now. As he'd helped her into the car earlier, he'd realized—with some alarm—that she'd lost quite a bit of weight. It wasn't like she'd had any to lose to begin with, but Grandma Fay said Bree had been sick for about a month now, unable to keep much of anything down and throwing up even when she hadn't eaten anything.

How she'd managed to hide that from her father and brothers should have been a mystery, but it wasn't really.

About the only time any of them paid attention to her was when it was time to eat and they wanted to know what she'd prepared for dinner. As soon as the meal was finished, they'd all bolt from the table, either to watch a show, play video games, or to target practice on their back property. Carson knew because he and Anna had been there on many occasions and witnessed this exact scenario.

More than a time or two Bree's brothers had teased him because he preferred to stay in the kitchen to help the girls clean up instead of heading out to the yard with the men. He'd always brushed their comments off and used the excuse that he wanted first dibs on the dessert—not a complete lie. Bree was a great cook. She'd had to learn early and had been doing all the cooking since she was thirteen, when her mother died.

Good-natured ribbing from Bree's brothers was a thing of the past. Now, if they didn't murder him on sight, they certainly wouldn't talk to him. Not such a terrible loss, except that they were Bree's family—his family soon too—and keeping peace between them was going to be important.

It was all Carson could do not to lean his head forward and bang it in on the steering wheel or drive them both off the bridge into the river. For the first time in his life, he began to understand the despair that might lead someone to end his life. It would be so much easier than facing everyone and everything.

Except that then he'd be facing his mom. And Bree's mother too. This life wasn't the endgame. He'd be accountable here or there. And while he was still here, he'd better do everything in his power to fix this mess. He hated the thought that his mom might know about this, that she might be watching him and be so terribly disappointed.

"I'll make it right," he vowed, pounding a fist instead of

his head against the wheel. He glanced over at Bree, knees tucked up to her chest, dried tear tracks on her face as she slept uneasily. Pity and regret swelled within him, overshadowing his own misery. He softened his voice. "Somehow," he promised, "I'll make this right."

Two

"WHERE ARE WE?" Night had turned to gray morning, but they were still driving. Knees cramped, Bree changed positions slowly, ever aware of her roiling stomach. She glanced at Carson, staring straight ahead, two hands gripping the steering wheel in the classic three o'clock and nine o'clock driver's ed position. Except he'd never looked this focused or intent—even when they were logging behind-the-wheel hours with their teacher all those years ago.

"Almost there." He glanced at the dashboard. "Another twenty minutes maybe."

"Almost where?" It seemed too much to believe they were anywhere together at all. He was supposed to be getting ready to marry Anna right now. But if they'd been driving since just after midnight, there was no way he could turn around and get back in time for his wedding now.

"Chattanooga. When I stopped for gas last night, I booked a room for us at a Holiday Inn Express. You can rest while I go downtown and see about a license and finding someone who can marry us today."

Bree felt a queer tickle in her stomach that wasn't nausea. He'd been serious last night. Carson was really going to marry her and rescue her from this nightmare—sort of. It was still a nightmare for both of them. By now Anna would know what had happened. Bree's eyes stung. *She'll hate me.* Anna was the closest thing to a sister Bree had ever had. Anna's mother had always treated Bree as one of her own as well. She'd received nothing but love from that family, and this was how she repaid them.

"Are you sure?" Bree placed a gentle hand on Carson's arm. "You don't have to do this."

"Yes, I do. We both do." He glanced at her. "We've already broken Anna's heart and hurt her family and others. But our child is the most innocent of all, and we aren't going to hurt him or her."

Though he didn't sound happy about it, Bree still took courage from his words. Carson had always been one to do the right thing—or try to, anyway. Everyone failed sometimes. The night he had, she should have been better, should have been watching out for him, knowing his emotions were a mess and his heart fragile. If he'd been himself that night, had been thinking clearly like he usually did, they wouldn't be here right now.

The thought made her a little sad, and her guilt multiplied. *I wouldn't be marrying him or carrying his child.* She never would have had the opportunity for either but would have remained his friend, as she had all the previous years, on the sidelines while Anna and Carson's romance bloomed.

Once or twice, Bree had thought things might turn out differently. At their junior prom, she'd have sworn that Carson had wanted to kiss her. She'd been very aware of the change that had come over him that night. From the moment he first saw her on the stairs, his eyes had opened, literally, and it was like he was seeing her for the first time. It was as if, instead of seeing Bree, the permanent fixture in his life, frequently at his and Anna's side, he'd realized she was her own person. That she had things to offer the world too. Things he might be interested in.

She'd never forget the way he'd taken her hand at the bottom of the stairs and brought it to his lips like a southern gentleman of old. When he'd raised his head again, his eyes had held a tender gaze she'd never seen from him before.

"You're beautiful," he'd said. Not "you look beautiful tonight" or "that dress is beautiful on you." He'd told her *she* was beautiful—always. And from that night on, Bree had believed it.

With this newfound confidence she'd also had many more dates than she ever had before, including one to her senior prom the following spring with fellow student Robbie Marsh. That night hadn't been nearly as magical as her junior prom, when she'd had one of her best friends at her side and holding her hand all night. But Carson had surprised her during her senior prom as well, trading partners mid-dance so that Anna paired with Robbie and Bree danced with Carson for nearly one entire slow song—the same one that they had danced to the previous year, when she'd have sworn he almost kissed her.

This time, of course, they didn't sway quietly and hold each other closer than they should. Instead they talked and joked and laughed throughout the song—mostly at poor Robbie, who looked disgruntled at the arrangement. Anna hadn't seemed to mind at all. She was like that—gracious, generous, kind.

Trusting.

I've repaid her so poorly. The first tear of the day started its trek down Bree's cheek. She dashed it away, hoping Carson hadn't noticed.

"You okay?" He sounded genuinely concerned. Breanna couldn't understand how he didn't hate her. She hated herself right now, and for the first time since he'd told her she was beautiful, she didn't feel that way.

"Should we stop?" he asked.

Stricken, she stared at him, remembering the one other time he'd asked that question. To both their demises, she'd told him no. Now she couldn't bring herself to say the word.

"I hate myself," she whispered instead.

"I know the feeling." His Adam's apple bobbed as he swallowed. "Last night, when you were sleeping, I thought about driving off the bridge into the river. We could have just been swept away in the current."

"Why didn't you?" His confession alarmed her, not for her own safety but that *his* misery and despair were so great he would consider suicide.

"My mom—and yours." He glanced at Bree. "Sure we would have been swept away, but our problems wouldn't. They'd only be worse. I hate thinking my mom knows about this and what she must feel—how disappointed and sad she must be. But it was a mistake."

Bree winced inwardly at the reminder. *He regrets every part of this. He doesn't love me—not the way he loves Anna. Not in the way a man should love the woman he's going to marry.*

"I never intended to get you pregnant, Bree. I didn't come to your house that night hoping to seduce you. But if I drove us both off that bridge, that would have been intentional. I would have purposely ended your life, our child's, and mine. And I'm not sure that's forgivable. I want to hope that what we've done already is, but I can't imagine facing our mothers if I did worse."

He was blaming himself too much. Bree turned away and stared out the window at the dreary morning. *He didn't intend to seduce me.* She held in a choked laugh. Carson was so good—too good for her. He'd been so grief stricken that night, she didn't think he should be held accountable. Or at least not as accountable as she was. She'd known clearly what was going to happen the minute he'd finally stopped crying, released her, and raised his tear-stained face to hers. They'd both hesitated a few, interminable seconds—seconds she should have used to move away, to get off the sofa, to say something else comforting, to break the spell that had come over them both. But she hadn't done any of those things. She'd wanted him to kiss her. And when he'd bent his head forward just the slightest bit, she'd moved hers to meet him. She'd felt his lips against hers, as soft and sweet as every single kiss she'd imagined from him over the long years she'd loved him.

Her longing mingled with his immense need for comfort and reassurance had proved a fateful combination. One kiss, then two and three hadn't been enough for either of them. It had seemed to her that they'd waited their entire lives for this. She, at least, had been wanting it—wanting Carson—for years. And he'd come to *her* for comfort, hadn't he? That had to mean something. He could have driven a few hours to see Anna. *But instead he sought me.* How easily Bree had rationalized what they were doing, how lost she'd been in his lips and touch. How desperate for affection, especially from him. When, half-delirious, he'd murmured a question of whether they should stop, she'd been hasty to assure him that wasn't necessary.

Haste makes waste. One of Grandma Fay's oft-repeated adages rang through Bree's mind. In this case, haste had made a baby. *Not a waste.* Bree placed a hand over her concave stomach, worrying again for the child inside. If she'd felt half-starved these past weeks, unable to keep anything down, how was her baby able to grow? She wanted him to grow, couldn't wait to feel him moving, to see him born, to hold and love him.

Our baby. Carson's and mine. And now I can keep our baby, because Carson's going to marry me. The happy thought was followed instantly by another gush of self-loathing.

It was more than what she'd done, more than breaking both of her best friends' hearts, more than stealing Anna's fiancé and ruining her wedding. Bree hated herself because, deep down, she'd wanted Carson for herself, and now she had him.

She clutched the bowl in her lap, certain she was going to be sick again.

"I'll be right back." Carson left the engine running and stepped out of the car. He inhaled the rain-scented air deeply, grateful to be away—for a minute or two—from Bree and her misery.

And what about Bree? Can she get away from this? He'd dealt with their situation for one night, whereas Bree had been paying the consequences for their actions the past couple of months. *I deserve to be miserable. As miserable as I've made each of the two girls I love.*

With grim resolve Carson entered the lobby and registered for a room. He'd only purchased one. As it was he had to pay for last night, though they hadn't even been here. He and Bree would be married by the time they slept here tonight. And it wasn't as if anything other than sleep was going to be happening—if that. Exhaustion settled in his bones after the long night's drive and the stress of the past several hours. But he wasn't at all certain he'd be able to sleep, even if he had the time.

He returned to the car with the room keys and found Bree's eyes closed again, her dark hair draped over the reclined seat, contrasting sharply with her pale skin. Carefully he took the bowl from her lap and tossed its contents into the nearest bushes. She hadn't thrown up much—her stomach was probably too empty—but she'd convulsed for probably an hour straight, every gasp and heave and sob tearing his heart out. He'd done this to her, to Bree, an angel of a friend who'd done nothing to deserve any of this.

He regretted speaking angrily to her at her house last night. He still felt angry, but mostly with himself. Taking it out on Bree was the absolute wrong thing to do. He didn't know how he was going to show her he was sorry, but at least he could show her she wasn't alone anymore, by marrying her today.

He drove around the side of the building and parked near the entrance. Their room was on the first floor, and Carson wheeled their luggage inside before returning for Bree. His honeymoon suitcase had been packed and ready in the trunk of the car. Bree had been mostly ready to leave as well, as she'd been planning to go to Mississippi. Grandma Fay had helped her gather the last of her things.

Carson supposed she had included a dress for Bree to be married in. He, on the other hand, had nothing but shorts and T-shirts, swim trunks and sandals in his bag. His tux was still on its hanger at his dad's house. When he went out to arrange things, he'd have to stop at a store and buy something suitable to wear.

Ridiculous, considering he had a closet full of suits at his apartment. But then this entire situation was absurd and unbelievable. Right now he should have been getting out of the shower, with only a little over an hour until he left for the church to marry Anna. But by now his dad would have found the letter Carson had slipped through the mail slot just after midnight. Knowing his dad, he was probably already over at the Lawrences' house, apologizing profusely for his son's behavior and offering comfort. That was the thing about his dad. There was never any time for his own grief or troubles, and rarely time for his family's.

Old resentment rose in Carson. Wasn't his dad responsible for at least a bit of this mess? During the long months of his mother's illness, Carson didn't think his dad had been around enough. There was always some other family in crisis, always one of his flock who needed him.

"What about Mom? She needs you too," Carson had shouted at his dad one day, when he'd been preparing to leave to visit an elderly member of the congregation.

"Mom has you and Charlie here with her," his dad had said. "Old Mrs. Gunderson has no one. Mom understands."

She might have, but Carson never had, especially on the night of their mother's death when Dad had left her hospital bed, shortly after she passed, to drive an hour to a different hospital where the young daughter of another family in his congregation was awaiting surgery.

He'd needed his dad that night. Charlie had too. He'd dealt with Mom's death by driving two towns over and getting drunk. But at least Charlie had the presence of mind to call Carson instead of attempting to drive himself home. His mistake had been bad but not fatal.

It was that early-morning phone call that had awoken Carson to the reality of his own situation and the stupidity of his own actions. He'd come to Bree for comfort and had ended up with much more, half-dressed and curled up on the couch with her at three a.m.

Remembering her now, the way she'd looked as she'd slept in his arms, softened Carson's anger as he opened the passenger door. "We're here, Bree."

She groaned in her sleep and tried to tuck her knees up higher. Carson leaned over, closer to her. *Wake up, sleepyhead* was on the tip of his tongue and nearly escaped before he held it back. Sixth grade summer camp he'd first said that to her, after the boys had pranked the girls by toilet papering the outside of their cabin. He'd hollered through the window at Bree, then shot her with a can of silly string when she sat up on her bunk.

She'd paid him back good the next afternoon, catching him unaware while he was trying to bait a hook near the fishing hole.

Something cold and wet smacked the back of his head a second before a dead fish slid over his shoulder into his lap. "Wake up, sleepyhead, or should I say, fish head?" She'd laughed as she ran away, faster than he could catch her.

"Wake up, sleepyhead," he'd said to her at a junior high swim team practice, just before he'd pushed her into the pool and earned himself an extra twenty laps for doing it.

"Wake up, sleepyhead," she'd whispered urgently, bumping his elbow out from its position of support when he'd nodded off during their AP history class. She'd probably saved him from detention that day.

And so it had gone over the years. The last time he'd said it to her was the night before they'd slept together, when she'd opened her front door, eyes little more than slits, hair tousled, and wearing only pajama pants and a tank top. Grief stricken as he was, his brain had immediately noted Bree wasn't wearing a bra.

"Wake up, sleepyhead," he'd said, attempting a light tone, though his voice trembled. "I need to talk." She'd seen his tears then and knew what they meant. Everyone had known the end was near for his mom. She'd been sick for so long. Bree understood that, too, though their mothers' illnesses had been different.

"I'm awake," she'd said. "I'm here." She'd opened her arms to him to prove it.

When he'd had to wake her at three the next morning,

filled with heavy regret over his actions, he hadn't used their teasing phrase. It hadn't been a time for teasing, and this wasn't either.

"Breanna, we're here." He touched her shoulder, and she came awake at once. Confusion clouded her eyes as she looked up at him, then took in their surroundings.

"You're still here." Her hand touched the side of his cheek.

Carson resisted the urge to lean into her touch for comfort. Breanna was good at comfort and at listening. But it was his turn to be here for her.

"I am." He forced a smile. "I'm not going to leave you, Bree. We're in this together."

Her return smile was accompanied by misty eyes. He took her hand and gently pulled her from the car and guided her to their room.

He gave her the bed nearest the bathroom and left the other, near the door, for himself. He pulled back the covers and tucked her in, like she was a little girl, blankets up to her chin. "Get some sleep. I'm going to find out about a license and when and where we can get married. It's barely nine, so you should be fine to sleep for a few hours."

"Thank you, Carson." She rolled over on her side and curled up again.

He set the abhorrent bowl on the nightstand. "Can I get you anything while I'm out?"

"Crackers," she whispered. "Saltines. They're the only thing this baby seems to like."

"Right." *This baby.* She spoke as if it were here already. "Can you—can you feel it yet?"

She shook her head. "No. But I feel his presence, his spirit. He's very real to me." Her eyes closed, and she smiled almost peacefully.

Carson wished he could feel the same.

Three

ONE OF HIS father's favorite and oft-repeated sermons was that the true measure of a man can be determined by how he acts under duress. *Integrity is what a person does when in a crisis and no one is around to see him.* How often he and Charlie had heard that from Dad, both from the pulpit and at the dinner table.

You're not around now, Dad.

Carson wanted to think that in the next few hours, he did a fairly decent job being a man and owning up to his mistake and taking the only steps he could to make it right, or as right as possible. He had no illusions that things would ever be completely whole again. His dreams—from marrying Anna to raising their family in Holiday—were never going to be.

Unfortunately, another of his father's favorite sermons was about how a person's thoughts, as well as his words and deeds, would ultimately condemn him. If that was truly the case, Carson was in trouble. He couldn't seem to stop thinking about Anna, even as he made preparations to marry Bree.

Ten o'clock. He would have been at the church now, maybe getting his first glimpse of Anna in her wedding gown. Instead he was entering the clerk's office in another state, to find out about getting a license to marry another woman.

Ten thirty. Would their vows have been complete by

now? Would he have lifted Anna's veil and kissed her as his wife? Carson pictured her face, even as he spoke with a clerk about the possibility of a wedding that afternoon.

Eleven o'clock. Pictures. Carson groaned as he drove across town and remembered the expensive photographer Anna had arranged. *No refund there,* Carson supposed. He added sending a cashier's check for a few thousand dollars to Anna's parents to his list of must-dos.

Twelve o'clock. The wedding luncheon. He'd almost forgotten about that, about the guests who weren't going to know what had happened and had probably shown up at the church and/or the luncheon. Carson grimaced as he stared at his reflection in the dressing room mirror. No suit could make someone as guilty as he was look good.

Who had gone to the church to tell everyone? Anna's dad, probably. What about those who had traveled for the wedding? Had they hosted the luncheon anyway, to feed everyone? Carson's actions hadn't just affected Anna and Bree and their families but a lot of other people too. Probably the entire town, in one way or another.

He jerked off the suit coat more roughly than necessary and jammed it back on the hanger. The measure of the man he was, the integrity he didn't have, was clearly visible in the mirror before him. He was a horrible human being who had not only thrown his future away but taken a few others down with him.

A fresh infusion of anger boiled inside of him as he dropped $300 for a suit he didn't need or want. He left Dillard's, got in his Camry, and sped back to the hotel, just wanting to get this day over with and get out of town. Maybe they wouldn't stay the night tonight. Maybe they'd drive to his apartment in Birmingham. Since there would be no honeymoon, he could show up for work on Monday. If Bree's dad came after him with a gun before then, so much the better.

A flash of light and the wail of a siren made his heart jump. Carson looked in his rearview mirror to see a police car trailing him. Swearing under his breath, Carson pulled over to the side of the road and removed his license from his wallet. He opened the console and dug around for the car's paperwork stored inside. He found it beneath a bag of stale licorice and the white ring box holding Anna's wedding band. He tossed the box and licorice on the seat, unfolded the registration, and rolled down his window as the policeman strolled leisurely toward him.

"You're in quite a hurry there, son. What's the rush?" The officer held out his hand, and Carson handed over his license, registration, and insurance.

"Mind's a bit preoccupied. I'm getting married this afternoon," Carson said. "I must have lost track of the speed limit. I'm sorry."

The officer leaned in, noting the suit bag draped over the front seat. His gaze flickered to the ring box. A slow smile grew on his face. "Well now." He straightened and seemed to consider a minute, then handed Carson's license and papers back. "I think, given the circumstances, that a warning might be enough. Can't say I wasn't in a hurry on my wedding day too." He grinned at Carson.

"Slow it down, son. Enjoy the day. You only get married once, so try to savor each minute if you can. Next thing you know, it'll be your twenty-fifth anniversary, and you'll have a daughter of your own who wants to get married." He shook his head and turned to go. "Don't be in a hurry. It all comes fast enough."

Yeah. I know. "Thank you," Carson called, relieved and grateful for this little break. He shoved the papers back in the console, then reached for the licorice and ring box. He held the latter a moment, wondering what he was supposed to do with it now. Anna had the solitaire engagement ring that went with the set, and it wasn't like he was going to ask for that back. But it wasn't like he could use this ring.

Bree needs a ring. A married woman, and one pregnant at that, ought to have one. But it couldn't be this one, and there wasn't time to find another now. They needed to be back at the courthouse in two hours.

Given the state he'd left Bree in this morning, he was going to need every second to get her up and moving and ready. Rings, for both of them, would have to wait. The best he could hope for now was that she'd be able to part from her bowl long enough to say "I do."

But as he pulled into traffic, the officer's advice rang in Carson's mind. *Slow down, savor each minute. You only get married once.* This wasn't the way to start a life together, but he was right. Carson wanted to get married only once. Bree had to feel the same. Difficult circumstances or not, he had to do what he could to make the day special.

Breanna paced nervously in front of the hotel room mirror, her heels making indents in the plush carpet. Like the carpet, the rest of the room was nice—nicer than any place she'd ever stayed. This was thoughtful of Carson. He could have spent less money for a cheaper hotel. He could have driven them straight to the courthouse. *Could have turned around and walked out last night like I asked him to.* That he hadn't, but had abandoned his entire life as he'd planned it, for her—or for their baby, at least—made Bree love him all the more.

She had no delusions that love was returned and could only hope that someday they could possibly regain the level of friendship and trust they'd shared for so many years. Clinging to that faint possibility, she vowed to do all she could to be a good wife. But she wasn't Anna and never would be. Anna had always been prettier, taller, wealthier, had better clothes and better grades. She simply *was* better—in every way, as was evidenced by the current situation. Anna had been engaged to Carson and hadn't slept with him. It had probably never occurred to her that her best friend would.

Bree paused in front of the mirror and spoke to her reflection. "I did a terrible thing." Did that mean she was a terrible person? She didn't want to think so, though right now it sure seemed like that. "Somehow I have to make it up—to Carson, at least. But I can't be Anna." She could only be herself, the girl that Carson had sought comfort from, the one he'd felt something for, at least a few times in his life. To that end, she'd tried her best this morning to at least look like that girl, instead of the shriveled-up mess she'd been all through the long drive here.

Grandma Fay had packed some saltines, and Bree had forced herself to eat an entire sleeve of them. Those, plus a Sprite from the vending machine down the hall, had her feeling better than she had in a while. Once she'd felt steady on her feet and able to stand more than a minute without feeling faint, she'd showered and washed her hair. Since Carson still hadn't returned then, she'd dried and curled it, then dug out her cosmetic bag and done her best to make her overly pale face a little brighter.

Her grandmother had also packed the bridesmaid dress Bree was supposed to have worn to Anna's wedding today. It seemed somehow sacrilegious to wear it now, to her own wedding to Anna's groom, but then she'd already done the most sacrilegious thing she could think of, so what harm was wearing the dress going to do? It was the nicest thing she'd ever owned, a layered pale-pink chiffon with a fitted bodice and a long, full skirt that floated around her. Bree remembered the day she'd first tried it on at Anna's house. Anna's mother had made it, had sewn it lovingly for her, and Bree had felt almost happy that day when she'd put it on and looked in the mirror.

She'd been so grateful for the pretty dress and knew she was going to need it to bolster her courage on Anna's wedding day. It was sure to be difficult—the ending of her childhood fantasy about marrying Carson, and the beginning of Carson's and Anna's lives together. Bree had been so very careful over the years, so no one would guess her feelings for him. She certainly couldn't let them show on his wedding day.

After junior prom, a couple of people had mentioned how good she and Carson had looked together, as well as the fact that they'd looked pretty cozy as they'd danced.

Bree had quickly brushed those comments off, stating it was Anna's borrowed dress that had supplied all the magic but that the spell had definitely broken at the stroke of midnight. She was back to being just Bree, and Carson was back to being just Carson. There was nothing between them, except Anna—literally anywhere the threesome was seen together. Bree had even started dating Robbie shortly after prom, just to prove her point that dancing with Carson hadn't meant anything.

And look where lying to myself and everyone else landed me. Alone in a hotel in Chattanooga. She glanced at the clock. It was nearly one. What could be taking Carson so long? *What if he isn't coming back?* What if he'd changed his mind and left her, after all?

It would be no more than she deserved. Bree turned from the mirror and began stowing things back into her open suitcase, thinking through what she'd do if he didn't come back. There was still Mississippi. She could always—

The door lock clicked behind her. The handle jiggled.

"Bree? Is it all right if I come in?"

Carson. She nearly wept with relief. She didn't want to go to Mississippi. She didn't want to give their baby away. She wanted to marry Carson. Even under these difficult circumstances and this awful beginning.

"Yes." Her voice sounded all trembly. He was going to think she was sick again, but the butterflies in her stomach had nothing to do with being pregnant.

The door swung open, and he stepped inside, a garment bag held in one hand, the hotel room card, a paper grocery bag, and a bouquet of pink and white roses in the other.

"Hey." He stopped, staring at her, and the door swung back and hit him in the shoulder. He scowled, then stepped aside, allowing it to close all the way. His eyes returned to her. "You're up."

Bree nodded. "I thought I should get ready in case . . ."

"Did you walk to the store across the street to get saltines?" His eyes drifted past her to the open box of crackers on the nightstand. "I'm sorry. I should have bought those first and come back."

She shook her head. "My grandma packed them. I ate a whole sleeve," Bree boasted, as if that was some extraordinary accomplishment, then felt herself blush the moment the words were out. "I mean, that's a lot for me right now. But if I can keep them down, I'll feel better longer and . . ."

A relieved smile crossed his face, and he started toward her, dropping the garment bag on his bed as he came. "Eat as many as you'd like or can." He set the grocery bag down on the floor near her. "I bought twelve boxes. There are two more bags like this in the car."

"Oh my." Bree looked down at the bag filled with nothing but saltines. She felt a laugh rise in her.

Carson stopped a foot in front of her and held out the flowers awkwardly. "I don't have a ring for you."

"I didn't expect—"

"I know, but we'll get you one. There just wasn't time today, and you should probably pick it out—something you like."

I like you. Bree nodded and pressed her lips together to keep from crying. He was so thoughtful, so good. She really didn't deserve him. But she wanted him so much.

"I thought you should at least have a bouquet."

She took the flowers from him and pressed her face to the petals, inhaling the sweet scent and hiding her teary eyes. "Thank you, Carson. They're beautiful."

"You're beautiful, Bree." He didn't smile, but lifted her chin gently and looked into her eyes as he said it. She wanted to believe him, but mostly she wanted to be beautiful on the inside, to be a good person, worthy of him.

She held his gaze. "Are we going to be okay?"

He nodded, then took her free hand and kissed the back of it as he had those long years ago the night of prom. "We're going to be okay."

Four

Bree walked past elaborate water fountains and statues of civil war generals, toward the stately Hamilton County Courthouse in downtown Chattanooga. "What a gorgeous building. This isn't such a terrible place to get married."

"Not terrible at all." Carson caught Bree's free hand in his as it swung backward.

She glanced at him with a grateful smile. "Thank you for doing this."

"Thank you for not siccing your dad and brothers on me. It's no less than I deserve."

Bree paused before the steps leading up to the double doors. "As Grandma Fay said, 'It takes two to tango.' I'm every bit as guilty as you are." *More, actually.* "But can we try not to think about that for the next half hour? Can we pretend—" *That we love each other.* She broke off, before the fatal words could slip out.

"Of course." Carson gave her hand a squeeze. "After all, you only get married once."

His smile was tight, but he kept her hand as they started up the steps between the tall pillars on either side. At the top he motioned for her to go ahead, through the revolving door, and Bree stepped into a foyer as grand as the outside had promised.

The tall marble pillars continued inside, leading up to a rotunda with a domed ceiling of stained glass.

"Unfortunately the clerk's office isn't quite as impressive." Carson took her hand again and led her to the office, where they obtained a marriage license, then waited for their appointment time.

"We are incredibly lucky they're squeezing us in today. I'm pretty sure the judge is using his break between sessions to marry us."

"That's kind of him," Bree said, wondering what a judge must think of a couple who obtained a license and then wanted to marry immediately.

She was just starting to feel ill again when their names were called. *Hold off a little longer,* she silently begged her stomach or the baby or whatever it was that caused her almost-constant nausea. She thought she could bear almost anything—except throwing up at her own wedding.

They were led to an empty courtroom with faux-paneled walls. The robed judge was already there and smiled at them in welcome. If he was sacrificing his break for them, he didn't appear to mind too much.

"I'm Judge Patterson." He held out an age-spotted hand to each of them. Bree introduced herself after Carson. The judge was old, much older than she'd expected and certainly old enough to be retired.

"So y'all decided to get married on Valentine's Day." He took their paperwork and looked over it briefly.

"We did," Carson confirmed, sounding nervous.

"Wise." The judge nodded his head. "You get points for being romantic, and you'll never forget your anniversary. Just remember, she may expect *two* gifts on Valentine's Day instead of one from now on." He grinned at Bree, putting her more at ease, in spite of her roiling stomach and clammy palms.

"Thank you for accommodating us," she said, more grateful than he could possibly know.

"I had a feeling I should come in today." Judge Patterson smiled broadly. "I don't work the regular docket anymore—thank heavens—but I still retain my license to marry folks. After so many years spent with people who'd made serious mistakes and were often at their low point in life, I've earned the right to these happy celebrations."

Bree and Carson exchanged a quick, guilty glance.

"Being Valentine's Day and all, I suspected there might be a few couples who could use my services today. But we do need to hurry before they need this room again."

"Could you—could you marry us elsewhere?" Bree asked, struck with sudden inspiration, born of her dire need for fresh, cool air. The stifling room and walls that felt like they were closing in weren't helping her nausea.

Judge Patterson looked up from the papers. "What did you have in mind?"

"Outside?" Bree suggested. "The grounds are so pretty, and this room is—"

"Not?" he said with a smile. "Let's go. After you." He held his hand toward the door.

"Thank you." His willingness to move locations might just save her.

As if he knew she was feeling ill, Carson kept his hand at the small of her back as they walked.

"Are you going to be all right?" he asked in the second after they left the revolving door but before the judge had come through and joined them.

"I hope so." Her answer didn't sound particularly reassuring to her own ears, but it was the best she could do. Along with fighting nausea, she felt like she might pass out at any minute.

"How about over there, beneath those trees?" Judge Patterson pointed to an out-of-the-way spot on the lawn.

"Perfect." Bree mustered a smile and allowed Carson to guide her. At least the grass would be a softer landing than the hard floor if she fainted.

"Very nice. Excellent suggestion." The good judge stopped beneath the budding trees, opened his folder, and looked at Bree and Carson. "Now then, if you'll face each other, please."

Still holding on to Carson's hand, Bree turned toward him. She breathed in the cool air deeply and prayed it and the scent of the roses clutched in her other hand would be enough to keep her stomach calm and to keep her upright until the ceremony was complete.

"Though I perform many weddings, marriage is a dying institution," the judge began.

Carson raised his brows in question, and Bree gave a little shrug. Those certainly weren't the first words she'd imagined hearing at her wedding, but then she never dreamed she'd be getting married beneath a tree in Chattanooga, Tennessee, while wearing a pink bridesmaid dress.

The only thing she had imagined that was the same was the man standing across from her.

And that's all that matters.

"Young people today treat marriage much as they would a vacation or purchasing a house, getting a job, or any other temporary experience in life. Not—" Judge Patterson paused, as if for emphasis. "Not one of the great purposes of life itself. To have found someone to love and to have that love returned is one of the best gifts of the Almighty. May you, Breanna, and you, Carson"—the judge turned to each—"realize what a gift you have in each other. May this simple wedding be but a beginning to a grand life together, rich with enduring love and family, and especially each other."

From such an awkward beginning sentence, Judge Patterson's words and advice had turned beautiful. Bree felt touched that he would take the time to share it with them when this was just a simple civil wedding.

"Now then. Let's get down to business, shall we?" He cleared his throat.

Please. Bree tightened her grip on Carson's hand and tried to make sure her knees didn't lock.

Judge Patterson turned to Carson. "Do you, Carson Levi Armstrong, take Breanna Eleanor Wagner to be your lawfully wedded wife, to care for in sickness and health, to cherish and love in poverty and wealth, to have and to hold from this day forth?"

"I do." Carson spoke the words with a somberness that nearly broke Bree's resolve to go through with this.

What *was* she doing? This was all wrong. Carson didn't want to marry her. He didn't love her—no matter what he had just promised. He was in love with Anna and had been for practically his entire life. *How am I supposed to compete with that?* She wasn't. She couldn't. She never should have told him about the baby but should have let him go so at least one of them could be happy. Now she was going to make them both miserable. Carson, because he'd had to marry the wrong woman. *And I'll be miserable, too, because I know he'll always be thinking of Anna and wishing . . .*

"Bree?" Carson squeezed her hand gently and looked into her eyes.

She snapped hers back into focus and saw his slightly panicked expression. Carson inclined his head toward the judge, who looked at her expectantly.

What? Had she missed her cue? Her own panic erupted, and a cold sweat broke out on her forehead. *Don't faint. Just a little longer.*

"Please," Carson mouthed.

He wants me to say yes. He wants to marry me. She couldn't fathom why, but her overwhelming desire to make him happy was enough to prompt her to action.

"I do," she said quietly. *I do love you. I'll make this up to you somehow, I swear.*

"Splendid." Judge Patterson sounded relieved and withdrew a handkerchief to swipe across his brow. "By the power vested in me by the state of Tennessee, I pronounce you husband and wife. Mr. Armstrong, you may seal those promises with a kiss."

There was no veil to lift, no church full of friends and family to sigh at their first kiss as husband as wife, no reason for a kiss at all. Bree stood, unmoving and uncertain what Carson would do with this complication. She'd forgotten about this part of a wedding. It had been all about making things legal, keeping her father from killing them both, and giving their baby an honest name.

It had been all she could do not to sway on her feet and to say two simple words. But a kiss—

Carson's lips touched hers, and all else in the world faded away. Bree's eyes fluttered shut, and she leaned into him, into the warm caress of his mouth on hers, into his embrace pulling her close, and into the black oblivion that claimed her at last as she fell.

Five

"You know, sometimes when you put the cart before the horse, you end up needing to buy a buggy."

"Yep. We're gonna need one of those before the year is up. A few other things, too, I suppose." Carson met Judge Patterson's gaze without flinching while the paramedics attended Bree. They'd put her on a stretcher and hooked up an IV. She was dehydrated, among other things, they'd said. Carson felt foolish for not realizing sooner. There had been a can of Sprite on the nightstand by the crackers, but that was likely the only liquid she'd had since they left Holiday, and the soda would have only made things worse.

He should have realized that her increasingly pale face and wan expression hadn't been a sign of nerves but that she was about to pass out.

"How far along is she?" Judge Patterson sat on a nearby bench and motioned for Carson to sit beside him.

"Almost three months," Carson said. He didn't care who knew or what they thought. He only wanted Breanna to be okay.

"Worst of the sickness should be over soon. She'll feel better the second trimester."

"Good to hear," Carson said, praying the old judge was

right. He didn't want to think Bree was going to have to endure being this ill the entire nine months. He wasn't sure she *could* endure it—without being hospitalized.

"Mr. Armstrong." One of the paramedics waved him over. "Your wife would like to speak with you."

My wife. It didn't seem real. None of this did. It was like his worst nightmare come true, except that Bree was in it, and there was nothing bad about her—except what he'd done.

"Thanks for everything," Carson said to the judge, then tucked the envelope with the marriage certificate under his arm as he stood. He and Breanna still needed to sign the copy to be turned in today so everything would be official.

He crossed the short distance to the ambulance. "Hey." He crouched beside the stretcher so his face was close to hers.

She attempted a smile. "How was that for a moment we'll never forget?"

In spite of the gravity of the situation, he laughed. Or maybe it was the relief of seeing her awake and teasing.

"Oh, Bree." He leaned closer and kissed her forehead.

Her eyes flew to his, looking as surprised as he felt by the spontaneous gesture.

"It was my other kiss that did it, wasn't it?" he asked in mock seriousness, hoping to prolong the lighter mood between them. It was the best they'd shared since they'd embarked on their middle-of-the-night escape. "Kissing me was so dreadful you had no choice but to faint."

"Absolutely—*not*." She rolled her eyes. "Though your kisses are definitely enough to make a girl swoon."

They are? This was news to him. *Is Bree blushing?* He thought so, but maybe it was just some of the color returning to her face.

The idea that kissing him might make her swoon—in a good way—went a long way to reassure him. From the first, she hadn't seemed overly keen on this marriage, and for a few terrifying seconds during the ceremony, he'd thought she was going to back out. But then he supposed she must have felt *something* the night they—connected. Or at least she'd pretended to. He really hoped she had, and that maybe— months from now when they were past all of this and their marriage was stable—they might feel something together again. But that was only if he hadn't imagined that his affection was returned.

He'd wondered since that night if Bree had gone along with everything simply to comfort him. He'd been so distraught, and Bree was such a giving person.

And now look at her. His gaze shifted to the needle in her hand and the bag of fluid hanging above.

"I'm really sorry, Carson." Her hand without the IV in it reached for him.

"You don't have anything to apologize for, and besides, we were supposed to forget all that serious stuff and try to be happy today, remember?"

"I tried. I really did." Bree's eyes and nose scrunched up like she was getting ready to cry again. "This is so embarrassing. Whoever heard of fainting at your own wedding?"

Carson gave her a lopsided smile. "Could be worse. You didn't throw up."

"And she shouldn't throw up so much anymore, once she's had an injection of B6," one of the female paramedics said.

"Can you do that right now?" Carson asked. If one shot would make Bree feel better, what were they waiting for?

The paramedic shook her head. "She'll need to be examined at the hospital first."

"No." Bree's grip on Carson's hand tightened. "I don't want to go to the hospital. My father can't afford an ER bill right now. He's between jobs again, and we don't have any insurance."

Amid her protests, the paramedics raised the gurney so they could push it toward the waiting ambulance.

"This will cost hundreds of dollars, maybe thousands. I can't—" She tried to sit up.

"Don't worry about the money." Carson moved along beside her. "Your father won't have to pay for anything. I've got insurance. *We* do. You're covered now—Mrs. Armstrong."

Her mouth fell open with a tiny gasp, and he could see the name shocked her as much as hearing the word *wife* had shaken him.

"Speaking of which, I need your John Hancock right here, to make this all legal." He reached inside his suit coat for a pen.

The paramedics halted near the back of the ambulance.

"I don't want to go to the hospital, Carson."

"I know." He freed his hand to brush a tear from her cheek. "But I want to know that you're going to be okay. And I think you want to know that our child is too."

She nodded. "I do."

"So easily she says those two little words now," Carson teased and held out the papers to her.

Bree took the pen and signed her name. "Meet me at the hospital?" she asked, her voice forlorn.

He nodded. "Just as soon as I make sure these are filed."

She gave him a wobbly smile and handed him the papers. The paramedics loaded her into the ambulance.

"Hey, Mrs. Armstrong," Carson called just before they closed the doors. "It's really going to be okay."

Six

COULD THIS DAY *be any more surreal?* Carson followed a nurse through the hallway of the Parkridge East Hospital ER. Twenty-four hours ago, he couldn't have concocted this scenario in his wildest imagination. Yet here he was, a state away, married to a different woman than the one he'd planned to marry and visiting her in the hospital.

"Here you are, Mr. Armstrong." The nurse stepped aside so he could enter the tiny room.

"Thanks." Carson moved past her toward the bed, which took up most of the space. "Hey there," he said to Bree, who looked both pale and anxious, lying in a half-reclined position. The IV bag from earlier hung on a pole above, attached to the tube running down into Bree's hand.

Carson made sure to reach for her other hand. "How are you feeling?" Her pink dress was draped carefully over the chair, so he stood beside the bed.

"Better." She mustered a smile. "They gave me a shot to help with the nausea."

"That's great."

She nodded. "Someone is supposed to come in to check the heartbeat in a minute. Then I think I'll be good to go."

"Okay." Lame response, but he couldn't seem to think of

anything better. Carson shifted awkwardly from one foot to the other. He'd been so focused on the one thing he had to do today, so intent in his determination to see marrying Bree through, that he hadn't yet had time to consider what came after.

And he needed to figure that out quick.

"Mr. Armstrong?" A woman in scrubs entered the room.

"Yes. Carson." He would have held out his hand, but hers were full. He supposed hand shaking might be frowned upon in hospitals anyway, considering germs and all.

"I'm Dr. Morris. Your wife is doing much better, so we just need to check on baby, and if everything looks good, you'll all be free to go."

"We're going to *see* it?" A mixture of panic and excitement collided in his gut. *Ready or not . . .*

"Only if we suspect a complication. Unfortunately our ultrasound machines are being used at the moment, but there isn't a whole lot you can see at this stage, anyway. When you schedule with your ob-gyn, he or she will likely let you take that first look at baby."

"Right." Carson squeezed Bree's hand, offering support if she needed it, unsure how she felt about all of this too. It occurred to him that he hadn't asked her, beyond that initial question to make sure she wasn't considering an abortion.

Dr. Morris lowered the bed to a flatter position. She pulled the blanket down to Bree's hips and helped her push the hospital gown up, revealing her pale, flat stomach, including the mole on the left side of her belly button. Carson had seen it once before when they'd been swimming. Bree had never been one to wear a bikini, and she hadn't been that night either. One of the guys at the party they'd been at had been teasing Bree and following her around, trying to get closer to her than she wanted.

At Anna's sixteenth birthday party. Carson remembered like it was yesterday and also remembered hauling the guy across the deck and shoving him in a lawn chair after his hands got a little too grabby and tugged Bree's top up, revealing not only her belly button but that cute little mole. Carson recalled the rage he'd felt that other people there had seen it too.

Pulling his eyes from the mole now, he stepped back and sat down hard in the chair and on top of Bree's dress. Better that than to be staring at her exposed stomach and feeling the odd flip in his own as he did.

He hadn't seen much of her the night they'd made this baby, but he remembered how soft her skin felt. *Not the thing to be thinking of right now.*

Instead he concentrated on Dr. Morris, holding what looked like a walkie-talkie or small radio in one hand, her other hand pushing what almost looked like a short microphone or wand over the goo she'd smeared on Bree's stomach. This way and that it moved, with no resultant sound, no anticipated heartbeat. Dr. Morris's mouth turned down. She moved the wand lower, opposite to the tension in the room that was rising with each passing second. Carson glanced at Bree's face and caught her worrying her lower lip. Out of long habit, he brushed his finger across it and whispered the phrase both he and Anna had spoken to Bree over the years. "Keep those nice for kissing."

Bree nodded but didn't look at him.

Dr. Morris moved the wand lower. A faint blip sounded on the monitor, and she stopped, pressing harder.

Come on, Carson silently urged the unseen heart. *Let everything be okay.* He glanced at Bree again, her face pale and tense.

"Where are you hiding?" Dr. Morris murmured, rotating

the wand slowly. A second later the blip sounded again, above the static, then turned to a quick, steady whooshing beat.

Carson leaned his head forward in relief as the tension left his body. Yesterday he hadn't even known about this child, but today—this day that felt like a month already—the baby seemed real. It was certainly real to Bree, the way the pregnancy was making her so sick and had completely upended her life. And Bree—and making all this up to her—very much mattered to him.

"Found you." Dr. Morris smiled as the heartbeat continued strong. "There's your baby, Mom and Dad." She glanced up at them.

Dad? That was even trippier than calling Bree Mrs. Armstrong. But he couldn't deny the relief he felt at hearing the heartbeat. He squeezed Bree's hand again. This time she looked up at him with a teary smile.

"Is everything all right?" she asked Dr. Morris. "Should it be that hard to find?"

"Sometimes, especially when you're not very far along, it can be tricky to find the heartbeat. Baby is still tiny, and yours is sitting a little different than most, but I don't think it's anything to worry about."

"So we can go, then?" Bree asked the question Carson had wanted to but didn't dare for fear of sounding like an insensitive jerk. If Bree needed to stay in the hospital longer, then he would too.

"Yes." Dr. Morris wiped Bree's stomach with a towel and pulled the blanket up again. "I'll let them know you're ready, and someone will be in with your paperwork shortly."

"Thanks." Carson and Bree spoke at the same time.

Dr. Morris left, and a nurse came to remove Bree's IV. Carson held her other hand through the process, wincing along with her as the tube came out.

"So," Carson said when they were alone again. "There really is a baby in there. You didn't just eat too many tacos."

She pulled her hand away quickly, as if he'd offended her. "It's been *years* since that happened. What, were we ten or something?"

"Twelve," Carson corrected. "You were having a growth spurt and were always ravenous. I remember your mom was concerned that you were starting to eat like your brothers."

"Yeah, well that didn't last long. As soon as I had to take over the cooking, eating wasn't so fun anymore."

"I'm sure it wasn't." He wanted, suddenly, to touch Bree's face in a tender caress. She'd had such a hard time of things for so long, and here she was, unexpectedly pregnant and married by default. It didn't seem things were about to get easier for her anytime soon. Somehow, he needed to make sure they did.

"You ready to spring this joint?" He rose from the chair.

"Yes. I hate hospitals." She pressed the button on the side of the bed to raise herself to a sitting position.

"The feeling's mutual."

They exchanged a bittersweet, knowing look, filled with the kind of empathy that only two people who have lost their mothers, and lost them young, to a ravaging illness, can understand.

Carson turned away as Bree started to push back the blanket. He kept his gaze averted, listening to the quiet sounds of fabric moving as she changed.

"Will you help me, please?" she asked after a minute had passed. "It's difficult to zip this dress by myself. It must have taken me over five minutes this afternoon, hopping around with my arm twisted behind my back."

"Sure." He faced her as she turned away, her long, dark hair scooped up in her hands, revealing her bare neck and back where the zipper gaped open. Carson placed one hand at her waist and with his other pinched the zipper tab between his thumb and index finger. Slowly he pulled it upward, the teeth weaving together and sealing the sight of her beautiful body from his all-too interested eyes.

She was his wife now—in name at least. He had a lot of work and a long way to go if he ever hoped to earn the right to touch her again. He hadn't had that right in the first place, and now he had a good seven months to contemplate the result of his serious breach of conduct. It was a bad enough thing to happen to anyone, to do to or with anyone. But that it was Bree made it so much worse. Because she deserved so much better.

"Carson?"

Startled from his thoughts, he realized his hand was still at her waist, though he'd finished zipping the dress.

"Sorry." He dropped his hand and stepped back.

"Thank you."

She kept her head down as she sat in the chair and put on her shoes. Carson wished he could see her face. Did she feel anything for him when they were together? Did being near him affect her at all the way that being near her affected him?

These last few hours had wreaked havoc on both his mind and body. It had hit him as they'd stood outside beneath that tree, faced each other, held hands, and spoken their vows. Bree was going to be his wife! They were going to be married. For a few blissful seconds that joyous thought had taken over all else, and he'd felt almost giddy with happiness.

But then she'd hesitated with her vow, and rational thought and reality crashed down again, reminding him that Bree hadn't necessarily chosen him as the man of her dreams. She was making this deal out of necessity—possibly to save him from being murdered by her dad and brothers.

Not only that, but he'd shattered Anna's heart, too, by marrying Bree instead. Carson wouldn't have believed it possible to go from such an amazing high to the lowest low in less than a minute. But he had and did again as he held out his hand and helped Bree from the chair.

She swayed on her feet a second and leaned into him. Carson wrapped his arm around her and followed his natural instinct to kiss her temple. He liked the way she fit into the crook of his arm perfectly. Her hair smelled like it had the night of the prom. It felt as good to hold her now as it had then.

All of this pleased him and gave him hope. They might have started out all wrong and might not have much now but each other, but it seemed like that might be enough—for him, anyway. Winning Bree over might be another matter. One he intended to set himself to at once.

Seven

IF THEIR WEDDING had been unconventional, their wedding night was even more so, yet somehow Bree felt happier than she had in months. Some of the burden she'd been carrying had lifted. For better or worse—and it most definitely had to be worse—Anna knew the truth now. Carson did, too, and it seemed he'd not only forgiven Bree's part in the fiasco but had joined forces with her to make the most of their circumstances.

It was *the most* part that Bree kept thinking of now, from her side of the room. On the other side, on his own bed, Carson relaxed against the pillows, a box of Chinese takeout in his hands—and on his shirt and shorts as well. She'd challenged him to use the included chopsticks to eat his meal, and the results had been both entertaining and messy.

For her part, Bree was simply happy she could stomach the smell of chow mein without having to go worship the porcelain god. The shot, plus the fluids they'd given her at the hospital, had her feeling better than she had in weeks. That she wasn't alone, wasn't as terrified as she had been, but had Carson on her team, definitely had to do with her improved spirits and health as well.

From the corner of her eye she glanced at him again, appreciating how handsome he was. She wished she'd been able to enjoy their wedding more. He'd been right in front of her then, and she was supposed to look at him. But she'd been too busy trying to stay upright to enjoy the eye candy that was now her husband. She hoped he'd wear that suit again soon. Maybe someday they could dress up again and get some pictures together.

"Time for another bite," Carson ordered, staring at her with an exaggerated, stern expression until she brought a piece of chicken to her mouth. She hadn't felt up to eating Chinese, but he, and the ER nurse, had insisted she expand her diet beyond crackers. Fortunately the Chick-fil-A nuggets, fries, and frosted lemonade were thus far well received.

"Good girl." Carson slouched against the pillows again. "Another episode?"

"Of course." Bree felt an absurd rush of happiness as she sipped her drink and listened to the *Scooby-Doo* intro for the third time in the last hour and a half.

They'd needed to do something celebratory when they returned to the hotel. Usual wedding night activities were out of the question—for several reasons—and of course there was no reception with guests, cake, or dancing awaiting them.

But still, they'd done something significant and gutsy and brave. They'd finally been honest and were taking the right steps. Surely that deserved some sort of celebrating. And if not, well, they needed to relax after the stress of the last nearly twenty-four hours.

Carson had suggested they watch a movie, but a quick flip through the channels hadn't yielded anything they wanted to watch. No romantic comedies tonight or movies about weddings or wedding crashers or wedding planners or anything to do with getting married. No action films that might upset the balance in her easily upturned stomach. Bree especially hadn't wanted to risk any movies with intimate scenes that might do more than embarrass her. She didn't need a reminder of what had landed them in this situation, and she doubted Carson did either.

Cartoon Network to the rescue with a *Scooby-Doo* marathon. She'd been surprised at how much she was enjoying herself. It had been years since she'd watched Fred, Velma, Daphne, Shaggy, and Scooby unmask the bad guys, and it brought back a host of pleasant childhood memories.

"I can almost taste your mom's chocolate chip cookies as I watch these," Carson mumbled around a bite of chow mein. Now that he'd given up the chopsticks in favor of a plastic fork, he was shoveling his dinner in like a half-starved man.

"Me too." Bree smiled at the memory. The three of them often rotated houses after school. Carson's mom was into health food and usually served Fig Newtons and fruit for an after-school snack. Anna's mom's specialty was pecan bars. They had a tree in their backyard, and she always had plenty of pecans on hand.

But Anna, Carson, and Bree had all agreed that Bree's mom's chocolate chip cookies were the best. They could smell them baking a half a block away. They were always fresh-out-of-the-oven warm and served with ice-cold glasses of milk. Bree had the recipe memorized now, though to her they never tasted quite as good as Mom's. She wondered what Carson would think, if they'd taste the same to him. Her dad and brothers never seemed to notice a difference and usually polished off an entire batch the same day she baked them.

The idea of baking cookies for Carson instead of her brothers buoyed her spirits even more, and she hoped she'd keep feeling well enough to bake for him soon.

"Those were some good cookies," Carson said. "Just hearing the word *Scooby Snack* seems to conjure them."

"I wish," Bree said. "Mom would always bring the whole

plate out. She never cared how much we ate." She imagined herself seated on the couch beside Anna, with Carson on the other side. They'd always sat wedged together, both for easier access to the cookies on the coffee table and because they were simply that comfortable with one another.

Her happy mood fled suddenly. Their days of chumminess were over. Never again would the three of them pile on the couch beside one another. Anna might never speak to either of them again. And if she did, it wouldn't be as one friend to another.

Bree glanced at Carson and noted that his expression had changed too. *I'm sorry* hovered on the tip of her tongue again. But he'd asked her to quit saying that. They were both sorry, he'd said, but the time for apologies had passed. Now it was time for actions that would make things better—eventually. But Bree wasn't certain things with Anna could ever be better. And why should they?

Here I sit with Carson, while Anna is at home with her heart broken. Bree's self-loathing returned with a vengeance.

"Want to go sit in the hot tub?" Carson asked, as if the oppressive mood had reached him too.

"I can't," Bree said regretfully. "It isn't good for the baby."

"Oh." He sounded disappointed.

"I can swim, though. The pool is heated, isn't it?"

"Yeah. I think so." Carson looked over, a hopeful expression on his face.

"Let's go," Bree said. This certainly wasn't the Caribbean he'd planned to swim in on his honeymoon, and she wasn't Anna, but they could at least get wet and have some laughs. Plus, she usually won whenever they played Marco Polo.

"You cheated. I know it." Carson hoisted himself out of

the pool to sit on the deck and count. He was it again. There was no way Bree kept catching him without peeking.

"Did I cheat?" Bree turned to the group of kids gathered around who were playing with them.

They all shook their heads and called out an emphatic "No!"

"You're a slow swimmer," a seven-year-old named Mark said to Carson. "It's not your fault. Your mom just needs to get you more lessons."

Bree bit her lip, holding in a laugh.

Carson pointed to her. "You're going down, Mrs. Armstrong. Because these strong arms"—he raised his in a pose intended to show off his muscles—"are going to get you." Strong arms had been a joke between them forever. When he and Anna and Bree were just four years old, he'd boasted that his name meant he was strong and he could pick them both up—and he had, even though Anna had been taller than him at the time.

Instead of calling him by the name across his jersey, as most guys were called, he was always "Strong Arms" on the football and soccer fields. Carson had tried to keep himself in shape and live up to the name.

He stood to begin counting as he swung his arms back and forward, then clasped his hands together and cracked his knuckles. "Going down." He grinned at Bree.

"We'll see."

He closed his eyes, counted to twenty, and called out his first Marco. He slid into the pool and headed in the direction of Bree's voice.

When he thought he was close, he called again.

A girl's voice called a timid "Polo" right behind him, but he pretended not to hear and struck out toward Bree, on the opposite end of the pool now, if he judged her voice correctly.

When he reached the deep end and called once more, she

answered from the side he'd just left. She was a good swimmer, but the pool wasn't that wide that she should be able to get past him each time. Plus, he hadn't heard any splashing.

I know your game. He started swimming in the direction he'd just left but after a few strokes called, "Fish out of water."

To his surprise there was no response. Certain they were *all* cheating and conspiring against him, Carson opened one eye a crack but didn't see anyone on the deck. He felt a current beneath him and looked down to discover Bree, with all the kids following her, skimming the very bottom of the pool.

Instead of moving toward her at once, he stared for a few seconds, admiring the way she looked in a swimsuit. Bree wasn't tall, and she'd become almost too thin with this recent weight loss. But he still found her every bit as attractive. Before, she'd been a perfect fit when dancing, a perfect fit—

Carson slammed on the mental brakes. He wasn't going there. Not now. Not for a long time. But he hoped it wouldn't have to be—not ever. Bree was his wife now, and he hoped they'd have more children beyond the one they were expecting. Even more than that, he hoped someday their marriage would seem real, that they'd develop a genuine affection for each other as husband and wife.

Bree's casual comment about his kissing making a girl swoon gave him hope. *Not the time to test that.* Right now he'd be happy to hold her in his arms for a minute.

"Fish out of water," he called again, scrunching his eyes closed just as she surfaced. When there was again no answer, excepting several childish giggles, he called once more. "Marco."

The chorus of "Polos" came as expected, and he took off fast, only to switch tactics and rocket straight to the bottom of the pool when he'd crossed about half the distance. Carson opened his eyes below the surface, reasoning it wouldn't be cool if he grabbed some little kid the way he intended to grab Bree. He spotted her below and dove deeper, stretching out his hands and wrapping them around her waist. She flinched in obvious surprise and flipped over to face him.

He kept a tight hold on her and swam them both quickly to the surface.

"And you say I cheat," she spluttered.

Carson backed her against the pool wall. "If the shoe fits."

"Since when is swimming on the bottom of the pool cheating?" She struggled to brush the wet hair from her face.

He moved one of his hands from her side long enough to help, pushing the dark, silky strands aside. "It's not," he admitted. "I just—wanted to catch you." *Wanted to hold you like this.* "I wanted to be with you."

"Oh." Her eyes widened.

Bree sounded a little breathless, and he hoped it was from more than the exertion of her swim. Being near her like this, touching her, was definitely affecting his breathing.

"You caught me, so do you want to let me go now so I can count?"

No. He didn't want to let her go. Not at all.

"Or was there something else?" She tilted her head sideways just slightly, the same way she had since she was a little girl. For some reason today, he found the gesture, and her pouty lips that accompanied it, both endearing and sexy.

His mind scrambled for an answer. He couldn't tell her the real reason he was reluctant to let her go: that he was seriously attracted to her, that he had been for years, that today he'd finally allowed himself to acknowledge that, and that at least part of him felt relieved and hopeful and maybe even happy they were married. All of that sounded wrong. Or at the very least it was too much, too soon. It would make him seem even more of a louse.

He was supposed to be on his honeymoon with Anna

right now. So what did having these feelings for Bree make him? *A faithless pervert.*

"I wanted to catch you ... so I could tickle you!" He reached down, grabbed her feet, and began a relentless attack.

"Carson, you—" Her hands flailed in the water as she tried to support herself. Her legs twisted and tried to kick, but he held her feet tight, stroking his fingertips along their sensitive soles.

Bree shrieked and laughed out loud, then dipped backward beneath the surface. Carson immediately released her, pulling her up and pinning her against the wall once more.

"Thanks for swimming with me," he said. She tried to look angry but instead burst out laughing again just as a child-size, bright-pink flamingo swim tube was rammed over his head and encircled him, pinning his arms to his sides.

"Let her go," the kids they'd been playing with shouted from behind him.

Carson allowed himself to be towed away by his captors. "You'll pay for this later," he called to her.

"We'll see." She propped her elbows on the narrow shelf behind her and leaned back against the pool wall, laughing as she watched the kids climb all over him.

Thinking of the way Bree had been curled up and sick in the seat of his car last night, and how frightening it had been to see her put in the back of that ambulance this afternoon, he felt inordinately happy to see her laughing now. It was nothing short of a miracle.

They were going to need a few of those if this marriage was going to work. And he was determined that it was.

Tonight had been good. *Scooby-Doo* and swimming wasn't such a bad beginning after all.

Eight

ANNA. BREE WOKE suddenly, heart pounding, stomach revolting—or threatening to. She did her best to ignore it for the moment as she tried to decipher what had woken her. *A dream?* A nightmare was more like it. She'd been at Anna's house, upstairs in her bedroom, and Anna had been crying.

I did that to her. She'd hurt her best friends—both of them. The thud of Bree's heart quieted. Its beat slowed, but the pain there didn't cease. Bree felt like crying herself, imagining how Anna must feel right now. *I hope she hates me.* Being hated was the least Bree felt she deserved. And angry Anna was easier to imagine than heartbroken Anna.

Let her get good and mad—at both of us. Then let her meet someone wonderful who will mend her broken heart.

"Anna, wait," Carson's anguished voice cried.

Bree's heartbeat sped again, and a different kind of pain struck. *He loves Anna, not me. You've got to quit pretending.*

He groaned again and kicked one leg out of the blanket, as if he were trying to escape.

"Carson?" Bree rolled over to face him and reached for her phone. Holding it up as a light, she peered across the space between beds to see Carson asleep on his side, the leg out of the covers flung carelessly over a pillow and the edge of the bed.

"Anna." From his lips her name sounded almost reverent.

Bree sucked in a breath as she stared at his face. Carson's eyes were closed, his forehead wrinkled, as if with worry.

Carefully she put her phone on the nightstand and lay back against her own pillow in a vain attempt to contain her tender emotions. He was asleep, after all. Yesterday he'd been nothing but attentive and kind. If, in his sleep, Carson's thoughts turned to the life he'd planned to have, she shouldn't blame him.

But knowing his subconscious, his heart, was really with Anna instead of her did hurt. A lot.

Even more than her stomach was starting to, though Bree could tell it was well on the way to a full-blown eruption again.

The hated and life-saving bowl was on the bed beside her, but instead of leaning over it, Bree forced herself to get out of bed, hoping not to wake Carson. On tiptoes she crept to the bathroom and shut the door. She turned the faucet on to mask the sound, then fell to the floor in front of the toilet a second before last night's dinner reappeared.

Carson woke alone—normal, but for some reason that didn't seem right today. For one thing, the room was too dark. He hit the button on his watch, and in that brief flash of light and view of the hotel room, his mind reviewed the previous day's events.

"Bree?" Her bed was empty. Carson sat up and threw back the covers, panicking until he stood, walked to the end of the bed, and caught the sliver of light below the bathroom door.

He walked over to it and knocked quietly. "Bree? You okay?" He waited a minute, and when there was no answer, he turned the handle and pushed the door open just a bit. It stuck on something. Carson pushed the button on his watch again, illuminating the small space. The door was caught on a towel. They were spread all over the floor, with Bree, curled on her side and asleep, on top.

He budged the door a bit more, bunching the towel as it opened. He considered picking Bree up and tucking her back in bed, but she'd obviously come in here because she was ill. Waking her and risking her being sick again when, for now, she was sleeping peacefully, seemed a poor idea.

Instead Carson brought a blanket from the bed and covered her up. He also brought a pillow, but maneuvering it in place of the rolled towel currently beneath her head proved tricky.

"What are you doing?"

"Trying not to wake you." Carson smiled sheepishly. "Not doing a very good job of it, apparently."

Bree didn't say anything else but closed her eyes as he finished the pillow/towel exchange. "I can help you get back in bed, if you'd like. It's probably more comfortable than this hard floor."

"Nothing is comfortable," Bree murmured.

"Be right back." Carson jumped up and ran to get her vitamins. He returned with the smaller one, the one that was supposed to help her feel less nauseated. "Take this. Hopefully it will work as good as the shot last night."

She opened her mouth, and he popped the pill inside.

"Want some water?"

"No." She shook her head. "Maybe never. No more Chick-fil-A for me either."

"I'm sorry."

"Me too."

Carson tried to think of something else to say. He

considered brushing the hair back from her face or holding her hand but decided now wasn't the time to be touching her in any way. He sat on the floor in the doorway and waited until he was certain she slept again. Then he backed carefully out of the room and shut the door.

His watch showed that it was five thirty in the morning. Too early to go down to breakfast—not that he wanted to with Bree lying on the bathroom floor, unable to drink even a sip of water.

But he also didn't think he could go back to sleep. If he'd ever been asleep at all. It didn't feel like it. Last thing he remembered they'd been watching Shaggy and Scooby being chased through a castle by a knight. Carson didn't remember turning off the television. Bree must have, and he must have slept at least a few hours.

More than she did. He sat on the bed and considered what to do next. He thought briefly about calling Anna but decided against that almost at once. He'd told her the truth and given her a sincere apology in writing. Saying the same wasn't going to help anything, especially when the wound was so fresh. Besides, he hoped she was in Atlanta and then on her way to the Caribbean later today.

Thinking of that and not being there with her made him feel sick and sad all over again. Carson leaned forward, resting his head in his hands. He wished—he didn't know what he wished. That he hadn't hurt Anna—definitely. But that would mean he wouldn't be here with Bree, and as depressing as their situation was, he still couldn't feel entirely regretful about it.

Next to Bree and Anna, the person he was most worried about was his dad. Carson picked up his phone, turned it back on, and looked at it a long moment, uncertain now was the best time for that call either.

Maybe not. But Charlie . . . His brother would be able to

tell him how things were at home. Heedless of the early hour, Carson called him.

"Charlie?"

"What time is it?" was followed by a groan and the sound of Charlie fumbling with things on his nightstand—his glasses, probably.

"It's early," Carson said. "Sorry." His voice was unapologetic. How many times had Charlie woken him in the dead of night, either to talk or request a ride?

"Didn't think I'd be hearing from you," Charlie mumbled. "Aren't you supposed to be in the Bahamas or something?"

"Caribbean," Carson corrected. "But I put the tickets with the note I left for Anna. Marrying Bree wasn't a honeymoon type of occasion."

"Nope." Charlie chuckled. "Sounds like you already had the honeymoon."

Carson supposed he deserved that. "Not helpful. I'm calling to check on Dad. How is he?"

"Funny you should ask," Charlie said, without offering further detail.

"What do you mean?" A nagging unease stirred in Carson's gut. The night before last, when his world had imploded, he'd thought about going to his dad. It wouldn't have been a pleasant conversation, but Dad might have had some good advice. He would have known what to do, and that guidance might have been reassuring. It also might have been better for his dad to have heard the situation in person than to read it in a note.

But there hadn't been time—or so Carson had convinced himself. And the thing was, he'd already known what his dad would say, what needed to be done, what the right thing was, precisely because Dad had been teaching him those things his entire life.

That didn't ease Carson's concern or his conscience right

now. "Is Dad all right? Was he really upset?" Had Anna's family, or Bree's, taken their frustration out on him?

"I think it shook him pretty ba—ad." The last word widened, turning into an audible yawn.

"What makes you say that?" Carson asked. Of course it had shaken his dad. Not to mention embarrassed him. A few hours from now he'd have to stand in front of his congregation, every single member of which would know exactly what his son had done.

Carson stood and began pacing the narrow space between the beds.

"Well." Charlie spoke around another yawn. "He read your note yesterday morning, then stood by the mantel talking to Mom's picture."

"Nothing unusual about that." Another person talking to his deceased wife's picture might be weird, but their dad did it all the time. Carson kind of liked it, actually. It almost made it seem like Mom was still there with them.

"Yeah, but what he said was kind of weird."

"Which was . . ." Carson stopped and ran a hand through his hair in frustration. On some level he could tell Charlie was enjoying this. He was usually the one who messed up. Now that their roles were reversed, he probably felt like gloating.

Though I never did. Instead, he'd helped Charlie out of his mistakes more than a time or two.

"After Dad read your note, he stood there a minute, almost like he was listening. Then this odd expression grew on his face. It was almost a smile."

"What?" A smile? Charlie had to be making this up.

"I swear on Dad's Bible I'm telling the truth."

"Tell all of it, then, and be quick." Carson stared at the bathroom door. Bree could wake up at any minute, and he didn't want her more upset than she already was.

"I'm trying. You keep interrupting," Charlie whined.

Carson bit his tongue.

"Dad gets this slow smile. Then he walks over to Mom's picture, and he says, 'I suppose I should have listened to you . . .' He pauses. 'Suppose you were right. If I didn't know better, I'd say you had something to do with this, and a fine mess it's left me in. You'd best help me out. I'm going to need your wisdom on this one, Darlene.' Then Dad turned to me and said he was going to the cemetery to talk to Mom and he'd be back later. He asked me to return your tux to the rental place, and that was it."

"That makes no sense at all." Dad wasn't a big believer in visiting cemeteries. He said the dead weren't really there, their spirits had long departed, and he didn't need to stand over a grave to pay someone respect. Carson's worry increased. Maybe his actions *had* pushed his dad over the edge. "He didn't say anything else? He didn't mention going over to Anna's to do damage control or offer comfort or apologies or anything?"

"I think the apologies are your department, bro. Though it's too little, too late now, if you ask me."

"I didn't," Carson growled.

"Not that you could apologize, anyway. Anna's left town."

"She did?" Carson hoped she'd taken her mom or sister or cousin with her to the Caribbean. It wasn't much, but at least he'd know he'd paid for them to have a week in paradise to start to recover. "So Dad just left? Did he say anything when he came home later?"

"I don't know. I wasn't here. But he did say something as he left the house yesterday morning. He was still muttering to himself—or Mom. I swear it's like he really talks to her, you know. You don't think—that because he's a clergyman—that he can actually see her or hear her or anything, do you?"

"I don't know." Carson had wondered that himself. "He lives close to God. So maybe—"

"Well he was talking to her again as he left, and he said something like, 'If you end up being right, I'll be happy to hear I told you so.'"

"Right about what?" Carson felt more worried than he had been before he called. "It almost sounds like Mom expected this to happen—expected me to mess up royally."

"If the shoe fits," Charlie mumbled.

"That's low. Even from you." Carson felt the old familiar urge to pummel some sense into his brother.

"It was. I'm sorry," Charlie said, offering a rare apology. "You were always Mom's favorite. She wouldn't have thought you'd ever do something like this."

Not making me feel any better. Carson heard the undertone of sadness in Charlie's voice and forgot about himself for a minute. "You were her favorite, Charlie. You were her baby. I was the older one who always got you into trouble." They both knew the latter wasn't true—beyond their years of playing in the mud and sneaking frogs into the house, anyway. Carson had been guilty of both of those and several other boyish pranks. But for the past several years he'd done all he could to keep Charlie out of the serious kind of trouble. *And here I am, in it myself.*

"I think Dad had us both beat." Charlie still sounded melancholy.

"Yeah. You're right. He and Mom had a pretty amazing relationship. We had a good example of what marriage should be."

"Good luck following that." Charlie's voice held a flippant tone now. "This conversation's gotten boring, and if I hang up on you now, I can get a few more hours' sleep before church."

Wouldn't that be nice. For as tired as he'd been, Carson had slept terribly last night. Hopefully tonight would be better, in his own bed again.

And Bree . . . Where was she supposed to sleep? His apartment only had the one bedroom.

"Thanks for talking to me, Charlie. Keep an eye on Dad, okay? And call me if he gets worse or does something weirder."

"Will do. Enjoy your honeymoon. We'll see you around sometime, I guess."

"Yeah . . ." Carson's voice trailed off, noncommittal. He didn't know when they'd be back in Holiday again. He couldn't exactly show his face there for a while, and Bree wasn't going to be any more welcome than him. "Don't do anything stupid, okay? No drinking."

"Fine."

"I'm serious, Charlie. Dad's got enough on his plate right now." *And so do I.* "But if you ever need something, you know you can call, right? I'd still come."

"I know."

"Good." Carson wasn't sure whether or not to feel relieved. Had he just asked Charlie not to drink and then given him permission to, practically in the same breath? But what else could he do? Charlie needed to know he still had someone. "Take care."

"You too. Tell Bree I said hi." Charlie clicked off the call, leaving Carson alone with his thoughts and the pleasant sound of Bree vomiting on the other side of the bathroom door.

Nine

"YOUR PLACE IS really nice." Bree nibbled a saltine as she sat on a stool at the counter in Carson's apartment. She'd survived the two-and-a-half-hour drive from Chattanooga to Birmingham and was feeling only mildly nauseated—better than this time yesterday.

"*Our* place," Carson corrected. "For another three and a half months, at least."

"Then what?" She glanced around the room—plain brown sectional, bare walls, no dining table.

Carson followed her gaze. "It's a bachelor pad, I know. But check out the size of the television. Think of how frightening some of the monsters from *Scooby-Doo* will look on that thing."

Bree laughed. "You always find the bright side." She loved that about Carson. He always found a positive with everything, every situation.

His mouth turned down in a mock frown. "Are you saying you have to look for a bright side with this apartment?"

"No." She shook her head. "This is *much* nicer than my house, and we both know it." She wasn't sure if the carpet in the house she'd grown up in had ever been replaced. And there were so many things broken or needing repair that she'd given up making lists for her dad. Their furniture was old, the towels and sheets threadbare and stained. Pretty much everything about the house said "worn out." *Kind of like Dad is.* He'd stopped caring about the house and just about everything else after Mom died. Twelve years was a long time for a house—and its occupants—to go without care.

"Well, hopefully this won't be too bad for a few months." Carson's words brought Bree back to the present.

"It's only a one bedroom, and you can have that. I'll take the couch so I can binge Cartoon Network late without keeping you up."

"Hmm. We'll see." Bree had no intention of taking his bed or his room. The couch looked comfortable enough. "Your lease runs out in June?"

"Yeah. We were—I was thinking of buying a house after that."

"I know." Bree swiveled around on the stool to face him. "Anna told me you were looking at some in town—in Holiday. She wasn't certain she wanted to live there and commute that far—if she even took the job in Mobile." Better to tell Carson what she knew. Better that they talk about the elephant in the room, which, soon enough, would be herself waddling around in maternity clothes.

"I didn't mean to remind you—"

"It's going to be hard to forget for a while—that you planned to marry my best friend but got stuck with me instead."

"I did not get stuck with you." He sounded almost angry as he marched over to her. "I made the choice to do the right thing, to try to make the best of our mistake."

"Ouch." Bree placed a hand over her pained heart, then slid it down and held it protectively over her stomach. "I don't want our child ever hearing that, Mr. Armstrong." She glared at him. "I know that I'm the mistake, but this baby should never, ever feel that he or she was."

"Bree, I didn't mean—I'm sorry."

"Ah—" She held a hand up to silence him. "No more apologies. Your words."

"I need to take that back, then," Carson said. "I'm allowed to apologize every time I say something stupid or stick my foot in my mouth."

"Fair enough." Bree turned away and resumed nibbling the saltine.

Carson walked over to the cupboard and took out two glasses. "You aren't the mistake either. What we did—together—was."

She nodded but didn't say anything, not trusting herself to continue that conversation. It might have been a mistake on his part, but she'd known all too well what she was doing that night. Sick as she'd been in the weeks since, and as terrible as she felt about everything, Bree wasn't entirely certain she wouldn't make the same choice all over again. She'd seen her one opportunity to hold the man she'd loved for as long as she could remember and to be held by him in return, and she'd taken it. Though at the time, she'd believed it would be for only a few hours. She hadn't foreseen beyond those first few kisses and that they would both get carried away, swept up in a powerful tide of emotion.

Carson, at least, had an excuse for his instability that night. Hers could be attributed only to desperation and to the hope of creating a memory she'd cherish the rest of her life.

Now they both had a bit more than that to cherish.

"We're also going to have to talk about things too." Bree steered the topic to somewhat safer waters, or at least those that wouldn't endanger their day-old marriage. She knew she'd have to confess her feelings and motivation of that night to Carson sometime. But not yet, not when everything was so very fragile. "We can't tiptoe around the fact that you love Anna, that we both hurt her terribly, that we shamed our families and disappointed the entire town and can probably never go back there again."

Carson sighed. "You're right. About all of that. Except maybe not ever returning to Holiday. That's our home, and people forget."

"In a town of seven hundred and sixty-five? We're bigger news than a hurricane."

"Yeah. Probably." He sighed again.

Bree softened her voice. "I know you wanted to live there. Anna told me how you had your heart set on it."

He nodded. "She didn't, though. But she had that job offer, and I'd hoped . . ."

"You hoped for a lot of things, and now they're all gone." Bree slid off the stool and walked around the counter toward him, the instinct to offer comfort strong. It was what had landed them here in the first place, but she couldn't seem to care about that now. Carson was hurting, and if it was in her power to ease his pain, she wanted to.

"We're going to be okay." She paused a couple of feet away. "*You're* going to be okay too." She stepped forward, closing the gap between them, then circled her arms around his waist and laid her head against his chest. *I love you, Carson Armstrong.* She couldn't tell him that yet, but she could be strong for him. Her love would be steady. Enough for both of them, enough for all three when the baby came, though she desperately hoped Carson would love their child too.

It had been his mom who'd always said, "Love will find a way." *Let it find a way now,* Bree silently prayed. *Let us find our way.*

Ten

CARSON ROLLED OVER and looked at his phone. 4:02 a.m. Voices drifted from the other room—Bree's and one other he didn't recognize. *What?* He threw back the covers and stumbled out of bed. Who could she possibly be talking to? Was someone here? *One of her brothers, or her father?* It wouldn't have taken much for them to look him up and find his apartment.

As he crossed the dark room, he stubbed his toe on the wheel of his suitcase. He sucked in a breath and waited a few seconds without moving, fearful for Bree. The voices were still muted. It didn't appear that they'd heard him. Carson grabbed his phone from the nightstand, in case he needed to dial 911, and a book in his other hand, thinking he could throw it at the intruder and buy a second of distraction. *I should have insisted Bree take the bedroom.*

She'd said she'd be more comfortable on the sofa, where she could access the bathroom and kitchen easily if she was sick or needed to eat in the middle of the night. He'd reluctantly agreed but still felt like a cad sleeping in a queen-size bed while she had only a couch. *And now if she's in danger—*

He opened his bedroom door slowly and peered into the hall. It was dark, but a light shone from the living room. Not wanting to startle Bree or reveal himself to whoever was with her, Carson padded quietly, stopping at the end of the hall to listen and then peer cautiously around the corner with the book raised in his hand, ready to throw.

Bree sat on the floor, facing away from him, a laptop open on the coffee table in front of her, and her barf bowl—as she'd named it—on the floor beside her. She wore a clip on microphone and appeared to be talking to someone online. He stared at the scene a few seconds before full realization set in.

No one. Is. Here. Carson leaned his head back in relief and felt the adrenaline release. He lowered his hand. But who was she talking to at this hour? Maybe it *was* her father, trying to persuade her to come home.

Carson took another step closer, listening. *A child's voice.* Not her dad or brothers, then. His relief was complete, and he felt like an idiot, sneaking around his own apartment with a paperback for a weapon.

"Yes." Bree nodded. "You're right, Daiyu. I am someplace different this morning. I got married and moved this weekend."

Bree's voice had a smile to it, and Carson wished he could see her face. Was she happy about their marriage? He wished he knew, but she hadn't given him much to go on, excepting their brief play at the pool—when she'd seemed almost like her old self—and last night when she'd surprised him by giving him a hug and offering the reassurance she'd been so eager for herself all weekend.

He savored the memory for a minute, remembering the feeling of being held by her and holding her close. He was pretty sure she'd intended a brief hug, but he hadn't wanted to let go at all. It was the most physical contact they'd had since the night they created the baby she was carrying. And while he still felt every bit as attracted to her, last night the emotions enveloping him had been far different.

That night they'd been caught up in an unforeseen passion that had quickly engulfed them both. He understood the comparison to a flame or fire now. How many times had his dad warned him about that very thing, yet he'd succumbed and let it consume not only himself but one of his best friends as well.

Last night he hadn't even thought about kissing Bree. Having her in his arms and being in hers had been enough. Knowing that they were in this together, that come what may, it was the two of them against the world—if need be—made the trials of the last couple of days survivable.

I want us to do more than survive.

"Are you ready to begin?" Bree spoke into her microphone. The face on the screen nodded. Carson forced his mind to the present, and his bleary eyes focused. Bree was talking to a little girl.

"Great. First we're going to review some verb conjugations. Then I have some new vocabulary for you. I think you're going to love these words."

Bree was definitely smiling now. Carson caught a glimpse of her upturned mouth as she turned to the side to take a sip from her water bottle before beginning.

Carson stepped back into the shadow of the hallway and retreated to his room, though he doubted he'd sleep. What was Bree doing at four in the morning, teaching some kid online? She hadn't mentioned anything about this last night. He shut the door and lay back on his bed, listening to the muted voices, closing his eyes briefly and nodding off, only to look at the clock again at 4:45, 5:20, and 6:15.

At last the apartment was quiet. He thought he heard the click of a laptop being shut and got out of bed to check.

Bree was just taking off her microphone.

"Hey."

She jumped, clearly startled, though he'd spoken softly. "Good morning." She had a smile for him, too, and it eased the ache in his heart a bit.

"Did I wake you? I'm so sorry if I did."

"What were you doing?" Carson dropped onto the couch, and, bringing her bowl, Bree came and sat sideways on the other end, pulling her legs up to her chest and tucking her feet beneath her.

"I teach English to Chinese students five mornings a week. I should have told you. I'm really sorry I woke you."

"No worries. It was time for me to get up anyway." He didn't mention that he'd been awake since four a.m. "What, uh, time do you start teaching? How many students?"

"Only one at a time." Bree lay her head against the arm of the overstuffed couch. "I start at three thirty, and I teach five students."

"Three thirty?" He stared at her like she'd lost her mind. "Monday through Friday? How long have you been doing this?"

"Four and a half years." Bree stifled a yawn. "It's early here but not in China. It's not so bad getting up at three, once you're used to it. And I always wanted to be a grade school teacher. This is a tiny bit like that."

"I remember that you wanted to teach." Carson thought suddenly of the senior snippets in their high school yearbook. All graduating seniors were given space for a short paragraph beside their pictures to write their hopes and dreams. Bree's paragraph had mentioned being a teacher. What else had she said? He tried but couldn't remember. He wondered if Charlie could find the yearbook at home for him and read it over the phone. "Why *didn't* you become a teacher?"

He felt like an idiot the minute he asked the question. Everyone in Holiday knew Bree hadn't gone off to college or even had a job. *Except for this one, apparently.* There weren't a lot of employment opportunities in Holiday, and her father hadn't wanted her to move away while her brothers were still at home. Her dad had never really recovered from her mother's death and was a frequent customer at the one bar in town. Carson had seen him there almost every time he'd gone in to get Charlie and drag him home.

Bree's dad had a hard time keeping a job very long these days. It hadn't been that way before Bree's mother passed, but since then he'd been a mess—a ball of grief that had slowly unraveled, leaving only threads tenuously holding their family together. It was Bree who kept things going at their house. Bree, who did all the cooking and cleaning and shopping and laundry and gardening and even car repair. He'd helped her change a belt just last summer.

And now it seemed she maybe did even more than that.

"You never became a teacher because you were too busy taking care of your dad and brothers."

She shrugged. "Someone had to. But I'm still going to become a teacher—someday." She glanced at her stomach. "I suppose it will be a bit longer."

Carson sat up quickly as sudden inspiration struck. "Why don't you start college *now*? Here in Birmingham? You could start at Jefferson State and then transfer to the University of Alabama next year. I'll see if I can extend the lease, or better yet, we can find a bigger apartment. You could start spring term in a few weeks."

"It's not that simple." She reached for a blanket that had fallen to the floor. Carson beat her to it and picked it up, then stood to place it over her.

"Why not? If you're worried that it's been a while since you've been in school—don't. I can help you." He remembered that she'd earned her associate's through online courses about the same time he and Anna had been graduating with their bachelor's degrees. "Besides, you've already done your generals, and you're smart. Studying and memorization will come back to you, and you'll get the hang of it."

Bree looked up at him, her mouth twisted with a hint of exasperation. "I've done a bit more than my generals, Carson. I've done everything except my practicum—student teaching. I've been going to school almost nonstop, albeit slowly, mostly a class or two at a time, since we graduated from high school."

"Oh." Why hadn't he known this? What had he been thinking, anyway, offering to help *her* with classes? Bree had always been a better student than him. Anna had been the valedictorian the year they'd all graduated, but it was Bree who'd been awarded the faculty scholarship. "That's right. You had a scholarship. But you never mentioned using it. You never went away to college. Except that one summer."

At least he didn't think she had. Though he'd been gone a lot in the years since high school, he still felt like he and Bree had stayed connected, talking and texting. It had been every day at first, then a few times a week, then in the last couple of years a few times a month—usually. They always saw each other when he was home. Yet, she hadn't mentioned college or classes, tests, anything having to do with school, for a long time. *Did I ever ask her?*

"There are other ways to attend a university, aside from physically going to one. You should know that, Mr. Web-developer-have-laptop-can-work-from-anywhere."

Bree pulled the blanket up closer to her chin and snuggled into the couch pillows as if preparing to go to sleep. She did look pretty tired. *And just pretty.* Considering the hour, she didn't at all look like she'd either been up since three thirty or barely rolled out of bed. She'd pulled her hair back into a low ponytail, put a little bit of makeup on, and dressed in a pretty blouse and a pair of jeans that showed off her figure.

Carson forced his gaze from the curve of her hip to her eyes just starting to close. "How come you never told me?" *Why do I know nothing about my wife—one of my best friends?*

"There wasn't much to tell." Bree opened her eyes enough to look at him. "Almost everything was online, except for the summer I went to stay with Grandma Fay. I managed fifteen credits on campus then." Bree smiled wistfully. "I really did love it, but my dad and brothers weren't doing so well at home, so I came back."

"You shouldn't have," Carson said. "You deserve to go to school, Bree, to do the things you want to do, to have dreams."

"I will finish, and I do have dreams. I've saved over twelve thousand dollars from this job. When I have fifteen, that will be enough to support myself while I do my student teaching."

Twelve thousand dollars saved, over the course of four years—a miracle and a pittance at the same time. Carson easily guessed what she let remain unsaid. The online teaching job probably didn't pay all that great, but no doubt Bree saved every penny she made—except those she used to keep her family afloat.

"What's your dad going to do without you—and your income?"

Bree's eyes widened. "Still perceptive, I see."

"Not that much." Carson shook his head, disgusted with himself. "Since I didn't even know you were going to school."

"That's just it," Bree said. "I wasn't really *going*. Not like you and Anna were. It was much better for me to listen to your stories about everything happening where each of you were—Anna and her sorority, you and your funny roommates, the professors you loved, the football games and parties, how it felt to be one person on such a big campus, internships, landing your dream job. I loved hearing all of that. It helped me experience it a bit, even though I wasn't there."

"Well you're going to be there now," Carson declared, rising from the couch. "Take a nap. Get some rest. I'll make breakfast in a bit—don't worry—nothing with an aroma to upset your stomach. Just toast and some fruit. Then we're going to see what we can do to get you set up to do your student teaching."

"I can't go to school when I'm pregnant."

"Sure you can," Carson said. "You taught this morning, didn't you?"

"Yes, but I threw up twice between students."

"So throw up between classes instead, or when your students are at recess or something. You can do this, Bree. You really can. You shouldn't be limited to teaching a few kids in China but should have a whole classroom of your own right here. Think of all the good you could do—all the fun you'd have."

"It would be fun, wouldn't it?" She sighed.

"Will be," Carson corrected. "I've worked with the university on a few projects lately. I'm going to make some calls and see if we can get a bit of help from inside."

Bree didn't have a response for this, but she still appeared uncertain.

"Wouldn't you like that?" Carson asked, worried he was pushing her. "Would you like to spend spring and summer student teaching and then be able to graduate in the fall?" He imagined her walking across a stage in a cap and gown while he sat in the audience cheering her on.

"What about the baby?"

"You're only what—about eleven or twelve weeks pregnant? You've got time to finish before the baby comes. And after, if you want to teach, I can adjust my schedule so you can, part time at least. I can stay home with the baby too. We can make this work out. Have a little faith."

Their eyes met, hers crinkling slightly. "You sound like your—"

"Dad," Carson finished, having realized it himself the second the words were out of his mouth. If he had a dollar for every time his dad had said that to him over the years. "Well, he is a pretty great guy. Pretty smart."

"He is." Bree's gaze softened, full of hope and . . . Carson wasn't sure.

"Maybe you're right."

He grinned. "Words every husband dreams of hearing."

She returned his smile. "Don't get too used to it."

Eleven

Saint Patrick's Day

"A WORK PARTY?" Bree picked at her baked potato. Her stomach had been feeling better the past week and a half, but the idea of going to a big, swanky event where she didn't know anyone other than Carson made her feel ill all over again.

"The owner of the company comes from strong Irish stock. He hosts a big party every March to celebrate Saint Patrick's Day and his heritage, along with the company's achievements over the year. It's a lot of fun—great food, good music, dancing..."

"If you're talking Irish step dancing, this could be a disaster in the making."

Carson grinned. "No. Sometimes they have entertainment and there's a performing group, but the employees aren't expected to have any talent in that realm."

"That's a relief." Bree took a long drink of water and tried to shake off the feeling of foreboding. Once upon a time—several times, over a decade of them—she would have loved the idea of Carson inviting her to an event like this. For years she'd secretly dreamed of going on dates with him, but the only real date they'd ever had was the junior prom when Anna was at home with the flu.

But now . . . This would be the first event Bree attended as his wife. What if she became ill during dinner? What if everyone asked about their courtship or honeymoon?

Because Carson wasn't in the office every day or even every week sometimes, no one at his work knew about the last-minute bride switch—or about the baby they were expecting and that would arrive well before they'd been married nine months. Carson had made sure to stay away from the office all during the week he and Anna were supposed to have been on their honeymoon. When he'd returned he'd acted as if everything was normal, not seeing the need to tell anyone what had actually transpired in the past week.

Bree understood why he'd done that, and she was grateful—mostly. But someday she hoped the truth wouldn't be so awkward and painful for both of them. In the meantime, an event like this seemed a perfect opportunity for someone to realize that his marriage wasn't exactly as he'd planned.

What if someone noticed she didn't look like the pictures Carson had kept on his desk for so long but had brought home his first day back to work? Bree had found them in the trash when she went to take it out the next day and had spent a good hour by herself sobbing. Viewing the evidence of Carson and Anna's love had felt like a knife twisting into her gut. Hers was going to be a slow, painful death, the poison of guilt trickling daily through her veins, spreading, blackening her soul.

It was no less than she deserved for ruining both of her best friends' lives. She didn't want to ruin Carson's any more by making a spectacle of herself at some fancy dinner. Surely someone there would notice she wasn't the woman he'd brought last year.

"I don't have anything nice to wear." That was definitely true. The bridesmaid dress she'd gotten married in was still the nicest thing in her wardrobe, but if Carson suggested she wear that, she might punch him.

"Can you go shopping for something? Tomorrow after class?"

"Maybe. I'll have lesson plans to prepare, though." The term had started a week ago and was already more intense than she had imagined it would be.

"Breeeee ..." He held out her name, using his whiny, nasally voice that dated back to their childhood whenever she'd had a toy he wanted.

She laughed. She couldn't help it. "Fine. I'll go buy a dress." And some shoes. Heels to make her look taller. Maybe she should dye her hair blonde too. *As if that would convince anyone I'm Anna.*

"What's wrong?" Carson reached across the table, then hesitated, grabbing the salt instead of her hand. "I can tell when something is bothering you."

Some of the time. She'd had to work hard over the years to hide her feelings from him. To not could have resulted in disaster. *Kind of like it did.*

Bree picked at her potato again, wishing she'd thought to mask her feelings a bit better tonight. But he'd surprised her with this party request. *Might as well tell him the truth.*

"Won't someone think it's odd that I'm not Anna? That you're with someone else and not the fiancée you brought last year?"

"No." He sat back quickly, as if stunned at her words. "I never brought Anna to this party. She could never come. She was always in the middle of an excursion or an internship— something. No one from my office has ever met her."

"Oh." Bree gave an audible sigh of relief and offered him a wan smile. Anna hadn't been an entirely perfect fiancée. That shouldn't have made Bree happy—and it didn't, because she could tell that on some level Carson had been hurt by Anna—but it did ease her feelings of inadequacy the tiniest bit. Enough that Bree felt she could attend a swanky dinner on the arm of her new husband. "In that case, I'd be delighted to go, Mr. Armstrong."

Carson straightened his tie, then reached in the closet for his dress shoes. Bree had been in the bathroom since he'd arrived home twenty minutes ago, and he was starting to worry she might be sick. She hadn't thrown up for a while, but that didn't necessarily mean she wouldn't again.

He left his room and stepped out into the hall, pausing in front of the bathroom door, debating whether or not he should knock and ask if she was all right. Before he could decide, the knob turned and the door opened.

"Carson." She jumped a little at seeing him so close, and her hand, complete with newly polished nails, covered her heart. "You scared me."

"I'm sorry. I didn't mean to. I was just—" What had he been doing? All rational thought seemed to leave his brain as he stared at her. The vanity light shone down like a halo over her crown of rich brown curls, swept up elegantly in some fancy hairstyle, reminiscent of prom so long ago.

An emerald-green evening gown clung to her in all the right places, emphasizing a body that none of his coworkers would ever guess housed a developing baby. If she'd gained any weight yet, it wasn't at her waistline. The dress had a shimmer to it when she moved that matched the sparkle of her earrings and necklace. His eyes drifted down the length of the delicate chain to the hollow of her neck—and beyond.

His throat felt suddenly dry. *A man in a desert desperate for a drink.* It was all he could do not to fall at her knees to worship her.

Exactly what he had better do if ever there was a next time

between the two of them. He reined in his lustful feelings as a heavy dose of shame and remorse overrode any passion he might have been feeling about Bree. He'd not treated her well before, and he never wanted to make that mistake again. His actions *had* been like those of a man in a desert, desperate for a drink from the well. He'd been selfish—and rushed and clumsy and awkward. He knew he'd hurt her—physically then and emotionally still.

Making that up to her—if such a thing was even possible—was going to take a lot, and it certainly didn't include sweeping her off her feet and carrying her to the bedroom when she'd dressed for an evening out.

"Carson? What's wrong? You're looking at me funny." Bree turned back to study her reflection in the mirror. "Is this lipstick too much?"

"No." *Yes. Let me take care of that for you—with my lips.*

His conscience was going to have to work overtime tonight. "Your lipstick is perfect—like the rest of you. You're beautiful, Bree. All my coworkers are going to be jealous."

"Good." She flipped off the light and sauntered into the hall with a confidence she didn't usually show.

He caught her arm as she passed. "Thank you for agreeing to come." He'd never had a date to this party before. The past two years he'd asked Anna, and always she'd had some other commitment that took priority. This year he wouldn't have to come up with an excuse for being dateless. This year he'd have the prettiest woman at the party at his side. "It means a lot to me."

Bree's expression softened from mischievous to tender. "Of course. I'm sorry I was hesitant at first. I'm happy to come with you."

They stood close another moment, his hand on her arm, her expression not quite readable in the dim light of the hall.

Her lips pressed together, rubbing the dark gloss alluringly. His gaze lingered on them longer than was gentlemanly while he continued to fight urges similar to those he'd felt that fateful November night.

Fearing they'd never get to the party, he released her. "After you." He held his hand out, indicating she should go ahead.

Bree crossed the living room, heading for the front door, while Carson groaned silently. *That dress.* This view wasn't any harder on the eyes than seeing her from the front. It was going to be a long night.

Twenty minutes later he wasn't sure he'd ever felt so euphoric as he helped Bree from the car and they strolled into the lobby of the Grand Bohemian Hotel.

Bree leaned close to whisper in his ear. "Do you realize that you're practically strutting?"

In response he stuck his neck out farther and bobbed with each step. "Let me enjoy my moment of glory, will you?"

Bree laughed. "Glory?"

"Yeah." He bent his head near to hers. "Walking into the office party with my beautiful *wife.*" He gave her a quick kiss on the cheek and enjoyed her resulting blush.

They'd arrived fashionably late, about fifteen minutes into the evening. Carson spotted his boss and steered Bree toward him. "I need to introduce you to a couple of people. Then we'll eat."

"No rush." She pressed a hand to her stomach.

"Nervous or sick?" he asked, concerned.

"Hard to tell. Right about now they both feel the same."

"We'll hurry with the introductions, then." Carson said hello to a few people as they made their way across the large room and introduced Bree when they weren't interrupting another conversation. They stopped a few feet away from the CEO, Connor Sheehan, who stood with his back to them, sporting a navy-and-green Irish dress kilt, long black dress socks, and a jaunty cap. Not everyone could pull off that look, especially in a place often dominated by bolo ties, but Connor did. Carson wouldn't be surprised to find him wearing that ensemble featured on the cover of *GQ* someday.

"Connor doesn't just dress like that for Saint Patrick's Day. He wears a kilt to the office pretty regularly too," Carson explained to Bree.

"I like it," she said, turning slightly to face Carson. "You should try it sometime. Maybe for the next company party."

"Wouldn't your brothers have fun with that," Carson said. They'd taken opportunity to razz him enough about everything else over the years. But he doubted they'd feel friendly enough toward him to joke about anything for a good long time.

"Carson. Good to see you." Connor came toward them, leaving the group he'd been talking with. "This must be your lovely wife—Anna, isn't it? So sorry we were out of the country and couldn't attend the wedding." Connor extended a hand toward Bree.

She accepted it, dazzling them both with a smile. "*Bre*anna," she said casually, not missing a beat. "It's so nice to finally meet you."

"No excursions this year, eh? Have you decided on that job down south yet? The West Coast would make a long commute for your husband, even if it is only a few times a month that we need him in house."

"We'll be staying in the South," Bree said.

"Excellent." Connor looked at Carson. "I'll keep that in mind when it's time for promotions. Now that I know we get to keep you . . ."

Breanna looped her arm through Carson's. "He's definitely a keeper." She tilted her head, giving Carson an adoring, heart-stopping smile.

"You're a smart lady, and he's a lucky man." Connor clapped Carson on the shoulder. "Nice to meet you, *Bre*anna. Have a wonderful time tonight. Be sure to try some of the colcannon and have a Guinness or two." He turned away, hand already extended to the next couple waiting to greet him.

Carson took Bree's hand, threading their fingers together. "You were brilliant. Thanks."

She let out an exaggerated breath and sagged against him for a second. "Glad to have passed muster."

"Oh, you more than passed." He tugged on her hand, pulling her toward the center of the room. "Let's dance."

"Now?" The panicked look he'd seen yesterday returned to her eyes. "We haven't even had dinner yet."

"Eating for two already, are you, Mrs. Armstrong?" Carson whispered in her ear. "Don't worry. I promise to feed you. And the food at these things is always great. But dance with me first—please."

"All right, Mr. Strong Arms. Just no sweeping me off my feet in front of all these people."

As if I could. It was going to take a lot more than twirling Bree around a dance floor to win her heart.

Only two other couples were dancing, but he wouldn't have cared if there hadn't been any or if there were a hundred. He wanted to hold Bree, and dancing seemed an opportunity too good to pass up.

He reached for her other hand, pulling her close so they stood facing each other. "It's been a long time," he said, referring to more than the last time they'd danced. In the month since they'd married, they seemed to have grown further apart instead of closer, each almost tiptoeing around the other, as they tried to figure out how to act, how to be married.

Carson had found himself going into the office a few

times a week instead of working from home—giving his coworkers the legitimate excuse that his wife was a distraction.

"I may have forgotten how to dance," Bree said quietly, almost shyly. Now that his boss was out of earshot, the act was over, and her reserve seemed to be returning.

"Let me remind you." Carson placed a hand at the small of her back and pulled her close. Keeping hold of her other hand, he tucked it between them, near his heart. He hoped he could remind her of other things, too, tonight. Like how much they used to confide in each other and how much fun they used to have. He'd even settle for watching an episode of *Scooby-Doo* together from opposite ends of the couch.

The evening of their wedding seemed a long time ago, in another place. They'd settled into the routine of an old married couple who'd grown distant all too easily and quickly.

Bree moved stiffly in his arms, matching his slow steps but keeping her body rigid and aloof, much the same way she'd been with everything lately. Since she had started school, she seemed to be getting home later and later, almost making him regret that he'd insisted she take the car each day. He'd wanted her to be safe, and with his flexible schedule it wasn't a big deal for him to use his MAX pass to get to and from work.

What he really wanted was to reconnect with Bree, to feel the easy camaraderie they'd shared for so many years. Several times he'd felt they were on the brink, but always something held them back in that distant, *safe* zone.

Safe from me. Carson didn't think Bree was afraid of him—exactly. After all, she'd agreed to marry him. But she certainly had reason to be wary. Stacked against their years of being best friends was that one night that felt like a concrete wall between them. Until they figured out how to breach it, and how to deal with their guilt about Anna, he wasn't certain they could regain the ground they'd lost. It terrified him to think of losing any more.

He'd lost Anna already, had made that painful choice and was coming to accept the consequences of it. The only consolation in that decision was that it had meant he had Bree, that they were in this together. In those initial moments, hours, and days of realization and panic and regret, she'd been the one constant, the reason he kept hope that everything would end up all right in the end.

But without her . . . It all fell apart. Emotions that had nothing to do with physical desire made him want to hold her as close as he could and never let her go.

The best he could hope for tonight was that holding Bree in his arms—in a very public, safe setting—might convey a little of what he felt.

The music changed to a slower beat, and he took his chance, wrapping his arm around her a little more and bending his head closer to hers. For a second Bree seemed to freeze, then it was as if a chink of armor fell away or a piece of the wall between them tumbled down. Carson felt, rather than heard, her sigh. Her body softened, becoming more pliable, molding against him.

The side of her face brushed his for a second, then returned to stay there so they were dancing cheek to cheek, possible only because of the heels she wore. He remembered wishing for this when they'd danced at prom, but he hadn't dared to initiate such closeness. As it was, he'd been playing with fire, just holding her in his arms. The thought of touching her face—and then possibly, accidentally, her lips—had been both terrifying and exhilarating and had haunted him all that night and many more after.

He'd wondered for years if it might possibly have been the same, or something like it, for her. "Did you know I wanted to dance like this with you at prom?"

"You did?" She leaned back just a little, as if searching his face for the truth of that statement.

"Yeah." Carson forced himself to look in her eyes and not at her tempting lips. "I—something happened that night. Between us. Or for me, at least."

Bree nodded, and her smile seemed sad. "I know. I felt it too." She moved again, so her face was close to his once more. Carson hugged her a little tighter, discouraged she hadn't said more, hadn't let him know if his feelings had been or were at all reciprocated.

"I wanted to do this," Bree whispered, a few turns later. Her hand left his shoulder and made its way behind his neck, brushing the base of his hair. "You've always had the most gorgeous curls."

"The compliment every guy dreams of hearing," he joked, though her confession had his heart soaring.

Bree laughed. The intimacy of a moment before fled, and he was sorry for it.

"It's true," she said. "Don't you remember when we were little and I was always touching your hair? Then we got older—and it would have been weird if I was sitting behind you in class, petting your head."

Weird, but he would have liked it. But that would have caused all kinds of problems with Anna. "I had no idea you were having hair envy all these years." What else didn't he know?

"Not envy, exactly." Bree's fingers continued their gentle, tickling touch. "I didn't wish for those locks for myself, but I always thought of what adorable children you and Anna would have—with her blonde hair and your curls." Bree's eyes welled with sudden tears.

An infusion of guilt that had far more to do with Bree than Anna surged through him. "Brown hair is beautiful too."

Carson stopped swaying, caught Bree's gaze, and held it. "I didn't date Anna for her hair color, and I didn't marry you for yours. Did you date Robbie because of his rainbow hair?"

"No. " She shook her head. "I dated him so people wouldn't talk about the possibility that you and I were going to be a thing after prom."

"You did?" Was that really the only reason? "I mean, did you even like him?"

"As a friend." Bree shrugged. "He was always very kind to me, and it was nice to have my own dates once in a while, instead of being third wheel to you and Anna all the time."

And now? Did she still feel like a third wheel? Somehow Carson knew, without asking, that she did, that Bree didn't feel like she belonged in this marriage or with him. He felt the same way himself sometimes—a lot of the time. He'd never imagined being married to Bree, but for as long as he could remember, he had planned on being married to Anna.

But he wanted to imagine it, to figure it all out and make it work.

Bree's hand had ceased touching his hair and slid back to its proper position on his shoulder.

Carson began moving again, slow, solid footsteps around the floor, with hers matched, one foot between his two and her other foot barely outside his shoe. *So close and yet...* "There's only the two of us now." It was just going to take some getting used to.

She stopped suddenly, a look of wonder crossing her face as she gazed past him. Carson turned to look but saw nothing out of the ordinary.

"You okay?"

"Shh." She squeezed his hand, then stood perfectly still.

"What are we waiting for?" he whispered.

"The baby—it *moved.*" Her smile contained all the glee

of a child finding just what she wanted beneath the tree on Christmas morning.

"It did?" Carson stepped back to look at her stomach.

"Don't." She pulled him toward her, wrapping both arms around his neck and leaning close. "You don't want anyone to think—"

"That my wife is carrying our child?" Carson began turning them slowly again. "People are going to find out sooner or later, Bree. And you know what? I'll be happy when they do. I'm not ashamed of this baby—or you. Tonight, introducing you as my wife was seriously awesome."

Her gaze softened. "Thank you. That means a lot."

"Can I feel the baby move at home?" he asked, almost pleading. She'd gone to her first OB appointment without him, without even telling him until it had passed. He'd been hurt but tried not to make a big deal about it. How was he supposed to convey that he wanted to be a part of this? To be a real father?

"Maybe." She turned her head away, as if suddenly shy about something.

Again he wondered if she wasn't a bit afraid of him now. "Please don't shut me out, Bree. Let me go through this with you—as much as I can. I was wrong about there being just the two of us now. We're three—you and me and our child. We may have started things off wrong, but that doesn't mean we can't be a great family."

Twelve

BENEATH CARSON'S WATCHFUL eye, Bree chugged the entire glass of ice water.

"Poor kid, the cold shower treatment already," Carson teased, then rubbed his hands together gleefully. "All right then. Let's get this party started."

"Patience." Bree swung her legs up on the sofa, lay back, and closed her eyes, trying not to think about the last time she'd lain on a couch with Carson so close. "He doesn't always move. It's not an on demand kind of thing."

"How do you know it's a boy? Did they tell you that at your appointment?"

"No. I would have told you sooner or had you come with me if they were going to do an ultrasound. That appointment is next month."

"Oh. Good." He sounded relieved.

Bree opened one eye a crack and peeked at Carson, perched on the edge of the coffee table, hands extended as if he were a catcher expecting a fastball. She had a sudden vision of him at the hospital, with the same pose, waiting to catch their baby. The thought of him being there with her was both comforting and horrifying. Though they'd made a baby together, he'd never actually seen her without clothes on. So how was she supposed to handle him seeing her give birth? Yet how could she go through it without him?

The recently familiar flutter inside her started again. She chanced another look at Carson, still staring intently at her unmoving stomach. He hadn't noticed anything. It was tempting to tell him there wasn't any movement tonight. But he'd seemed genuinely interested—envious, almost—that she could feel the baby now. She supposed letting him touch her stomach was as good a place as any to start their journey to togetherness at the hospital labor and delivery room. Sooner or later, she had to get comfortable with him touching and seeing her.

"He just moved." Bree reached up and took one of Carson's hands. Her other hand tugged her shirt up slightly. "Right here." She placed his hand on her stomach, just below her belly button, then kept hers over it. "Hold very still. Hopefully he'll move again."

Carson nodded but didn't say anything. Bree resumed her eyes-closed position, this time reveling in the feeling of his warm hand against her skin. Such a simple thing, yet it had her all pleasant and tingly, her insides quivering with even stranger sensations than those caused by the baby.

It was a good thing she was lying down, because his touch made her light-headed too. *Swoony.* Apparently there was some truth to all those romance novels she'd read as a teen.

The baby moved again, a little stronger this time, probably pushing back against the external pressure of their hands.

Carson turned his face toward her, his eyes wide with wonder. "I felt—"

The fluttering came a third time. The little guy was putting on quite a show tonight. *Trying to impress his dad.* Bree smiled, this time imagining Carson with a chubby toddler in his arms.

"Incredible." Carson's grin stretched wider. "This is awesome. Can we do this every night?"

Bree felt herself blushing. Could they sit close with his hand on her stomach every night? "Sure." It might kill her. "After my lesson plans are done." The past three days since his work party, she'd put him off with that excuse. Somehow she thought it wasn't going to be as easy to avoid from now on. If only he realized what he was doing to her, what sweet torture this was.

If only he'd kiss me like last time...

What came after hadn't exactly been amazing—frantic fumbling in the dark on her old sofa wasn't her dream of romance. But the kisses that came before... Even after she'd found out she was pregnant, she hadn't been able to say she completely regretted that night.

Which makes me a terrible, horrible person. The thought of Anna was enough to quell Bree's growing desire tonight and to make her regret promising Carson they could do this again.

"Show's over." She tugged down her shirt and brushed his hand away. "I'm glad you felt him, though."

"Me too." Carson's eyes were shining. Or maybe it was the lamplight. She couldn't be sure.

"Is it wrong of me"—he leaned closer, over her—"to hope this baby is a girl and looks and *is* just like you?" He brushed a kiss across Bree's forehead, sat back and watched her a minute, then stood abruptly and headed to the kitchen. "Want some ice cream?"

Bree tried to answer but couldn't. Her throat constricted, and her own eyes stung. Carson was so good. If only she deserved him.

Thirteen

Easter

"BREE?" CARSON SET the takeout bags and his laptop case on the counter. He'd promised to bring home dinner tonight, as Bree had a big day tomorrow, teaching in front of not only the fifth grade class and the teacher she was working with but evaluators from the university as well.

"Hello," Carson called again. Their car was in its parking stall, so he knew she was home. *Asleep, maybe.* Poor girl was always tired. This baby wore her out, and he wasn't even born yet. As soon as he was, though, Carson vowed he'd do his part to alleviate Bree's burden. Their baby wouldn't be a burden at all. It really would be a bundle of joy—for him at least. And hopefully for Bree as well.

He crossed the living room and turned down the hall into the bedroom, hoping she'd finally taken him up on his offer to use the bed. Though he felt awful about her sleeping on the couch, he hadn't pushed her to take the bedroom, afraid that she feared something more than sleep happening if she stayed there. Like everything else between them, it was a fine line they walked.

Sometimes, occasionally, it seemed they were perfectly balanced and connected, like those few moments at his work party when they'd danced. Other times—too many of them—he felt Bree's reluctance to be close to him and felt her pulling away when he tried. So he didn't try too often. *In time,* he told himself. It would all work out in time.

Carson passed the bathroom, noting the light beneath the door. He paused, not wanting to intrude on her privacy but wanting to let her know he was home. Unsure exactly what to do, he took a few steps back so he stood at the edge of the living room once more. "I'm home, and I brought food," he called loudly.

No response. He stepped closer again, listening. The fan wasn't running, so she should hear him. "Bree? Everything okay?"

Silence. Forgetting protocol and privacy, Carson knocked on the door. "Bree? Can you let me know you're all right?"

When she didn't answer this time, he turned the knob and pushed the unlocked door open. The red stain on the tile caught his eye first. In the fraction of a second it took to follow it to Bree, unconscious on the bathroom floor, he had his phone out, his thumb punching 911.

He fell to his knees and reached for her arm, then checked for a pulse, pressing hard until he felt the faintest throb against his fingers. *Thank you, God.*

"Nine-one-one. What is your emergency?"

"My wife is on the floor in a pool of blood. Send help. Quick."

"Dad."

"What is it, son? What's wrong?"

Short-lived relief washed over Carson at hearing his father's voice. Though he'd done a stupid, terrible thing and then hadn't spoken to his dad in nearly two months—the longest in his life they'd ever gone without speaking—the connection between them wasn't broken.

"Where are you, son? Tell me what you need, and I'll be there as soon as I can."

Tears flooded Carson's eyes. What he needed was his dad's arms around him, strong and sure and safe, just like they'd been when he was a little boy. Instead, he had an awful favor to ask this man he loved and respected more than nearly anything or anyone. "Can you—can you go over to the Wagners' house and tell Bree's father—" *What?* Carson pressed his forehead against the waiting room wall and worked to hold back the sob at the edge of his throat. *That she might die because I got her pregnant?* That her last lucid minutes might have been spent alone, on a bathroom floor, as her baby's life and then her own ebbed away? "Tell him to come," he choked out. "Bree—emergency surgery."

Somehow he managed to sputter the name of the hospital and enough details that his father understood. They hung up, leaving Carson feeling entirely alone again, in this waiting room full of strangers. For a full minute he kept his phone pressed to his ear, as if drawing the last dregs of strength from the call and the giant of a man who'd been on the other end.

Not a literal giant—his father had a slight build that both Carson and Charlie had passed up years ago. But what their dad lacked in stature he more than made up for in spirit and wisdom. He always seemed to know what to say, what to do, what the right thing was, or—in cases where wrong had been done—how to make it right.

It was too crowded to pace, so Carson slumped in a chair, then leaned forward, elbows braced on his knees, and put his head in his hands. Why hadn't he called his father sooner? Weeks ago? Or better yet, sought his counsel the very night he and Bree had eloped. *Instead of eloping?* No. He felt confident that marrying her had been the right thing to do. But if he'd confided in his father or faced up to their mistake and stayed in Holiday, she might not have been alone today. She might have made it to the hospital in time to save their baby. *And herself.*

Now it was too late for their child, and maybe too late for Bree. The paramedics hadn't minced words as they pushed him out of the way and worked over her feverishly. She'd been close to death. Only a miracle might save her now.

Carson jumped up and practically ran across the room. "Where is your chapel?" he asked the nurse seated behind the counter. Before she'd finished giving directions, he was taking brisk steps.

"Thank you," he called over his shoulder, somehow remembering that in times of personal crisis he still needed to show kindness and gratitude. How many times had his dad, by example, taught him that very thing over the years? *Especially at the hospital when Mom was dying.* When Dad had every reason to feel angry or overly emotional, to not care about others or their problems, he'd still taken the time to. Dad had also taught him that he was never truly alone—unless he wanted to be.

If you remove yourself from God . . . You're only making life harder. He will always be with you, if you'll only ask.

Inside the tiny chapel, Carson slipped into a pew and bowed his head. He hadn't meant to abandon God any more than he'd meant to abandon his father. He'd let both down. Avoiding them had seemed less painful than facing them. Only now did Carson realize what a mistake that had been and how he'd been floundering—even before today—going this alone. He needed both God and his father in his life to help him make this marriage work. Even more, right now, he needed heaven's blessing for Bree.

He needed a miracle.

Fourteen

CARSON PACED THE oval waiting room, down, around, and back again. At two a.m. he had the place to himself. It was better than the ER waiting room he'd first been in, better than a few hours ago when he wasn't the only one awaiting news of a loved one in surgery. The others had come and gone—one with good news, one without. A father's heart attack had been caught in time. Quick thinking, an aspirin, and an emergency bypass had saved his life. He was going to make it.

But the other family had lost their son tonight. Words like *multiple gunshot wounds*, *spinal cord*, *brain damage*, and *fatal*—whispered among the extended family who'd arrived after the fact and the devastating news—were going to haunt him a long time, as was the image of the wailing mother beating her fists on the hospital floor.

Carson wondered where he figured into this. Where was Breanna on the scale between being fatally shot and having a survivable heart attack? The only words they'd thrown at him so far—and those were from the paramedics—were *placental abruption* and *hemorrhage*. He understood enough to know she'd lost the baby. That broke his heart, but he thought, eventually, they could live with that. What he couldn't live without was Bree.

"Mr. Armstrong?"

Carson paused his pacing and turned toward the voice. An older man in scrubs walked toward him. A mask hung loosely beneath his chin; his eyes were tired, his countenance sober. Carson reached for the nearest seat and braced his hand on the back. "My wife? Do you know anything about Breanna Armstrong?"

"She's just out of surgery."

"Is she going to be okay? When can I see her?"

"One question at a time." The man stopped in front of him and extended his hand. "I'm Dr. Ford."

Carson shook his hand briefly, resisting the urge to hang on to it like a lifeline. This man had just been with Breanna.

"Your wife survived the surgery, but she's not entirely safe yet. We don't often lose women to pregnancy or childbirth anymore in this country, but this was a close call."

She could still die. Carson swallowed and nodded, indicating he understood.

"Her placenta abrupted, meaning it separated from the uterus wall and caused profuse bleeding. Because the placenta was lower than the baby—a condition we call placenta previa—once separated, it dropped into the birth canal."

Essentially suffocating the baby. He'd read a bit during his hours waiting. Carson's eyes welled with tears. "I know. We lost the baby. But how is Bree? Will she be okay?" They could have another child someday. This would hurt for a long, long time, but they could get past it.

"To stop the bleeding, we had to perform an emergency hysterectomy."

"All right." Carson swiped a hand across his face. Whatever parts Bree didn't have now, he'd still love her just as much.

"Mr. Armstrong, your wife won't ever be able to get pregnant again. She won't ever carry another child."

She won't—A fresh set of tears coursed down his face. *Never. She's just lost the only baby she'll ever carry.* How was he supposed to tell her that? *Please let me have the chance to tell her.* Carson brought a hand to his head and started to turn away, wanting privacy to fall apart. "I just need Bree to be all right. Can I see her?"

"Not yet," Dr. Ford said kindly. "She's in post op, being monitored very carefully for the next few hours. She's had two blood transfusions, and if we don't have any additional bleeding, she should start to wake up and—we hope—be all right and have a full recovery."

"Hope?" Carson didn't feel much right now.

"It's not a guarantee," Dr. Ford said, quieting his voice even more. "She lost a lot of blood quickly, putting her kidneys at risk for renal failure. Her other organs may have been affected too. Without knowing exactly how long they were without the necessary blood supply and oxygen, we can't say for sure yet how her recovery will go."

"But she *will* recover." Carson met Dr. Ford's gaze. It wasn't a question this time. He wasn't asking but insisting. Bree had survived the surgery. Surely she would be all right. Or as all right as a woman who'd just lost the first and only baby she would ever have could be.

"You should go home and get some rest. It could be hours still before she's released to a room and you're allowed to see her."

Carson shook his head. "I'll wait."

Dr. Ford nodded, as if he'd expected as much. "Good night, then."

"Thank you," Carson said, as he turned to walk away. "Thank you for saving Bree's life."

Fifteen

Carson held Bree's limp hand between his two. *The worst is over.* They'd stopped the hemorrhage, Bree had been released from post op to the intensive care unit, and she was breathing on her own. *We've made it this far.* He brought Bree's hands to his lips, pressing a kiss against the top of her pale fingertips. Along with seeming almost translucent, something else about her left hand struck him. *I never got her a wedding ring like I promised.*

Bracing his elbows on his knees, Carson hung his head, ashamed that he had just now, in this moment of horrible crisis, remembered that promise. They'd settled into their new lives, if not comfortably and happily, then at least routinely, and he'd all but forgotten about getting her a ring in the weeks since they'd wed.

Because it's never felt like a real marriage.

The honesty of that thought was like another well-deserved slap across his face. Why hadn't it felt real? Likely because he hadn't put in the effort. Initially he'd wanted to please Bree, to somehow make up for his horrible mistake. Pulling some strings and getting her a last-minute spot for her practicum had felt like a victory and job well done. Knowing how much she'd wanted to complete her schooling, he'd been patting himself on the back for that one for several weeks now. But, good turn though it was, it didn't exactly make a marriage. Or make up for not buying her a wedding ring. Or her having to marry him in the first place.

I'll do it. As soon as Bree was well enough they'd go shopping, and he'd let her pick out any ring she wanted. They'd go on a honeymoon too. Hawaii or Europe—wherever she wanted to go. He wondered what she'd choose. Having never really been anywhere, what would she want to see first?

If you'll just wake up. Carson raised his head and stared at her with eyes bleary from lack of sleep—two straight days and nights now. He was going to have to go home soon. If nothing else, they'd probably insist he had to shower for hospital standards or something. But he couldn't leave. Not yet. Not until he talked to her. Not until he told her how much he cared for her and how sorry he was.

I'm so sorry, Bree. So, so sorry. Please give me a chance to make it up to you. Scooting his chair closer, Carson laid his head on the side of her bed, near her hand still clasped in his own.

He was dreaming. He had to be, except it was more of a nightmare, with Bree's father standing over him, shotgun leveled straight at Carson's head between his eyes.

"Now, Reginald," Carson's dad was saying. "Killing my boy isn't going to make anything better."

"It'll make me feel a sight better," Reggie spat, his spittle landing in a blob on Carson's arm.

"I'm sorry," Carson said. "I never meant this to happen." He swiped at the tears streaming from his eyes, not caring if he appeared a coward. He didn't care what Bree's father thought or even if her father shot him, other than that would mean he wouldn't be with Bree. And Carson needed to be with her. More than that, he *wanted* to be with her. Today, tomorrow. Forever. Somehow he had to explain that.

"I went to your house that night because I knew Bree would understand." She always understood him. He'd always been able to share his troubles with her, bounce ideas off her, and share his triumphs. She was a fantastic listener, always waiting until he'd finished saying what he'd come to say before offering advice or condolences or even congratulations. And then her responses always seemed to be exactly what he was hoping for, what he was looking for, be that approval or a solution to a problem or an excitement equal to his own.

Or true understanding of his grief.

She was the epitome of what a best friend should be. He could trust her with anything. He felt safe with her. Bree knew him well, faults and all, and yet had never once turned him away, had never denied him anything. Even when it cost her so dearly, as it had last November.

As it was still costing her now.

A few feet away, Reggie chambered the shotgun.

As if experiencing the phenomenon of his life flashing before his eyes in the seconds before he was to depart this earth, Carson saw a series of images—a scene from nearly every year he'd lived. Bree appeared in each. Anna was in many as well. But it was Bree that Carson noticed, seeing her as he hadn't before, noting her reactions, her kindness, her behavior toward him as it changed over the years from those early days of pushing each other on the swings and holding hands wherever they went, to the way—beginning in about the seventh grade—that she hung back and let him and Anna take the lead. The hand holding stopped—between him and Bree, at least. It was about this time that her mother died, and her carefree childhood gave way to the weight of grief and responsibility.

His mind conjured the image of Bree squished between him and Anna in a fierce hug, sobbing as if her heart were broken. Because it had been.

It would be again, once more, when she woke up. *If she wakes up.*

Carson turned away from Reggie and his shotgun and stared at Bree, her brown hair spread across the pillow, her eyes closed in deep, unnatural sleep. What if she never woke again? What if she joined her mother and his? What if his selfishness had cheated her out of the life she deserved?

His mind skipped ahead several years from middle school to their junior prom. His senses came alive with memory, the visual feast that had met him when Bree came down the stairs, the realization that Bree, his best friend, was a stunning beauty. He remembered the awkward moments followed by the hum of awareness and tension between them as he helped her into the car and they drove to the dance. Her sweet scent enveloped him, along with the thrill of holding her hand in his as they walked into the gym and then moved around the floor to almost every dance. He recalled the nearly overwhelming desire to kiss her, the realization that he cared for her as more than a friend, and the enormous problem that created.

All too soon the night was over, and the scenes that followed flashed by quickly. Instead of searching himself out in these, Carson sought Bree, noting—as he perhaps hadn't before—the expressions on her face, her reactions and actions. She was careful, thoughtful, always contemplating before she acted on something. She watched him. She watched Anna. She made an effort to stay out of their way.

Carson relived their double date the summer after prom—he and Anna, Bree and Robbie. He caught the hint of sadness in her eye, her forced smiles and laughter, and the way she became skittish whenever Robbie got too close or tried to take her hand or put his arm around her.

She wasn't like that with me.

Was it possible...

What if, way back then, Bree had been fighting off the same attraction he'd felt? What if she'd cared for him as more than a friend?

But no—after prom she'd never given him any indication.

Or maybe he just hadn't noticed. Had he ignored the clues, the furtive glances, the occasional meeting of their eyes, her blush, and the feelings of his own euphoria that followed? He had noticed the way she'd hung out with him and Anna less and less and the careful distance she kept between them whenever he happened to be alone with her. Which hadn't been often, until that night last November.

When she'd opened her arms and held him close and let him cry like a baby. And then when she'd let him kiss her— and so much more.

"I repaid her so poorly," Carson mumbled. "I never meant to hurt her—to hurt you, Bree. That's the last thing I wanted. I love you."

The truth settled over him like both a warm blanket and the light of dawn after the darkest night.

"I *love* you," he said again, louder this time. It shouldn't have felt like such a revelation, but it did, lightening his heart and infusing him with hope. He loved Breanna Wagner! *Breanna Wagner Armstrong. My wife.* He felt suddenly like shouting it to the world, like a recent convert to Christianity might stand and proclaim that he'd been saved. He felt saved—or like he might be, if only Bree would wake up and he'd have another chance to get this marriage thing right, to show her how he really felt about her. He *had* to have that chance.

Please, God. Don't take her now. Not when he finally understood and could declare the feelings that had been locked so deep and so long in his heart.

It had *always* been Bree—the girl who'd been able to pump higher and faster than him on the swings, the one for whom he'd spent hours creating special valentines in grade school. Bree, who'd raced him when they swam—and was always just a hair behind—Bree, whose laugh he loved, whose smile warmed his soul, whose heart he'd yearned to make his for so long.

Why hadn't he realized it sooner? How could he have possibly forgotten?

Anna. He'd cared for her too. She'd always been the one to lead them to exciting places. She promised a life full of adventure, and that enticed him, so he'd chosen her. It was more pleasant at Anna's house, more interesting. Her parents liked him and were fun to be around—unlike Bree's solemn father and her family's depressing circumstances.

Anna was going places. She loved the ocean and planned to make it her career. She was smart and had big ideas. She didn't contemplate like Bree. She jumped without looking first, and to teenage Carson, that had been thrilling. He'd followed her lead, believing the world outside Holiday held so much more.

When what he'd really wanted, what and who would fulfill him most, had been right there all along. It seemed so clear now, as if someone had placed a lens in front of his eyes that corrected his previously flawed vision.

The lens was freeing, showing him the path he should have been following all along and the one he should follow from here on. Anna was a branch off the main path, a significant detour, but not the way he was to go or the woman he was to be with. Now that his mind understood, he felt free to follow his heart, to love Bree completely, with no regrets, no looking back, no guilt.

"I love you, Bree." Carson pressed his lips to her ringless hand once more. "Please wake up so I can tell you—before your father shoots me."

"I'm not going to shoot you, son."

A rough hand, heavy with care, landed on Carson's shoulder. He turned toward it.

Reginald Wagner stood beside him, beside Bree's bed in the hospital room—not a shotgun to be seen. Carson raised his head from his arm and the drool pooled there to meet his father-in-law's eyes. He started to stand, but Reggie shook his head.

"Stay. Your place is right where you are. Beside Breanna."

Carson nodded and forced his constricting throat to swallow.

"I've been where you are." Reggie nodded to the chair and Carson. "I know what it is to see the woman you love suffer and then … to lose her." His eyes grew bright as Carson's grew large at the incongruous sight of the roughest-edged man in town fighting off tears.

"I can see you love my little girl." Reggie's hand fell away. "We can hammer out the details later. For now that's enough."

Sixteen

"It's been too long." Carson rested his forehead against the pew in front of him. "She should have been awake by now." That wasn't his assessment but what he'd gathered from the murmured conversations among the ICU doctors and nurses taking care of Bree.

Her organs, including her brain, had been deprived of oxygen too long. That she still hadn't woken up, two and a half days post-surgery, wasn't good. He wasn't leaving the hospital until she did or until—he wouldn't think it. Giving her father a few minutes alone with her now, before he had to leave to return home to his boys and his current job, had been difficult enough for Carson. If Bree woke up and came home, he doubted he'd ever work another day in the office again but would set up an office at home so he could always be nearby.

"Never lose hope." His dad turned on the bench to face him. "That's Satan's plan. The Lord's is all about hope. Many times it seemed your mother wasn't going to make it—through surgery, through her treatments—but I never gave up."

"She *didn't* make it the last time," Carson said bitterly, then immediately regretted the words and his tone. "I'm sorry, Dad." He lifted his tear-stained face to his father's.

"I see it a bit differently," Dad said. "I think she *did* make it. In fact, I know it. Your mother lived a full and wonderful life, and she was a good and generous person. It was simply time for her to move on to bigger and better things, a better place."

"Our place wasn't so bad." Carson's throat burned again. When had he turned into such a crybaby? He wasn't even certain who he was crying for at the moment—Bree or his mom? "We still needed her. *I* needed her. Charlie really needs her."

Dad nodded. "I do too. But maybe that's why she had to go—so we could turn our hearts elsewhere, looking both outside ourselves and inward, finding spiritual strength in the supreme source."

Carson didn't have a response to this. He'd done the opposite these past weeks, definitely drawing inward, relying on no one but himself for comfort and guidance. *And look where that got me.* And he'd looked outside himself all right, thinking only of himself, when he'd sought out Bree the night his mother died. After yesterday's revelation, he could no longer say that was a complete mistake, but at least partly providence, though he wished he'd handled it better, wished he'd owned up to his feelings years ago and had taken the many opportunities given him and the proper steps to explore a deeper relationship with Bree. She hadn't deserved an unexpected pregnancy and a shotgun wedding—especially from someone she'd trusted her entire life.

"I miss your mother," Dad said, bringing Carson back to the thread of their discussion. "But I still feel like she's here with me—with us."

"It's not the same," Carson said morosely.

"No. It's not," his dad agreed. "But it's what we have to work with, and for me at least, it's working fairly well."

"How?" Carson sat up, attentive. How had his dad been coping after burying the love of his life? Whatever trick or secret he might know suddenly seemed like invaluable information, considering they were in a hospital chapel while a floor above Bree clung to life. *Tell me how I carry on if the worst happens.*

"Your mom and I communicated well while we were here together, so it's only natural that would continue. I knew her mind on things, and she knew mine—often before we'd spoken our thoughts aloud. There were only a few times we disagreed or times she surprised me. In my day to day since she's been gone, I still feel her presence. I know what she'd say if she were here. I look in the mirror in the morning and it seems she's there behind me."

His dad's smile didn't seem wistful but peaceful. "How do you know she's there?" Carson asked.

"She talks to me, or to my heart and mind at least. 'Not that tie, Marcus. You know it doesn't go with those pants.' When I'm planning my week I feel her guidance. 'We should visit the Winkle sisters more often. They're getting on in years,' she'll say. When I read the note you left me the day you were supposed to marry Anna, your mom was right there, too, saying, 'I could have told you this would happen. How many times did I tell you that Carson and Breanna were meant to be together?'"

"What?" Carson stared hard at his father. "She said that, or you imagined it?"

"Both." His father smiled sadly. "While your mother was alive, we had this discussion on more than one occasion. She could tell you loved each other, but you were too blinded by the potential of worldly opportunities to see it, and Breanna was too much of a good friend to both Anna and you to allow her true feelings for you to show."

Except Mom knew. Wow. Why hadn't she ever said anything to him?

Because I probably wouldn't have taken it well. He'd had his future so carefully planned for so long that he could guess what his former self would have said to a suggestion from his mother that he should change it all.

Carson remembered his early-morning phone call with Charlie the day after he and Bree had married: the odd, one-sided conversation Charlie had overheard Dad having with Mom's picture. "And what advice has Mom given you on all this now? Since it happened?" Carson asked.

His dad shrugged. "To be honest she's been a little quiet on the matter—a tad gloating, perhaps, that she was right. After you and Bree eloped, I told your mom she had to help me out on this one, show me what to do, and so far I've really only had two answers, and they've been the same from both her and God." Dad stopped talking and faced forward, staring at the painting of the Savior hanging at the front of the chapel.

Carson waited without speaking. He'd learned long ago there was no point in asking his dad to speed a conversation along. Like Bree, his dad was contemplative.

"I was told to show you both love and patience. In that order. Same advice I'm giving to you now." Dad slapped a hand on Carson's knee, then stood, a little slower than Carson remembered him standing in the past.

"That's it? That's all?" He needed more than that to get through this.

Dad smiled at him. "Have a little faith, son. It'll all work out."

Seventeen

CARSON WAS ALONE in the room with Bree when it happened. Reggie had gone back home to his job and his boys—surprising, as he'd not been particularly committed to either his employers or his children the past several years, and having a daughter in critical condition seemed an actual, legitimate excuse for missing work.

"Reggie's undergone a significant change since Breanna left home," Carson's dad, who—just as surprisingly—had stayed, explained when Carson asked about Reggie's sudden departure. "That, and hospitals frighten him. Being here reminds him of losing his wife, a trauma he's not yet recovered from."

"What about you?" Carson had asked. "Does being here remind you of Mom? Is it hard?"

Dad shrugged. "Not really. I remember her at home. For me, a hospital is a sacred place. Many enter this world and depart it in a hospital. I've witnessed both and felt the nearness of heaven."

Carson hadn't ever thought about it that way, hadn't felt any heavenly presence when his mom died. There had been only sorrow and overwhelming, drowning loss.

The terror of those final moments came back in an

instant when an alarm startled him from half sleep, and he looked up to see the flat line across the screen monitoring Bree's heart.

"Nurse!" He jumped up so fast his chair tipped back and hit the floor with a sharp crack. The noise coincided with a sudden spike on the screen and Bree's gasp of breath. Her chest heaved upward, and her eyes flew open.

"Bree." He leaned over her. Behind him, two nurses rushed into the room.

"Her monitor—" Carson gestured to the screen where the flat line was still visible. "I thought, but then—" He burst into tears.

Bree's open eyes stared at him. Her lips moved, but the sound was too faint to hear.

He swiped at his eyes and leaned closer. "What is it, Bree? Are you hurting?"

Her breath tickled his ear. "Carson."

He grasped her hand. More tears poured out of his eyes. He turned his face to the nurses, busy checking lines and taking vitals. "She knows me."

Bree's brow furrowed. Carson cupped her cheek with his free hand.

"You—" She paused, swallowed.

He leaned close to hear again.

"You. Look. Terrible."

He reared back, catching the twinkle of mischief in her eyes as one corner of her mouth lifted.

His laugh startled the nurses, who pushed him out of the way to continue checking Bree.

"She's all right," he told them, relief flooding every cell of his body.

Over the nurses' heads he caught Bree's eyes.

"*You* are beautiful."

"I've ruined all of our lives," Bree said flatly and by way of greeting.

Carson stopped mid-step. The door to Bree's new room closed softly behind him. He flashed a questioning glance at his dad, who'd stayed with Bree while Carson went home to shower and change.

"A doctor came by to check her," Dad said. "I had to leave the room. I asked him to wait to say anything until the two of you had talked, but apparently he didn't. I'm sorry." Dad rose from his chair and glanced between them both, a joint apology for both their circumstances and the doctor not having kept his mouth shut.

"Not your fault," Carson said, embracing his dad, seeking strength from those strong arms that had held him so many times and always made things better.

"Love and patience," Dad whispered in his ear. "In that order. She is going to need some time to emotionally heal."

Carson nodded. "Thanks." His eyes followed his father as he left the room. Only when the door had closed softly once more did Carson face Bree, who was sitting up in bed, her eyes downcast. Offering a silent prayer for guidance, he pulled the chair closer to the bed and reached for Bree's hand, but she moved it away.

"I've ruined all our lives," she said once more. "Yours, Anna's, mine."

"I don't feel too ruined right now," Carson said honestly. "In fact, since you woke up this morning, I've felt about the happiest I've ever been."

She looked at him, her grim expression a mixture of hurt and confusion. "I lost the baby. You're happy about that? Relieved, I suppose."

"*No.*" He shook his head, reached across the bed, and captured her hand. "I've been bawling my eyes out for days—worried and sad. About both of you. It's just that I'm so happy you're here. With me. That you didn't—"

"I wish I had died." She tried to pull her hand away, but he wouldn't let her.

"You don't mean that," he said. "I know you're sad now, but it'll get better. We'll get through this, Bree."

She shook her head, then turned away from him. "Didn't they tell you? I thought you understood. I can't have more children. Ever. You would have been so much better off with Anna. I never should have said anything to you. I shouldn't have told you I was pregnant."

"That would have been the worst mistake of all." Carson squeezed her fingers gently.

"It's not too late to get our marriage annulled. We haven't exactly been living as husband and wife."

Carson felt like he'd been slapped. "Is that what you want? Look at me, Bree. *Please.*"

She wouldn't but kept her torso and neck twisted away from him in a position that had to be uncomfortable. After a minute he sighed, released her hand, and leaned back in his chair.

Annulled. Was she serious? Was that what she wanted, or did she think he'd want it, now that she couldn't have more children?

Minutes ticked by on the clock above the door as he considered his next move carefully, what he might say or whether saying anything right now would just make this worse and he should just keep his mouth shut and wait.

Times like this it would have been really good to have another woman to talk to, to ask advice from. Someone like Anna—or his mom.

Mom? He thought about what his dad had said, about still feeling her presence. It was worth a shot. He glanced around, a little weirded out at the thought of calling on the dead. But still . . . if she could maybe send him an impression. Something to help Bree.

If you're anywhere near and could help me out here . . . Mom?

Warmth enveloped him, settling over his shoulders and across his back, like a jacket fresh out of the dryer—the way his mother used to send him off to school in the mornings every winter. He hadn't thought about that in years, the way she always sat with him and Charlie at breakfast, which was always something fresh and healthy, never a box of cereal or something off a store shelf. He remembered how they made their lunches—similarly healthy—together, the three of them. Then, right before they had to leave for the bus, she'd always pull their jackets out of the dryer, toasty, sometimes too hot to zip up, after a few minutes tumbling around inside the metal barrel. He'd always been warm the whole way to school.

Details. His mom had been all about them—hundreds, probably thousands, of little things to show her love.

I can do the same. Maybe Bree didn't need a healthy, homemade lunch packed for her every day or her jackets pulled from the dryer before she left for school, but there had to be other things—lots of them—that he could do to show how much he loved her, to prove it, and to help her understand that she hadn't in any way ruined his life or hers, or even Anna's. If anything, Bree's pregnancy had saved them all—he and Anna from realizing too late that they weren't the best for each other, that they were better as friends. He and Bree from missing out on a wonderful life together.

If she feels the same way about me that I feel about her.

That was still a big *if* that he didn't know. His job was

doubly hard, then. He had to show Bree that he loved her, and he had to wait and see if she might love him as well.

Carson felt a cold sweat break out along his forehead. He was in this marriage for the long haul, fully committed, in 150 percent. But that didn't mean Bree was. Especially now when she regretted telling him about her pregnancy, which meant she likely did regret their marriage as well.

How was he even supposed to start?

He contemplated a few minutes more, then stood and walked around to the other side of the bed, only to have Bree turn the other way.

"That's okay," he said. "You don't have to look at me. If you never wanted to see my face again, I wouldn't blame you." He moved to the end of the bed, neutral territory, not too close or in her face, but where he hoped Bree might at least glimpse him occasionally out of the corner of her eye.

"I need to apologize"—he held up a hand when it looked like Bree might be about to interrupt—"really apologize, like I should have last November." Carson took a breath, then proceeded, choosing his words carefully, doing his best to say what was in his heart.

"I'm sorry for the way I acted that night. I took advantage of your kindness, your generosity. I was selfish and didn't consider you or your feelings or the consequences as I should have. I'm sorry for the way I treated you, for hurting you then and now, Bree. I wish that I could take my actions back, but I can't, and now they've cost you dearly. I'm not sure I can ever make that up. It's impossible, really, since the opportunity to bear a child has been taken from you."

He wished Bree would say something—anything. She ought to be angry with *him*, furious. She hadn't ruined anyone's life, but he had certainly impacted hers. He didn't want to think that he'd ruined it, not completely, though he could certainly see how Bree could feel that way right now.

"You can't carry another child or give birth to one, and there aren't enough words to express my regret about that," Carson continued. "But I won't say that you can't be a mother or I can't be a father. Someday, when this is long past, I hope we can be at a place to welcome a child into our home. But neither of us are ready to talk about that today, so I won't, other than to say that I'm not giving up—and I hope you won't either—the idea of being a parent.

"What matters the most, right now, is me being your husband and you being my wife. We married because of the baby, and now that baby's gone. But that doesn't mean our marriage is over. I don't have any regrets about marrying you, Bree. Instead—wrong as it was to start things off the way we did—I'm grateful, so very grateful for that little one we lost, because he brought us together."

What had become a daily dose of tears started down his cheeks. This time he let them fall, welcoming the bittersweet memory of his hand on Bree's stomach, feeling the flutter of their unborn child inside of her. Carson knew his pain could be only a fraction of the loss she must feel, but he mourned that child too. Surprising and incomplete as his appearance had been into their lives, Carson had still wanted him and looked forward to his arrival.

"I'm glad to be the one here at your side, Bree. So glad I'm your husband and praying you'll continue to be my wife. I'm sorry it took this tragedy to wake me up, to make me examine my feelings and figure out what I really wanted, but I'm so glad that it did. When you were asleep, when I thought you might not recover—I realized a lot of things, the main one being that I married the woman I was supposed to. It's always been you, Bree. I wish I'd had the courage to act on my feelings sooner. We could have had these past years together, and I'll always regret that we didn't. But I don't want to waste any more time. I want to go forward together from here, with no apologies between us for our feelings, no apologies to anyone else that we're together. If it's you and me against the world, then so be it. I don't really care what anyone else thinks. *You are my world.* I just want us to be together."

Out of words, he stopped, shoved his hands deep in his pockets, and stared at the floor, watching as a tear splashed on the linoleum.

"Carson."

He looked up. Bree's voice sounded as broken as her heart must be. Her face was wet with tears, and she held her arms out. He was at her side in an instant, carefully gathering her close, feeling her arms around him, holding tight.

"I thought you would hate me," she sobbed.

"Never." Carson pressed his lips to her forehead.

"I hate myself. If I hadn't—"

"You didn't do anything." Carson held her tighter.

"That night—"

"Shh. We don't ever have to talk about it again."

"We do. You need to know."

He pulled back to better see her face.

"When you kissed me, Carson, when we started—I knew what we were doing, where it might lead. I knew it was wrong, that you belonged to Anna, that we weren't married and you would never be mine. But I'd wanted you to kiss me for so long, for so many years had wanted you to hold me like you were. It was wrong of me, but I didn't think I'd ever get another chance; I thought I might have at least that one memory. And so I—"

"Let me get carried away and do what I would." *Bree has feelings for me too!* In the midst of their deep sorrow, he felt a spark of joy.

"You were grieving," Bree said. "I was the one who should have stopped us."

"We both should have," Carson said. "But it doesn't matter now. It's in the past, and we're going forward from here." His hands gripped her arms, and he looked into her eyes. "I love you, Bree. Especially you. Only you. Please say that you'll be my wife, that we'll spend our lives together."

For the space of a second he held his breath until she nodded.

Bree reached up to touch his face. "I love you, Carson. I always have, and I always will."

Eighteen

Mother's Day

I WILL NOT cry today. I will not cry. If she kept telling herself that, eventually it had to be true, right? Though Bree doubted it would be true today.

"Breakfast in bed for my beautiful wife." Carson entered the room, a glass of juice in one hand, his laptop balanced on the other with a plate, napkin, and fork on top.

"Best I could do for a tray," he said, setting the juice on the nightstand and the laptop on the bed.

They didn't own a tray or much of anything. No wedding meant no presents. That's what happened when you did things backward and then eloped. Not that it mattered. Their lack of material possessions hadn't even figured into life the past three and a half weeks and in her daily battle for physical and mental health. Carson had hardly left her side. He held her when she cried, drove her to her many appointments, made sure she ate well and took her meds. He'd been sweet and attentive, every bit as devoted and loving as his long proclamation in the hospital.

Bree loved him all the more for it but felt keenly her lack of contribution to their marriage, particularly today, the Sunday devoted to celebrating motherhood. *I'll never give Carson any children. If he stays married to me, there will be no one to carry on his name.*

Carson settled on the edge of the bed he no longer slept in and presented his offering—a plate of scrambled eggs, toast, and bacon, along with a cup of fresh-squeezed orange juice.

"You own a juicer?" she asked, surprised.

He shook his head. "But we own these." He held out his hands, flexing fingers that looked a little red. "Strong arms extends to hands as well. But yeah . . . a juicer would be nice. More than the necessary oranges gave their lives for that half glass of juice."

Bree smiled at him over the rim of her glass. "I'll do my best to appreciate the sacrifice." She took a drink. "Mmm. This is good."

"Mom's specialty. She believed a glass of fresh-squeezed orange juice could fix just about any problem. She was usually right."

"In that case, I'll drink it all." She took a long drink, then handed the glass back to him.

"Lots of problems this morning?" Carson set it on the dresser, then lay across the lower half of the bed, on top of the covers. He placed his hands behind his head and stared at the ceiling.

Bree munched her bacon and took a minute to appreciate the muscles visible beneath his T-shirt. His arms and hands weren't his only parts that were strong.

After a few bites, she answered, careful to keep her voice from wavering. If she started crying this early, it was going to be a long day.

"No more than the usual concerns. I can't have children, I'm missing most of my parts that make me a girl—which conversely makes me act *more* like one—and . . . it's Mother's Day."

Carson rolled on his side to look at her. "I'm guessing that's not going to be one of our favorite holidays—not yet, at least."

"Probably not." Bree swallowed a bite of eggs and concentrated on keeping her throat clear.

"I was wondering what you'd think about a drive today?"

She shrugged. "Sure." Anywhere but a church or a park or basically anywhere there would be mothers with their children. On second thought, maybe they should stay in.

"I thought maybe we could bring flowers to *our* mothers, or to their graves, at least."

"Oh. A long drive, then." All the way home—almost. She didn't see herself stopping in to say hi to her father and brothers. Not yet. But Carson's dad might be home, or at the church or the cemetery himself. "All right." She *should* go visit her mother's grave today. She should be thinking about her mom, instead of wallowing in her own sadness. And Carson would want—Bree stopped the fork midway to her mouth. It was his *first* Mother's Day without his mom. How could she have forgotten? Or been so insensitive?

"Of course we should go." She wiped the napkin across her mouth, then set the plate and his laptop aside. She pushed back the covers and rose slowly from the bed. Every day she felt a little better, physically at least. "I'll hurry and get dressed."

"Great."

Bree felt his eyes following her to the bathroom. She wondered what he thought of her now, her physical self. How could he be attracted to a woman who was hardly a woman anymore? It was one of the things she was having the hardest time with. As if losing their baby hadn't been enough, she couldn't seem to overcome the feeling that she'd lost an important part of herself as well.

"They were both so young." Bree snapped a blade of grass in half as she sat on the lawn between gravestones. It broke easily, with hardly any effort at all. It had probably taken weeks to grow that long and yet had broken with such little effort. Much as her family—even after years of her mother's tender care—had snapped at her passing. Her mother had been the strength, the fiber that kept them all together. Without her they'd withered, just as this blade soon would beneath the sun.

"Too young," Carson agreed. "No matter what my dad said about it being her time to go."

"Only the good die young," Bree quipped. "Guess I'm going to be around awhile, then."

"Hey." He frowned at her and stepped back from the headstone, his fingers trailing over the top. "You've got to stop that, Bree. No negative talk. Isn't that what the counselor said?"

"Yeah." She crossed her legs and leaned forward so she wouldn't have to look at him. The grief counselor wasn't really helping, but she didn't know how to tell Carson that. She'd never been one to talk about sad things. She didn't see how that made anything better. Maybe because there hadn't been a lot of talking about her mother's death, or even her mother at all, after she'd died. *Because Dad couldn't handle it.*

Am I acting like him now? It was a startling thought, a revelation too close to the truth—or possibly it was the truth. She loved her father dearly, but she didn't want to fall to pieces like him because of loss. She didn't want Carson to suffer because of her problems.

He plopped down beside her on the grass. "It's beautiful

here. Even at the cemetery." The white picket fence surrounding the churchyard and historic church was freshly painted. The tall pines were fragrant, and the large oaks had leafed out, shading much of the lawn and headstones. The street was peaceful, quiet now that the early church services were over. Everyone was at home, enjoying a Sunday dinner with their families.

She'd wanted it that way, wanted church to long be over, wanted the heat of the day with them when they visited in late afternoon, so there was less chance of being seen. As they'd driven through town, she'd kept her face straight forward, not daring to look left or right, lest any residents were out on their porches, pointing and gossiping about Carson and Bree as they drove past.

Thankfully, no one else had come to the tiny cemetery in the forty-five minutes they'd been here. She wasn't sure what she would have said or done—if she would have ducked her head and run for the car or hid behind Carson's back or burst into tears. None were good options, but her emotions were too raw to think of any positive way to handle whatever criticism might come their way.

How long will it take? she wondered. How many years would have to pass before they felt like they could at least visit, if not live here, like they'd both wanted? Did Carson miss Holiday as much as she did? Or more?

"I imagine the churchyard feels practically like home to you." Bree stared across the headstones to the side of the church, with its stained glass windows catching the afternoon sun. The house where Carson had grown up, the one his father and brother still lived in, was just down the street. But his dad, and therefore Carson, had spent almost as much time at the church as at their house.

"It does feel like home. Why did I ever want to leave?" he asked.

"I think most people do—at one time or another. We want to see what else is out there, experience the wonders of the world."

"Does that include you?" Carson turned his head toward her, awaiting her answer.

Bree shrugged. "I'd like to travel and see some different places, but I've always wanted to live in Holiday. It's charming and beautiful and—"

"—home?"

Me, she'd been going to say. It wasn't her home that she missed, exactly. That was a place she'd yearned to be free of for a while. But if her house were still as it had been when her mother was alive, if it were a pleasant and happy home, like Anna's had always been, then maybe she would have felt different.

But Holiday as a whole was where she wanted to be. She'd hoped to teach at the nearby elementary school, to marry in the church, to own a house here—on the river, preferably—and to raise her family.

Bree's throat constricted. She forced her thoughts to the positive, to what she could still have. Maybe not that church wedding or children, but she didn't need to rule out living here—someday, in five or ten years, when the scandal had hopefully blown over—and maybe someday she could even teach school, that is if residents would consider trusting their children with someone guilty of such a grievous sin.

Carson leaned back, looking up to the cloudless sky. "I really miss her."

Bree placed her hand over his on the grass. "I know. I loved her too. Your mom was a great woman."

"I had her longer than you had your mom."

"Doesn't make it any easier," Bree said. "Now we're two motherless souls, trying to figure things out. How are we supposed to do that without their guidance?"

Carson smiled. "I'm pretty sure we still have it. If we want it, and if we listen closely."

"Are you going to start talking to your mom's picture like your dad does?" Bree didn't really care if he did. She'd imagined talking with her mom more than a time or two over the years.

"It's more like listening and thinking about what she would do, what advice she'd give me. It's not as difficult or weird as it sounds." Carson glanced at her, as if to gauge her reaction. "I bet you've done the same without even realizing it. I mean, how did you learn to cook so well and take care of the house and your dad and brothers? You were barely a teenager when you had to take over all of your mom's responsibilities."

"I guess I remembered what she had done, and I suppose I listened for her too."

Carson nodded. "You've been a mother for a lot of years already, Bree. Your brothers are lucky to have had you."

"Probably," she agreed. "Though they don't necessarily see it that way."

"They might now." Carson chuckled. "Considering they've had to fend for themselves the past few months."

She wasn't sure whether to smile or grimace at that thought. She could only imagine what the house looked like without her there to clean it. It was a good thing she'd taken everything with her that she valued and wanted to keep.

"Anyway—" Carson extracted his hand from beneath Bree's and turned to face her. "I've been thinking about a gift I might give my mom this Mother's Day."

Bree glanced at the flower arrangement on top of the

grave. They'd stopped at a roadside stand on the way and purchased two, one for each of their mothers' graves. "A gift?" What else could one give a deceased parent?

"It's a gift as much for me as for her. But I know she'd be so happy with it—with us." He rose, then with one knee on the ground, knelt before her. "Breanna Eleanor Wagner Armstrong, you've already agreed to be my wife—and I thank heaven for that daily. Will you now wear this ring, as a symbol of our love and marriage, as a symbol to the world—and especially other guys—that you're taken, that you're mine?" He withdrew a box from his pocket, opened it, and held it out to Bree.

A round-cut diamond solitaire set on a silver band sparkled beneath the sun. It was simple—far more so than the extravagant setting he'd given Anna, the one Bree had secretly thought was a bit much. This simpler band and diamond suited her far more. It seemed perfect, even without an accompanying wedding band. Maybe that would come later. Or maybe she would always just wear this one simple ring. And that would be enough. Without any ring at all, Carson had already been enough.

"Say something—please," he croaked.

She raised her eyes from the ring to witness the uncertainty of his expression.

"I love it." Bree rose up to her own knees and almost shyly wrapped her arms around him. "It's perfect. Thank you."

A whoosh of air left his chest. "Phew." Carson brought a hand up to wipe his forehead. "For a second I wasn't sure you liked it or wanted it."

Or liked or wanted me, he might have added. Bree chided herself again for not being the kind of wife she wanted to be, for not having it in her lately to show him the love he deserved—the love he was always showing her.

"I adore it." *And you.* It was still difficult for her to say things like that out loud when, for so many years, she'd had to practice hiding those feelings. She leaned back and held out her hand for him.

"Close your eyes," Carson said, standing and pulling her to her feet as well.

Bree's brows rose in question before she complied, squeezing her eyes shut and resisting the urge to peek. *Is he going to kiss me?* In those moments when she emerged from the dregs of sorrow, it seemed that was nearly all she thought about. Worry about her father and brothers, the loss of her long-standing job and only source of income, even her concerns about finishing school all seemed to fade into the background, to a state of complete unimportance. All that seemed to exist and matter during those precious segments of time was Carson and that he'd chosen to stay with her, that they were husband and wife and surely would start to act as such sometime.

Maybe today. Just one kiss. It was too soon for anything else for her physically or emotionally. But if they could start with a kiss, if they could manage that hurdle of intimacy, she felt like they might be on their way.

But now he only held her hand in his, and she felt cool metal slip onto her finger. *A perfect fit.* She could tell before even opening her eyes. "How did you know my ring size?"

"I measured when you were in the hospital and still—out of it."

"You did?" He'd been planning for their future at a time it had seemed so bleak.

"You can open your eyes now." Carson closed her fingers into a fist, kissed the top of her knuckles, then let go.

Bree looked down and gasped. The solitaire on her finger nestled in the middle of *two* bands, one of which looked almost familiar. "Where did—"

"That one was your mom's wedding band." He pointed to the ring farthest back on her hand. "When your dad came to see you at the hospital, I asked him if I could have it—for you." Carson took her hands again. "The one on the front was my mom's. I think—I *know*, they'd want you to wear their rings, to make them yours. Wear them to remember, to feel their love and presence."

"Oh, Carson—" Bree didn't know what to say, so she cried instead, large, salty tears that dripped on their joined hands. It was the most precious gift she'd ever received, the most beautiful sentiment.

"That's why I gave it to you here, today. Our moms' motherhood journeys weren't exactly what they'd hoped for either. Neither of them planned on a terminal disease that would take them from their families too soon. But they each *had* a journey. They were both fantastic moms. They still are. And you can be, too, Bree. You *will* be. Somewhere out there, when the time is right for us, there will be a child—maybe more than one—who needs us as parents, who is meant to be ours."

Her tears came faster. She stepped into Carson's embrace, sobbing her heart out, feeling sad, but mostly happy. Feeling hope.

Nineteen

Father's Day

CARSON LEANED SIDEWAYS as the car turned, exaggerating his movement across the console to nudge Bree's shoulder and enjoy the heady scent of her perfume. "If you wanted to ride a roller coaster today, we could have stayed closer to town and ridden the Rampage."

"No coasters for you today. Though that sounds like a fun date." She pushed him back to his side of the car. "Stay on your own side of the vehicle, please," she quipped in a ride operator voice. "And no cheating. No peeking."

"Yes, ma'am." He didn't need to peek to know exactly where they were, no matter that Bree had blindfolded him, doubled back a few times, and taken every country road she could probably find. There were only so many ways to Holiday, and he'd driven all of them. Still, he didn't want to spoil her fun. Whatever she had planned for Father's Day—he guessed it was a long-overdue visit with his dad—he'd be grateful for. That she'd thought of anything at all, surprising him this morning with the ugliest tie he'd ever seen—a joke, Carson had realized when Bree's attempt at holding back laughter failed—and a tall glass of fresh-squeezed orange juice, courtesy of his real present, a juicer, had lifted his spirits higher than they'd been in weeks.

It had been a tough couple of months, but she was slowly coming back to herself. Now if he could just figure out how to get her to come closer to him—for everything from someone to talk to, to back rubs.

In the weeks since he'd given her the rings on Mother's Day, Bree had stopped going to grief counseling and started going to the gym instead. He'd hoped that meant she would turn to him more, but their conversations still skirted around the hard subjects. She'd stopped crying, but he wasn't convinced she'd stopped hurting. He certainly hadn't. Neither had he stopped needing her. Instead, on every level his need and desire seemed to be growing. He wished he knew if it was the same for Bree as well.

Being blindfolded the past couple of hours had only heightened his other senses. Her perfume was driving him crazy, and every word she spoke seemed a tempting invitation. He thought again of a thirsty man in a desert. He was two steps from the oasis but couldn't seem to reach it.

"Church services were good today," Carson said, trying to steer his thoughts to safer waters. He glanced Bree's direction, though he couldn't see her.

"They were." She sighed. "Not as good as your dad's, though. There's just something special about him—kind of like there's something special about his son," she added, in a tone that didn't sound in the least religious.

Her hand covered his, and Carson's heart raced at the simple contact. Whenever she said things like that, he felt like a dog who'd been thrown a bone—only to discover there wasn't much meat on it. He always hoped more would follow, but so far . . .

He waited, hoping she'd say more, maybe tell him what

she found special about him, but when she didn't, and when her hand returned to the wheel, he buried his disappointment and steered the conversation back to his father. "Not every congregation can have a guy like Mr. Rogers leading the flock." Aside from the distinction between zip-up sweaters and clergy robes, Carson hadn't seen a lot of difference between the two men as he was growing up, watching reruns on PBS and watching the live version at church on Sunday mornings.

"It would be really interesting to see your dad in front of a congregation like ours," Bree said.

Carson heard the blinker click on for a left turn and knew they were getting close to Holiday. "It's a bit rougher crowd in Birmingham than in Holiday."

"More people, more problems, more scope of solutions, too, I'd think." She sounded distracted, as if she were searching for something.

"Maybe." If only Bree realized she was the solution to his problems, his loneliness and longing. How to convey that to her remained a problem. They were married. They were together, and yet . . .

He attempted another subject to divert his mind. "Did you leave us any time for apartment hunting later today?" He bounced along with the car as they rolled over the bridge separating Magnolia Springs and Holiday. The two towns had grown right up together, with only the river separating them.

Bree didn't answer but instead made a sharp right turn onto a lesser-used road, obvious by the crunch of the gravel beneath the tires.

A picnic maybe? With both their dads? Just please not her brothers. Things had gone better with Bree's father than he could have ever hoped, but that didn't mean her knucklehead brothers wouldn't try something. *Like lighting me on fire for the barbecue.*

Another turn and the car slowed, then she parked it. She placed a hand on his knee, then leaned close to whisper in his ear. "Don't move, and don't peek."

Carson suppressed a groan. Did Bree even have a clue what she was doing to him? All those brief touches, plus the way she'd bossed him around all morning—using *that* voice? Or was it just him, his imagination running amok with what was surely not her intent?

Carson heard her door open, heard it close. A few seconds later his own opened. Bree reached across him to unbuckle his seat belt. Her hair brushed his face, and he gave an agonized sigh.

"What's wrong?" She turned her face toward his, her breath on his cheek.

"Nothing." His voice sounded strangled.

"It hasn't been that bad, has it?" She stepped back, then took his hand and pulled him from the car. "I'll make it worth it," she said, not waiting for his answer. "Come on. She kept his hand, tugging him along beside her, after she'd closed the car door.

More gravel crunched beneath his feet. Carson tried to figure out what road they might be on and couldn't. She'd succeeded in surprising him a little bit at least.

"There's a step up here. Careful." Bree held his elbow, guiding him.

He lifted his foot and placed it on something solid, yet wobbly. *Brick.*

Bree came around behind him and untied the bandana covering his eyes. It fell away, and Carson blinked, adjusting to the sunlight and the absence of her touch.

She moved to stand beside him, staring straight ahead, their shoulders touching. He followed her gaze, though he would have preferred to look at her, and found they were in front of a building that looked like it ought to be condemned.

For a minute he took it all in: sagging porch steps, broken shutters and windows, peeling paint, weed-filled yard. *The Bakers' place.* They'd been some of the founders of Holiday, but the last Bakers had moved away decades ago, shortly after World War II, if Carson remembered correctly. It had been after their son was listed MIA in France, and it was said the grief had killed his father. Mrs. Baker had moved away to live with her sister, leaving the house as a rental, though it seemed like it had also been vacant a lot.

"Want to go inside?" Bree asked, her tone different now—hopeful and excited.

Excited? Did he want to go inside and risk the roof falling on them? Not really. But he was smart enough to guess that would be the wrong answer. "Sure."

Bree took his hand and pulled him forward, over the path of brick pavers that was more weeds than brick anymore. She ran up the front steps like they were sure and solid, then punched the code on a lockbox hanging from the front doorknob.

A lockbox? Who would lock up a place like this? Vandals could probably only improve it. *Especially if they burned it to the ground.*

The box clicked open, and Bree extracted an old-fashioned key. She held it on her palm. "Look, even the key is charming." She placed it in the keyhole, then opened the door.

It creaked loudly, the way you'd expect someplace old and haunted to sound. Carson wondered vaguely if the reason it had been vacant so much was because it was haunted by Old Man Baker, searching for his missing son.

"I feel like we're walking into a *Scooby-Doo* episode," Carson said, following her inside.

Bree turned back at him, a frown on her face. "You don't like it?"

Uh-oh. "I—don't know. I haven't seen much of it yet." As Shaggy would say, he was starting to get a bad feeling about this. Only, in his case, it wasn't because he was worried about meeting a ghost.

Bree propped the heavy wood door open with a chair from the living room. "Some furniture is included too."

Yeah . . . that's where this is going. Apparently they *were* apartment hunting. Or haunted house hunting. Something like that. But she couldn't be serious—could she? For starters, they were in Holiday. Or on the outskirts, at least. Much as he preferred his dad's sermons, he couldn't imagine sitting in the congregation again and feeling the eyes of every single member on him. *On us.* He wouldn't subject Bree to that.

Bree dropped his hand and stepped forward over dusty floors into what was once probably a grand foyer. She stood at the base of a wide staircase, the curved banister covered in cobwebs now but still visible beneath the layers of webbing and dust and grime.

"The kitchen is over there, toward the back of the house, and there's a living room and a library up front." She pointed to either side of the stairs. "All four bedrooms are upstairs." She started up them, and Carson had no choice but to follow. At least the steps inside seemed solid enough.

They peeked in each bedroom, a couple of closets, and two bathrooms. Upstairs was in better shape than the foyer, the crown jewel of the second floor being the central space that overlooked the entry below and from which the bedrooms spoked. A five-foot stained glass window, with all the glass still intact, caught the sun, spilling color across the room. For a minute Carson stood within its glow, imagining what this room used to be, who and what the house's former occupants had been. It was intriguing to think about, and as a whole the interior seemed a lot better than the outside.

Back downstairs the kitchen boasted appliances from the fifties, which Bree again pronounced charming. The library, with its dusty, cobweb-covered shelves received even more enthusiasm from her.

There was no carpet—a good thing, Carson decided—but old oak floors throughout the house. When he knelt to brush the dust from a section, it didn't look too bad. Cleaned up and refinished, it could be beautiful. He was starting to catch Bree's vision. *Maybe.*

It would take a ton of work to make this place livable, and he wasn't so sure he was up for that. But it seemed like Bree might be. What if this was just the sort of thing she needed?

Now that her body was mostly healed, she needed something to do. Starting her student teaching again wasn't a possibility until fall. And even her online job was no more. In spite of her four years as a dedicated employee, it seemed there was no forgiveness for missing the classes she had when she'd been in the hospital fighting for her life.

No matter. She could find better employment now that she wasn't limited to working from the confines of home. Not that he was pushing her to get a job, but he knew she'd been bored, that she needed to do something. Too many hours on her hands with nothing to do wasn't good, wasn't helpful for combating the discouragement from all she'd been through recently.

The gym, the library, keeping their apartment spotless, and cooking dinner could only occupy so much time. He'd been trying to occupy the rest, when he wasn't working, and inch by inch he thought they were regaining lost ground. Board games at night, walks in the park to the local ice cream stand, trips to the farmers market on Saturdays, cooking together on the weekends. It was all good—building blocks putting their former friendship back into place on a solid foundation—but moving at the pace of snails was killing him. He wanted more than the friend he'd had his whole life. He wanted Bree to be his wife in every sense, to be his lover. He wanted to feel loved by her.

Maybe renting this house and fixing it up together would be a giant step or two toward being a real couple. *A place Anna has had no part of. Except that we're in Holiday.* Bree had shown bravery just by bringing him here. But could she really handle living here? Did he want to subject her to that now, so soon after everything that had happened? She didn't need anyone tearing her down.

Living in Holiday—even on the outskirts of town—could be the worst idea ever. A few unkind words, feeling shunned by those who used to be her friends, could all combine to tear down what progress they'd made together.

Carson observed Bree as she stood at a window in the library. *She's still so fragile. I have to protect her.*

"You haven't even seen the best part." She turned to him, a bright, childlike smile on her face. "Come on." Bree took his hand again and tugged him toward the back of the house. They stepped outside onto a large deck that extended out as a dock over the river.

"It's on the waterway mail route," Bree said happily, as if getting your mail delivered by boat was a highly desirable commodity. "Do you remember when we were kids and we used to pretend that?"

He'd forgotten, but her words and the sounds and smell of the river recalled the memory.

"You always got to be the mailman." Bree frowned at him. "Anna and I had to stand at the edge of the river with our shoeboxes and wait for you to bring our mail—never the other way around."

"It was my family's boat, and your parents hadn't given permission for you to be in it," Carson said playfully.

"Your parents hadn't given *you* permission to be in it either," Bree reminded him.

Carson grinned. "Yeah, but being the mailman gave me an excuse to deliver notes to you."

"And Anna," Bree said, her happy expression faltering slightly.

"Yes, but . . ." It was really coming back to him now. His eight-year-old self laboring at the desk in his upstairs bedroom, crayon in hand as he drew a picture of a boy and girl standing close together. He wasn't using the yellow crayon to color the girl's pigtails. It was the brown clutched in his chubby fingers. *Bree. It was always Bree.* He'd been wiser as an eight-year-old than he'd been as a teenager and through his college years. "Anna's notes were different—usually just a sentence or two, a fake bill or a letter from a pretend person. Yours had pictures and sometimes a story. Yours, I spent time on."

"I know." Bree's gaze softened. "I still have them," she said, surprising him. "I have everything you've ever given me."

And it all probably fits in a shoebox. Carson couldn't recall giving her much of anything over the years. He brought her hand to his lips in a kiss of apology, intending to change that. No reason he couldn't start mailing her notes now, no matter where their mailbox was.

Bree's eyes met his briefly. "A good memory, for sure." She smiled before her attention returned to the yard. Though the river ran close to the deck and made up the rear property line, the house also boasted a sprawling side yard shaded by oak and magnolia trees.

Carson stared at the overgrown lawn, wondering if yard services were included in the rent or if the tenants would be expected to maintain the place. He guessed the latter, and that the past several tenants hadn't done such a great job.

Aside from the massive and overgrown lawn, the trees were another thing too. Several were in desperate need of a trim, and he imagined the piles of leaves they'd make when they dropped. He'd probably be raking for weeks. They'd need to have a bonfire just to get rid of all the leaves.

A smile on her face, Bree left his side and sat on the bench that ran the length of the deck. He studied her profile as she watched the river, and wished she would watch him as intently.

"So, what are you thinking?" she asked, turning to him suddenly.

"That I'd like to kiss you," Carson blurted, realizing as he did that she'd been asking his opinion on the house.

Bree tilted her head up toward him. "Why don't you, then?"

Why don't I— Two giant steps and he was at her side, looking down at her, trying to discern if she really meant what she'd just said.

"Well," he said slowly, mind spinning and heart thrumming. "You did faint the last time."

Bree grimaced. "I hadn't eaten much, and I was dehydrated. We had a big breakfast this morning, remember? Eggs, hash browns, bacon, juice . . ."

"It was delicious." Kissing Bree would be even more so.

"So it's doubtful that I'll faint again." She moistened her lips and smiled up at him with what could only be encouragement.

Carson hesitated, the moment he'd wanted so many times over the past weeks right in front of him: their chance to start over, the right way. He couldn't mess this up.

Her smile faltered. "What is it, Carson? What's wrong—with me?"

"Nothing is wrong. Everything about you is right, Bree."

He held a hand out to her and felt relieved when she placed hers in it. He pulled her to her feet so she stood in front of him.

"I'm a little nervous, I guess." Not exactly a manly thing to say. His confession sounded ridiculous, but of course Bree didn't laugh at him. Instead her look softened with understanding.

"I've wanted to kiss you for so long," Carson continued. "And when I finally did, I nearly ruined everything."

She squeezed his fingers and moved closer. "And then you saved everything."

"Not everything—not our baby." His heart throbbed with sudden ache, even as he wondered why he'd had to be so stupid to bring that up now.

Bree's next breath came deep and sharp. "That isn't your fault any more than it's mine. But you're right. We've lost the opportunity to create a child together. But I hope—that doesn't mean—we've lost other opportunities together. Like being close. Like kissing."

Carson's free hand reached up to touch her cheek. "I've just been waiting for your permission."

Her eyes locked on his. "You have it."

"Good." Carson bent his head, closer to hers. "Because I really liked those kisses we shared last November."

"I loved them." Bree's eyes fluttered closed.

Carson pressed his lips to her forehead, drawing them away slowly, loving the taste of her already. His mouth moved lower to brush the tip of her nose. He leaned closer yet, tilting his head, feeling her quickened breath against his lips a second before they touched hers lightly. He paused, awaiting her reaction. For such a brief contact, his own reaction was out of control, heart hammering, blood pumping, head spinning. He had to be so very careful not to get carried away again.

She sighed. "Is that all?"

He grinned. "Hardly." He cradled her face in both hands and kissed her again. Bree's fingertips found his chest, then crept higher, to his shoulders. Her mouth moved against his softly, slowly, as if uncertain.

"How many boys have you kissed?" he asked the thought out loud. *Stupid again,* his brain warned him too late.

Bree pulled back slightly, opened her eyes, and looked at him. "Just one. You."

"You never kissed Robbie?" The image sent a surge of jealousy through him.

"He kissed me. I never kissed him back."

"Oh," Carson mumbled. He was an idiot. But then Bree had to know that already, given all the stupid things he'd done thus far. Somehow, miraculously, she hadn't left him.

"Am I doing it wrong?" Bree whispered, staring at his chin instead of looking at him directly.

The uncertainty in her voice nearly killed him. Carson's hands dropped to her waist. He wrapped both arms around her and pulled her close. "You're doing it *perfect.*" To say it was the sweetest kiss, and that this was one of the sweetest moments of his life, was not an exaggeration.

"I love you so much, Bree. I've wanted to kiss you just about every minute of every day these past few months."

She looked at him again, frowning slightly and confusion in her gaze. "Why didn't you, then? I've been waiting."

She's been as starved for affection as I've been. A small-town, southern girl through and through, waiting for him to make the first move. He wasn't sure whether to laugh at her exasperation or pick her up and swing her around "I wasn't sure you wanted me to. If I'd have known—"

Bree raised up on tiptoes and silenced him with her lips as her hands inched slowly around the back of his neck. Still holding her close, he lifted one hand, threading his fingers in her hair as the length of her molded against him. Their kiss moved swiftly from tentative exploration to pent-up passion, seeking release.

Like two starving people. She's been in the desert too. The revelation that she wanted this as well emboldened him. He wasn't sure where the reserved, contemplative Breanna had gone, but he wasn't complaining.

Her hands finally reached the back of his neck and clasped together. She pressed against him, and Carson leaned back—and kept going, stomach dropping, heart jolting, the feeling like a free fall on a roller coaster. It took a second and Breanna's shriek to realize he really was falling, with Breanna on top of him.

The decaying wood of the railing gave way with hardly a noise, the wood splintering and crumbling to dust around them. The floor of the deck rushed past, or rather, he and Bree rushed past it on their downward plunge.

Bree screamed, her eyes wide with a mixture of surprise and terror. He clutched her to him as they both landed in the river with a great splash.

He plunged below the water, Bree still on top of him, then came up spluttering a few seconds later, dragging her with him.

Carson tried to stand and found his toes barely touched the bottom. Bree coughed and tried to catch her breath as well.

"Wow." He shook water from his hair, then pushed hers aside so he could see her face. "That was *some* kiss."

Her look of shock gave way to laughter as she glanced up at the broken rail. "Swimming was *not* on the agenda today."

"No?" Carson clasped her to him, then with his free hand began paddling them toward the shore. The current wasn't strong here, but the river had moved them a few feet downstream already. He didn't want to be caught in it or catch a rare glimpse of one of the alligators known to be seen on occasion. The riverbed beneath sloped up to the grassy side yard Bree had been admiring, and soon they both could touch. Holding hands, they trudged from the water to the tall grass along the bank.

"My shoes," Bree wailed, pulling one muddied sandal off and flinging it aside.

Carson collapsed on the grass beneath one of the overgrown magnolias. "I'm cooler now at least."

"So much for mail delivery." Bree pointed to the broken section of railing, mailbox still attached, as it floated past.

"We were probably lucky it wasn't the roof that caved in on us." He placed his hands behind his head, wondering about the possibility of getting back to where they'd been headed a few minutes ago.

"Do you really think the house is that bad?" The laughter was gone from her voice. She kicked off her other shoe and sat beside him, cross legged, then began pulling up blades of grass.

"If by bad, you mean it should have been condemned and torn down half a century ago, then yes. I think we can safely cross this one off the rental possibilities list. Though I am curious to see what else you've found for us to look at."

"I wasn't showing it to you as a possible rental." Bree drew her knees up to her chest.

Uh-oh. "Bree?"

"I may have put earnest money down on it. Only five hundred, and I can still get it back."

Carson rolled to face her and leaned up on one elbow. "You wanted to *buy* this place?"

She nodded and swallowed. He could tell tears were close. He sat up and pulled her against him. "Tell me." *Why.*

"I knew how much you wanted to live in Holiday. Anna was always going on about how you planned to live in one of those grand historic homes in her parents' neighborhood, how you thought it would be a great place to raise a family."

Anna. The usual feelings of guilt popped up at hearing her name. But no longing accompanied it. No second guessing, no more what-ifs. Carson felt only grateful to be exactly where he was, soaking wet and muddy on the riverbank—with Bree. He was always going to feel bad about the pain they'd caused Anna, and it was a continual prayer that someday they could make that up to her, but the dreams he'd had of a life with Anna were no longer, and he didn't miss them.

Bree shrugged. A tiny hiccup escaped her mouth. A precursor to crying, usually. Carson held her tighter and began running his thumb across her palm.

"I can't give you a family, but I thought I could at least give you a house in Holiday. Maybe a little less grand but still historic."

He stilled all movement as the magnitude of her offering struck home. She'd move back here, face ridicule and criticism, for him. "So you did it for me?"

She nodded. "I know you miss your dad. And Charlie needs you. I thought—living out here—it might not be too hard. We don't have to get our groceries in Holiday. We could drive to the Piggly Wiggly a couple times a month to stock up. I could try to arrange for student teaching in Fairhope or even farther out. It'd only be a semester of commuting."

"What about church?" Carson asked.

"We'd go every Sunday, of course." Bree leaned her head against his shoulder. "We would arrive just before it started and sit in the back. Then, the second *amen* was said, we could leave quickly. If we sat in the back, it would be difficult for people to stare at us. Even if a few did, it would be worth it to listen to your dad each week again, to be near our families—or yours, at least."

Carson considered all she'd said—and done—a bold and selfless move. As much as the condition of the house concerned him, his bigger fear was how the people of Holiday, his father's God-fearing yet imperfect congregation, would treat her.

Anna had been the darling of the town, even earning the crown for Miss Holiday, Alabama not once or twice but three times. She was the only girl to have ever had that honor—three years running—during her junior and senior years of high school and again her freshman year of college. People loved her so much that they'd even voted her back after she'd gone away to school. He remembered having to persuade her to return for the summer parade.

No doubt he deserved to be shunned or worse for breaking her heart and therefore disappointing the town. But Bree didn't deserve that same criticism. It wasn't her fault he'd nearly married the wrong woman. Not her fault that he'd taken so long to see what his mother had known for years.

If Anna had been the darling of the town, Bree had been the recluse. In high school Anna had encouraged Bree to run with her, in the town royalty contest, but Bree had refused, citing the lack of a good dress to compete in. Carson realized that had likely been true, but it was also more than that. With her mother's passing, Bree had changed. She'd withdrawn into herself, no longer the gutsy, tomboyish, outspoken girl she'd once been. Only now was he seeing glimpses of the original Bree reappearing. He'd seen her off and on over the years, but mostly the girl she'd once been had stayed in the shadows.

Not content, not happy, he realized now.

"What do *you* want? Where do you want to live?" Carson asked.

"With you." Her voice sounded steady again. She'd kept the tears at bay.

"Same," Carson said. "It doesn't have to be in Holiday."

"We can't avoid it forever." Bree sat up and faced him. "Our families are here. Our roots are here."

True. "Maybe we could rent a place—"

"Where?" they both said together, then laughed.

"In case you were wondering, there are exactly zero apartment complexes in town."

He'd known that, of course. Just hadn't thought about it before speaking. "So it's this place or nothing?"

She shook her head. "There are a couple of other homes. More expensive. Closer to town. I like this one, though. I like that it's on the river, that it's away from everything. I like its potential."

"Potential to kill us," Carson teased. He kissed her forehead. "Tell you what. Let's see what the inspector says."

"He already said." Bree's smile was impish. "It's in the binder in the car. You can read everything at your dad's house—and ask him what he thinks we should do."

"I think I already know what he'll say." Carson stood, then pulled Bree up. "Tell the truth. Face your problems. Love one another." He tugged Bree closer and circled his arms around her. "I like that last one the most."

She tilted her face up to meet his, expectation dancing in her eyes. "Me too."

Twenty

"A LITTLE WARM for flannel, isn't it?" Carson's younger brother Charlie appraised Bree as she entered the kitchen.

Already self-conscious of her attire—an old pair of Carson's basketball shorts cinched tight and a worn flannel shirt she'd found in the back of his closet—Bree felt her face heat as she faced the three Armstrong men already seated at the table. "It's the best I could find that sort of fit." Her clothes, including her bra and panties, were in the wash, along with Carson's clothes, also muddy from their impromptu swim.

"You could have used something of Mom's." Carson rose to pull out her chair for her.

"I know." Bree hadn't wanted to do that to them—any of them—even after they'd offered. It hadn't even been a year since Darlene Armstrong's passing, and seeing her clothes on someone else might be a painful reminder of their loss that was already recent enough.

Bree slipped into her chair, and Carson sat in the one beside her. His dad looked around the table, beaming.

"It is so good to have my boys both here. And to have my beautiful new daughter with us as well. Thank you, Breanna, for arranging this."

"You're welcome." Her blush was back. She hadn't done

anything except make a phone call a couple of weeks ago and bake a pie last night.

Everyone joined hands—a ritual Bree remembered from nights like this long ago when she and Anna had joined the Armstrongs for dinner. She bowed her head as Carson's dad began to pray. His words rolled over her like a soothing melody.

"We thank thee, Lord . . . God's grace be upon all at this table . . . Let us feel thy love and forgiveness."

Carson's dad had spoken to her a lot about forgiveness and love when she was still in the hospital and blaming herself for all that had happened, certain she was being punished.

"God doesn't work that way," he'd explained. "He doesn't interfere with natural consequences, but neither does he wish upon us suffering. Like any loving father, he wants the best for each of his children. When we stumble and are hurt, heaven weeps with us."

She hadn't been convinced. Surely losing the ability to ever have children was because of her indiscretion.

"Not so." Carson's dad had taken her hand in his, the way her dad used to when she was a little girl, the way she wished he still would now.

"Was losing your mom a punishment for something she or you did?" Carson's dad asked.

"Of course not," Bree had said indignantly. "No more than Carson losing his mom, than you losing your wife, was."

He nodded. "We all face different hardships in this life. For some, those are disease or physical limitations. Others struggle with poverty. Many, particularly those born in third world countries, suffer both. It's part of the package of life." He stared past her a moment, as if summoning the right words.

"You're at a crossroads, Breanna. You can allow yourself

to become bitter—toward yourself or Carson or even God. You can allow your grief to turn to anger and blame. Those who do often reap lonely, unhappy lives. Or"—he paused, looking directly at her—"you can choose forgiveness and love. You can forgive Carson—"

"I don't blame him."

"*And* forgive yourself," his dad added with a smile. "You didn't let me finish. Forgiving oneself is often hardest but equally important. When Jesus told us to forgive seven times seventy, he didn't say, 'except for thyself.'" Reverend Armstrong's brows rose knowingly.

Bree shrugged and looked down at their hands on top of the blanket.

"Forgive yourself. Focus on what you *do* have still, which is the love of God and the love of a very fine man, one who hopes to spend his life at your side." He gave Bree's hand a final squeeze and left her alone to think on his words.

She had. That night and many after, then many mornings while walking or at the gym. Happiness, she was realizing, was a conscious decision. Or at least it was for her right now.

A less conscious decision lately.

"Amen," she echoed with the others at the table, then looked up, smiling at the men on either side of her. What could be happier than being here, in this moment, surrounded by people she loved and who loved her?

Except maybe Charlie?

He was exchanging a peculiar look across the table with Carson. A second later Carson leaned close to her.

"That top button was always loose on this shirt. That's why it was in the back of the closet."

Alarmed, Bree pressed her hand to her chest, over the escaped button, attempting to discreetly tuck it back through its hole while Carson's dad passed the potatoes. She'd chosen to wear a loose shirt, since she was currently braless, but she didn't want to *appear* loose.

Established that much already.

Stop.

The warm feel goods of a minute before vanished beneath another onslaught of self-recrimination. Careful to keep her expression blank, Bree served herself a generous portion of salad, all the while worrying over what she had started today.

If she couldn't get through dinner at her father-in-law's house without feeling this insecure, how was she supposed to survive living in Holiday?

"Foundation, structural, plumbing, electrical—those are big issues." Carson's dad closed the inspection binder. "Reroofing isn't going to bankrupt you. Neither would replacing a water heater or furnace. But if you've got a foundation that's sinking or your entire septic system needs to be redone, you're likely to be into that house far more than it's worth. Based on this report, at the very least I'd get a couple of contractors out there to give you some estimates before you make a decision." He leaned back in the chair that used to be his wife's favorite. Bree had seen her in it more times then she could count. Carson's mom had never been the sort to be idle. When she was sitting, it was always with a project or a book in hand.

"Thanks, Dad." Carson picked up the binder and stood.

Following his cue, Bree stood as well, feeling like she was sixteen again and about to break a serious rule.

"You've given Bree and I a lot to think and talk about." Carson reached for her hand; his was warm around hers.

"We'll probably need a few days to make a decision."

"No rush." Reverend Armstrong began rocking. "I would love to have you close, and it would be good for Charlie, but you need to do what's best for you both. It's unfortunate there aren't more properties to choose from."

"That's small-town life for you. Night, Dad." Carson towed Bree toward the stairs. They'd decided to spend the night here so they could go over to the house again in the morning and talk in person with the real estate agent. At $105,000 it was already an amazing deal for anything with access to the river, but the more they read about the house, the more it looked like the only value would be in the property. And if that was the case, Carson wanted to see what else was available in or around Holiday.

"Good night. Thank you for a lovely evening." Bree realized how silly that sounded, like the dialogue from a romance novel. But she was nervous and embarrassed and a dozen other emotions she couldn't quite name. How was this possible? That she was being *allowed* to go upstairs with Carson? To his room? To sleep there?

And would they do more than just sleep? Here? In the house he grew up in? This was all so wrong. But then, she'd just eaten dinner at his house while braless. Which reminded her—

She stopped, tugging Carson to a halt as well. "I think our laundry is probably done now."

"Probably not. Our dryer is old. It takes forever."

"Oh. Well, I could just check." At the least, she could go to bed wearing panties.

"It'll keep until morning. I like what you're wearing now." A corner of his mouth lifted in a teasing grin.

That's what she was afraid of. "All right." Reluctantly, she allowed him to lead her upstairs to his room. Once inside, Carson closed the door behind her and locked it.

Bree glanced around the room she'd seen only two other

times in her life—during both of which Carson hadn't been present. The first had been when she was thirteen. Her dad and brothers had been gone overnight on a hunting trip, and she hadn't wanted to go or to stay home alone. Normally she'd stay with Anna, but her family had been out of town as well. So Carson had asked his mom if Bree could stay over.

Bree remembered that weekend well—the lively dinner conversation, helping Carson and Charlie with the dishes, playing on the swing set in the backyard, and sleeping in Carson's room, while he bunked with his brother. She remembered walking around the room, looking at every picture, every swim team ribbon posted on the bulletin board, every trophy on the shelf. Even at thirteen he'd already been a strong athlete.

Even at thirteen, with her mother so recently gone, Bree had recognized that her home lacked what Carson's had. She'd cried herself to sleep here in this room that night, not only missing her mother but missing her father and the man he used to be, the home they used to have and didn't anymore.

The second time she'd been in Carson's room was when she and Anna had decorated it for Carson's sixteenth birthday. Their decorations had included a couple of rolls of toilet paper and streamers, about thirty balloons, and a can of silly string—a throwback from their younger summer camp days. Carson's mom had come upstairs to help them.

What Bree remembered most from both previous visits to this room, and all of the other visits to the Armstrong house, was the feeling of home. Even now, with Carson's mom gone, it still felt like a home. It was what Bree wanted the home she and Carson made to feel like too. But she'd certainly started out wrong.

"Penny for your thoughts." Carson faced her, taking her fingertips lightly in his.

Bree shrugged. "Memories. I was just thinking of all the good times I've had in this house. You're lucky to have grown up in a home like this, with your family. And now, I'm lucky to count them mine."

He smiled at her answer and pulled her closer, into his arms. Bree leaned into him, relishing the feeling of security he provided.

"I'm sorry the house I chose is such a disaster. I'll get the earnest money back tomorrow."

"I don't want to talk about the house right now." Carson kissed the top of her head, then held her away from him. "I want to talk about us, about what happened this afternoon at the house—before we went swimming."

She stared at his chin, anticipating the start of a difficult conversation. "You kissed me. And—it was wonderful."

"And ... *you* kissed *me*," Carson said. "And it was wonderful. And unexpected. I almost thought, for a minute there, before we fell, that—"

Bree felt another blush steal over her face.

"I almost thought you maybe wanted to do something more than kiss. Not right there, but eventually, that is." Carson spoke quickly, as if he wasn't certain he ought to have said anything at all.

Bree searched for the words to tell him how she felt. She didn't know if there was a way to explain or if what she felt was normal or still craziness from her out-of-whack hormones from first the pregnancy and then the hysterectomy.

"I want—" She faltered, afraid of saying the wrong thing. Why did being married to her best friend make it so difficult to confide her deepest feelings to him? Once, a long time ago, it had been easy. *But then, during those long years since ...*

"Yes?" Carson pulled her over to the end of the bed and sat beside her, shoulders touching, but nothing else.

Giving me space. She started with the easy part. "I *always* want to kiss you and for you to kiss me. Well, except maybe first thing in the morning."

"Duly noted," Carson said.

"I'm pretty sure we *couldn't* kiss too much," Bree said, wanting to make sure she at least got that point right. If, from here on out, they kissed each other every day, she'd feel they'd gained significant ground. She took a breath and continued, plunging into the heart of the issue. "I also want to be your wife, you know—do the things a wife does."

"*With* her husband?" Carson clarified. "Or are you talking strictly wifely things like making me meat and potatoes for dinner every night and bringing me my slippers and paper?"

"Stop." Bree shoved him with her shoulder.

Carson took her hand, loosely lacing their fingers together. Bree's heart seemed to speed up as she looked down at their entwined hands resting on his thigh. It didn't take much contact to send her senses reeling.

"With you," she said quietly, after a minute. "This probably sounds stupid, but I want to feel like a woman. Since the surgery and losing the baby, I feel like I lost that part of me, and the only way to get it back, to know I'm okay, that I'm still me, is if we . . . If we're husband and wife truly. But—"

"You're afraid."

She nodded, relieved to have said it and relieved he might understand.

Carson angled his body toward hers. He brushed a few strands of her hair aside from her face, then traced his thumb down her cheek. "Given my past behavior, I'm surprised you even want to kiss me. I was really surprised you agreed to marry me. I don't deserve you, Bree."

She shook her head. "Don't go there, please. The past is just that."

"Yes, but it's affecting our future together. The way I see it, we started with two big hurdles to overcome. The first is what we did to Anna. The guilt and remorse were just about enough to kill any chance we had. *Until*"—he looked into Bree's eyes—"I realized my mistake happened long ago, when I planned to marry the wrong woman. I will always be sorry I hurt Anna, and I hope that someday, together, you and I can find some way to convey that to her and somehow make it up, but I have no regrets about who I married. I'm so grateful to be here, at this very moment, and every one of them we have, with you. The only guilt I feel now is that I haven't been the husband you need me to be. I didn't know you wanted to be kissed. But I won't forget now."

As if to prove his point, Carson leaned forward and covered her lips with his. Bree's initial sigh of content soon gave way to building desire and the wish that she could somehow express that she needed more from him, but maybe not too much more. Not everything. Yet. Before she could figure out how to share any of that, Carson had pulled back again.

"The second and larger problem, the one we're still facing, is how to get past the way we began. I hurt you, Bree. More than that, my actions cost you an enormous loss. *Not* of your womanhood. Trust me, you're every bit the woman you've always been and more. But because of me, you won't get to bear a child now. That you haven't left me, that you've somehow found it in your heart to at least try to forgive me for that, is incredible to me. I thank God every morning when I wake up and see you're still there, in our apartment, that you're still willing to try to figure out how to get past everything that's happened and you're willing to try with me."

"Oh, Carson." Bree pulled her hand from his and took his face in her hands. His skin was soft, yet scratchy with a five-o'clock shadow. She remembered the way he used to ask her and Anna to check his face for hair growth. They'd both been shaving their legs for a couple of years at least before Carson found need to use a razor. Once, that had been the source of much consternation for him. How endearing she'd found his concern. How much she'd cared for him, even then.

"I love you, Carson. I'm not angry. And I don't want to be afraid. I just don't know how to begin."

"Like this." He wrapped his arm around her waist and pulled her close, then kissed her again, a slow, languid kiss. "I love you so much it hurts, Bree."

She knew just what he meant. Carson's lips parted, meeting hers once more. His mouth moved against hers, gentle at first, then gradually bolder. Bree slid her hands down to his chest, running her fingers over the front of his T-shirt and his pounding heart.

Their kiss built in fervor until they both collapsed backward on the bed, the springs squeaking loudly in protest.

"Keep it down in there." Charlie rapped on the door as he walked by, startling them apart. A minute later his bedroom door slammed.

"I may kill him for that." Carson leaned up on an elbow and looked down at Bree.

"Me too." She touched his face again, then ran her hand down his shoulder and arm, marveling that he was hers to touch, to love. "But I'm grateful too. We can't—not here, not the first time, the *right* time," she amended.

Carson nodded. "I know. It needs to be our place, or a special place, at least." He tugged her off the bed, then folded the covers back. He held out his hand, indicating she should get into bed. "If I promise to keep my hands to myself, can I hold you tonight? Can I sleep beside you?"

An infusion of relief flooded Bree. She hadn't realized she

was so worried. She didn't think she had been—a minute ago. She nodded. "I'd like that."

Carson turned off the light, walked around the bed, and climbed in the other side. He pulled the sheet up over both of them, then took her hand on top of it. "Good night, Bree."

"Good night," she said, happy that it was.

Twenty-one

CARSON WOKE IN the middle of the night to find himself curled around Bree. His hand was over her stomach—his oversize shirt had ridden up sometime in the night—and her thigh was between his.

He stifled a groan and slowly rolled away. *Cold water. A cold shower. Something.* He forced himself from the bed before he broke his promise to keep his hands off her.

He made his way through the dark to the hall, intending to head to the kitchen, but a light beneath Charlie's door steered him the other direction.

"Charlie? You awake?" Carson knocked on his brother's door.

"Go away," Charlie muttered from the other side.

"In other words, come in." Carson turned the knob and entered Charlie's room. The old bunks had been unstacked, separated into two twin beds, one on either side of the room. Charlie sat on the far one, his legs propped on the chair beside the bed, an open bottle in his hand.

"Looking for a drink?" His words slurred slightly as he pointed to what was left of a six-pack sitting on the desk.

"Really?" Carson glanced at the one unopened bottle, then crossed the room and jerked the chair out from beneath

Charlie's feet. "What the hell, Charlie? You told me you'd stopped."

"I told you I stopped going to bars. I never said I stopped drinking."

"You knew what I meant when I asked you. And here you are—under Dad's roof."

"Look who's talking. What were you doing under Dad's roof tonight?"

"Kissing my *wife* good night." Carson flipped the chair around and straddled it, needing something between him and Charlie right now so he didn't strangle him.

"Yeah. Your mistake is all right now. Do you suppose if I upgraded from beer to wine, my vice would be more acceptable too?"

"Bree's not a vice. There's no comparison, so leave her out of this. This is about you and drinking too much, throwing your life away and now dragging Dad into it."

"Would you rather I still went to the bars? Since you're not around to pick me up, I figured you'd rather me be safe at home in my bed, where I 'can't harm myself or anyone else.'"

That was what he'd said, and Carson meant it. He felt a moment of panic, thinking about Charlie getting himself home when he was soused. "No. You're right. It's better here. If you have to drink. But *why*? What's it going to take to get you to stop, Charlie? I love you. Dad loves you. You've got a great life ahead of you if you'll just live it."

Charlie didn't answer but took another drink, head tilted back until he'd drained the bottle. He held it out to Carson, who set it in the trash, then shoved the remaining bottle out of Charlie's reach.

"I don't know how to live it. I don't know how to be happy like you. I don't have a Bree or an Anna. I don't have a college degree or an awesome job."

"So get one. Get your butt to college and figure out what you like, what you're good at and want to do." Even more than Carson, Charlie had excelled at sports in high school. He'd dreamed of playing college ball—either football or baseball. He was great at both, leading their team to the state championship in their division, as the quarterback with the most passing yards. That same year he'd set a high school record for most innings pitched without a hit. But good as Charlie had been, when it came to college ball, his talent couldn't compete with the kids from the bigger 4A schools, coming out of programs that regularly churned out college and later pro quarterbacks. Charlie hadn't received any offers from his dream schools, and their mom had been too sick, her medical bills too high for him to go where he wanted without a scholarship.

"I can't do what I love anymore," Charlie said morosely. "I'm old and washed up."

Carson stifled a laugh. "Twenty-two is hardly old, bro. A lot of people start college at your age."

"No money." Charlie held up his hand and rubbed his thumb and fingers together. "Dad's still paying off medical bills."

"Yeah. I know." It hadn't crossed Carson's mind to ask his dad to help with the down payment on a house, but tonight Dad had told him he regretted that he couldn't offer them any money.

"I'll pay for it," Carson said on impulse, though he knew at once it was the right thing to do. "I'll pay your first year's tuition. After that it's on you—either a scholarship or a job or some combination of both."

"Nah." Charlie waved off the offer.

"I'm serious." Carson leaned forward over the back of the chair, looking at Charlie intently. "I figure it's either your tuition or your rehab. Your choice. The first will yield a higher-paying job when you're done."

"Why would you do that? You're trying to buy a house."

"I've got enough for both," Carson said, not entirely certain he did. *If not, Bree will understand.* "And I'm doing it because I love you. I want you to be happy. Mom wants you to be happy."

Charlie's eyes clouded with sudden tears. "I miss her *so* much. I wish—I wish I hadn't been such a failure when she died."

"You're not a failure, just maybe a bit of a failure to launch right away." Carson got up from the chair, tucked it beneath the desk, then sat on the bed beside Charlie. He pulled his brother close in a sideways hug.

"I've missed you too." Charlie sniffed loudly.

"Same," Carson said. He hadn't considered the impact his absence would have on Charlie.

"Yeah, right." Charlie shrugged out of Carson's grasp and turned his head toward him. "You're not missing anything, not married to Bree."

Carson grinned. "We've had a rough time of it, but she is pretty great."

"Pretty hot, you mean." Carson gave a low whistle. "I don't remember her ever looking like that, like she did tonight."

"She usually dresses a little better," Carson joked, feeling his temperature rise just thinking of Bree sitting beside him in his old shirt with the finicky button. It had taken all his self-control to keep his eyes where they belonged tonight.

"It wasn't the clothes. There's just something different about her—about you too. I never saw you like this with Anna. It's like you, I don't know. Like you're—"

"In love," Carson finished. It had stolen over him quietly,

then walloped him hard, a jolt like a firework going off right next to his ear when he'd nearly lost Bree. But when had it happened for her? She claimed to have loved him for a long time, but if so, she'd hidden it well. Now that they were both set free from past restraints, it felt like their love was just starting to flourish.

One look from her, the right word, one kiss and he felt ten feet off the ground. *It's only going to get better.* What was he doing in here, when Bree was across the hall in bed by herself? Carson stood.

"Think over my offer. We can talk more about it tomorrow. Night, bro." Carson left Charlie's room, taking the unopened bottle of beer with him. This he set on the floor in his room, then closed and locked the door once more. Instead of going right back to bed, tempting as that was, with Bree sleeping there, he went to the bookcase and pulled out his senior yearbook. It took less than a minute to find Bree's picture and senior snippet. Moving closer to the window and the moonlight filtering through the half-closed blinds, Carson pressed the pages flat and began reading.

I want to marry the man of my dreams, who will first be my best friend, and make beautiful babies with curly hair. We will live in a home on the river, where the mailman comes by boat to deliver the cards my sweetheart sends me. I'll teach second grade and have the cheeriest classroom in the school, and all the children in my class will find it a wonderful place to be.

Carson read the lines a second time then closed the book. How had he missed that? *Babies with curly hair . . . cards my sweetheart sends me . . . Man of my dreams . . . first my best friend.* Bree really had loved him a long time. He hadn't realized, until now, just how long.

Or how much? He thought again of all the wasted years,

when they could have been together. And how very nearly they weren't. *Thank you, God. And Mom.* Carson raised his eyes to the ceiling, wondering just how much divine intervention there had been.

He slid the yearbook back in its place on the shelf then climbed into bed beside Bree. He leaned over and kissed her cheek, then snuggled up against her, positive he was the luckiest man in the world.

Twenty-two

"I NEED TO go see my dad."

"That wasn't what I was hoping to hear you needed first thing in the morning," Carson teased. He nuzzled the back of Bree's neck with his nose, then caught her earlobe gently between his teeth.

She giggled. "I said no kissing when we first wake up, remember?"

"I'm not kissing. I'm nibbling."

"None of that either. Not in your father's house." She scooted away from Carson, off the bed before he could haul her back with his outstretched hand. Bree stood, looking down on him, his curls bent this way and that, sticking out at odd angles, and tried not to laugh. "Have I told you how much I love your bedhead look in the morning?" She'd seen it many times before, when Carson was wandering around the apartment in the mornings. It was even more adorable close up.

"Right back at you." Carson grinned. "And your tangles look even better when you're wearing an unbuttoned shirt."

Bree looked down. "Oh!" She clutched the flannel and whirled away from him, her fingers fumbling to secure the *two* buttons that had come undone. Behind her, Carson chuckled, and the bed springs groaned as he moved.

"You planted that shirt in your closet on purpose for me to find," she accused.

"If only I was that brilliant." He came up behind her and circled his arms around her waist. "Wish I could claim I'd thought of that. But I can't, and I promise I didn't touch any buttons during the night. But since they were undone . . . you can't fault a man for appreciating his wife, can you? You're beautiful, Mrs. Armstrong." He kissed her neck. "I promise to keep my hands to myself as long as you want me to, but I'm not sure I can control my eyes. Forgive me for admiring your shapely figure?"

"Maybe." His compliment and kiss made her blush.

"What can I do to make it up to you?" Carson bent his head and pressed his cheek close to hers. "Want me to take off my shirt so you can admire me as well?"

Bree snorted. "I knew that whole strong arms thing would go to your head sooner or later." She was starting to feel light-headed, between his nearness and just thinking about Carson with his shirt off, letting her admire him, touch him . . . *Not now. Not here.*

Not yet.

She forced her thoughts elsewhere and turned in his arms to face him. "Let's go over to my dad's for breakfast. I'll cook. We can stop at the store on the way and get the stuff for omelets."

"At Mulberry Mercantile?" Carson's brows lifted. "Are you sure you're ready for that?"

"No." Bree shook her head, feeling suddenly deflated. A simple thing like going to the store would no longer be simple if they lived in Holiday. "I wasn't thinking." The last place she wanted to go was to the store Anna's parents owned, the only one in Holiday. "Maybe we won't go over for breakfast. Or I'll just make pancakes. Or maybe biscuits and gravy—those are Dad's favorites. I bet he has the ingredients already."

"He may not have much of anything to cook with," Carson said. "And that kitchen may not be a place you actually *want* to cook in anymore. Maybe we should make something here and bring it over."

"Good idea." Bree frowned, thinking of the neatly organized and decently stocked cupboards she'd left behind. Carson was right. There was no telling what it might look like now, given her father and brothers' previously demonstrated lack of housekeeping. She dreaded what she might find. But she had to return home sometime. She'd spoken with her father on the phone twice since her surgery, but that wasn't the same as facing him and apologizing for what she'd done. He might not have been the best father, but she'd always believed he was doing the best he could, pushing onward through the sorrow that had never left him.

Carson pulled her closer and held her tight against him, as if he guessed the direction of her thoughts and the turmoil they caused. "It will be all right."

Bree nodded against his chest. "So you keep saying." She looked up at him. "And I believe you."

He smiled down at her. "I believe *in* you. Together we will, someday, somehow, make everything better."

Bree wrapped her arms around his waist and held on. "It already is."

The screen door at the Wagners' place wasn't on its hinges anymore but propped against the wall beside the door, looking visibly bent as if someone had taken his temper out on it. The faded, frayed welcome mat was nowhere to be seen, but the porch was surprisingly free of old leaves and debris, as if it had been swept recently. Carson didn't know what to make of the contradiction and had no idea what to expect, save for the worst, as far as a reception from Reginald Wagner and particularly his sons.

At the hospital a couple of months ago, Reggie had been cordial enough, hinting that he and Carson would talk about all this later. All that had mattered at the time was Bree and her tenuous hold on life.

All that mattered to Carson now was her happiness. He knew, or guessed at least, that some part of that hinged on an improved relationship with her father. But if Reggie wasn't open to that or was of a mind to make Bree feel bad about the past few months, then Carson had no intention of sticking around, and there was no way they'd live in Holiday if her own family couldn't be nice to her.

He stepped in front of Bree. "Let me go first. Just in case." In case one of her brothers opened the door and wasn't at his best. Or was. In either case, Evan and Blane were unpredictable.

Carson pushed open the front door and held it out of the way while Bree stepped across the threshold, her peace offering balanced carefully in her hands. She walked past him and headed straight for the kitchen, or as straight as one could walk, meandering among the clothes and dishes and video game controllers littering the floor. He pushed the door closed, then caught up with her, walking at her side, then entering the kitchen first where eighteen-year-old Blane sat at the table staring morosely at a bowl of cereal.

"Smell this milk, Evan. I think it's gone bad again."

"Probably," Bree said. "That's what happens when it doesn't get put back in the fridge."

Blane turned in his chair to scowl at her. "Well, look what the wind blew in. What are you doing here? You don't belong here anymore, and I didn't hear you ask to come in or even knock. Oh wait, maybe that's because you were already knocked—"

Carson jerked the chair from beneath Blane before he could finish the insult, sending him sprawling backward on the linoleum. "Apologize," Carson ordered.

"For what," Blane said, his eyes spitting fire. "I wasn't saying anything that's not true."

"It's all right, Carson." Bree's trembling voice belied her words.

"It's not all right for your brother to treat you that way." Carson reached down, grabbed Blane by his shirtfront, and hauled him off the floor. He was at least as tall as Carson, but his body hadn't yet made the jump from scrawny teenager to filled-out man. Carson slammed him into the wall below the clock that hadn't worked in years. "Breanna is my wife now, and anyone who is rude or insulting to her is going to answer to me."

"That's right."

Carson stiffened. From the corner of his eye he saw Reginald Wagner enter the room.

"Hello, Dad," Bree said.

Behind him, Carson heard her set the pan on the table. He listened to her halting steps followed by one of Reginald's heavier ones.

"You're here." Reggie's voice caught.

"I've missed you, Dad." Bree sounded almost like a little girl again, and Carson wondered if, back in this house and with her dad speaking softly to her, she felt like one. Since age thirteen, she'd been missing the dad she used to know.

Carson released Blane, moved a safe distance away from him, and turned to find father and daughter caught in a bear hug, Reggie's larger frame engulfing Bree's smaller one.

"I missed you, too, Breanna. Oh, how I've missed my baby girl."

Blane's mouth opened, as if to let go another sarcastic remark, but Carson shot him a silencing glance.

"You have something to say to your sister?" Reggie asked, looking over the top of Bree's head at his son.

"We missed your cooking." Blane slouched his thin frame against the wall.

"Something else," Reggie barked, his look turning ferocious.

"Sorry," Blane muttered.

"Now act like it. Go find your brother, and the both of you get back here. It appears your sister has taken pity on us and brought us something decent to eat."

Still slouching as he walked, Blane left the kitchen. Reggie stepped back from Bree but held her at arm's length. "You look good." He smiled. "Marriage agrees with you." He glanced Carson's direction.

"It does, Dad. I'm very happy." Bree caught Carson's eye across the room. Carson started forward, uneasy, uncertain how her dad actually felt about him. At the hospital he'd said they would sort it all out later. For all Carson knew that meant he'd send him out back as a target for his boys to practice on.

Reggie released Bree. "Carson." He gave a curt nod.

"Mr. Wagner." Carson held out a hand. To his relief, Bree's dad shook it with his usual firm handshake instead of a grip intended to crush bones.

"I brought your favorite, Dad. Biscuits and gravy."

Reginald's smile grew as he turned back to his daughter. "Blane was right. We *have* missed your cooking. Unfortunately, I'll have to eat and run or I'll be late for work."

"Oh?" Bree uncovered the dishes she'd brought and took a clean plate from the dishwasher.

"Yeah. I'm over near Foley now, on the maintenance crew for some of those fancy vacation condos they've got out that way. Been there three months."

"That's great," Carson said. Three months at the same job

seemed a significant milestone for a man who hadn't had steady work for years. Carson wondered if keeping the job was out of necessity, since the loss of Bree's income, or if something else had fostered the change.

"Maintenance, huh?" Bree placed two large biscuits on the plate, then removed the foil from the bowl holding gravy.

"I know." Her dad chuckled. "The irony isn't lost on me. I'm not so good at that around here. I have fixed a couple of things since you left, though. That dishwasher included. The drain just needed to be taken apart and cleaned. And the garbage disposal is new."

"Finally." Bree finished ladling a generous serving of gravy over the biscuits, then stood facing her father with one hand on her hip. "Is that what it took? Me moving out, to get a decent disposal and the dishwasher fixed?"

"I guess so." He gave her a sheepish look as he pulled the plate toward him. "The boys and I never appreciated how much you did for us all those years."

"I can't come back, Daddy. I'm married now."

Reginald nodded. "I know. And I'm not asking you to. Just come around once in a while. You don't even have to bring any food. We want to see you, is all."

"I think she should still bring food too." Twenty-year-old Evan walked into the kitchen. "Hey, sis."

"Hey, Evan."

"We'll come over when we can," Bree said, noncommittally. "We haven't decided where we're going to be living for the next year or so. Carson's job is still based in Birmingham, and I have to find out where I'll be assigned for student teaching."

"Heard you were looking at the old Baker place." Evan paused long enough to give Bree a brief, sideways hug before sitting down at the table to dig in.

"Who told you that?" Carson asked. *Who could have possibly seen us yesterday?*

"Sonny said he saw you poking around there." Blane grabbed two plates from the dishwasher and dropped into the chair beside Evan.

"His cabin's nowhere near the Baker property." Carson wondered if he should be worried about Sonny lurking around. The old man seemed harmless and had been living in these parts longer than he and Bree had been alive, but still . . . He didn't like the idea of the town hermit spying on them.

"Good fishing down that way. That bend in the river creates a nice little pool for trout." Reggie spoke around a large bite of gravy-covered biscuit. "Few weeks back the boys and I caught some foot-long speckled trout. They're in the freezer if you want to try some."

"Thanks," Bree said. "But we wouldn't have a way to get them home."

"Good fishing hole aside, if the Baker place is the best you can do for a house right now, I'd wait awhile," her dad said. "That thing's been likely to fall down any minute since I was a kid."

"My thoughts exactly," Carson said, earning a frown from Bree.

"Course it would be nice to have you close." Reggie polished off his biscuit. "But we'll take what we can get. We've missed you, and not just for your cooking. Though, this is delicious. Best thing I've eaten in months."

"Thanks, Dad." Bree seemed suddenly deflated and sad. Carson worried it was his fault for agreeing with her dad about the house. *Does she really want it that much?*

"I'm really sorry, but I've got to go." Reggie ran a hand over the crumbs around his mouth, then crossed the kitchen to put his plate in the sink.

"We should have come over earlier. I wasn't certain anyone would be up." She paused and took a deep breath. "I'm sorry."

Reggie waved her apology away. "It's okay. How were you to know my schedule?"

"Not that, Daddy." Bree sounded childlike once more. "I'm sorry about what I—" She glanced at Carson. "What we did. I'm sorry if I embarrassed you or caused you to feel ashamed or—"

Reggie turned from the sink, the stern look on his face effectively silencing them all. Even Blane froze, a biscuit halfway to his mouth.

"I wasn't happy when I found out you'd eloped." Reggie walked toward them.

Carson intercepted him before he could reach Bree. "I'm the one who needs to apologize, not Bree. If you want to be angry with someone, it's me, not your daughter. I'm the one who came over that night, who—"

"I'm aware of what you did, and I've no desire to hear the particulars," Reggie barked. His attention returned to Bree, standing behind Carson. "I was upset when I learned you'd eloped. I was angry, furious—" His hands clenched at his sides, then released as his head dropped. He let out a sigh that sounded more weary than someone letting off steam. "Furious with myself for not being here, for not being the kind of dad you could have come to with your problems, for being the kind of dad you ran away from instead of relied on."

"Oh, Dad."

Carson stepped backward, his hand held out until it found Bree's. He clasped it tight in his own and stood beside her, facing her father. At the table, both Evan and Blane had ceased eating and had their eyes glued to the three of them, watching the drama unfold.

"I was never ashamed of you," Reggie continued. "You've never given me reason to be anything but proud. You were always a good student, an obedient daughter. You worked so hard for this family and stepped up and did your best to fill your mother's shoes, putting your own dreams on hold for so many years. I knew you'd have to leave us someday. I was just surprised at the timing—only a little surprised that you caught Holiday's most eligible bachelor."

Reggie shot Carson a wry grin. "I always suspected it was more than the promise of dessert that kept you hanging out in the kitchen instead of in the yard with the boys."

"Yessir." Carson was starting to feel ten again too.

"I wish you two had started out different, but I can't say I blame you." Reggie ran a hand through hair badly in need of a cut. Carson remembered Bree had always been the one to give her dad and brothers haircuts. It looked like they'd either done the job themselves in her absence or hadn't bothered at all.

Reggie reached out and took her other hand. "When you were little and playing dress up, I remember thinking about the day I'd walk you down the aisle. Guess we both missed out on that." He shook his head in a motion of regret. "We didn't have that daddy-daughter dance together. I didn't get to see you all dressed in white. But I've had more memories than your mother did. Should have had a lot more." He shook his shaggy head again. "But that doesn't mean we can't have other good times ahead of us. Heaven knows we're overdue for some around here."

Bree released Carson's hand and stepped toward her dad, who swept her into another fierce hug. "I love you, Dad."

"I love you too. I'm happy you got yourself out of here, got a good fellow. He'll do right by you." Reggie glanced at Carson as he spoke, and Carson gave an answering nod.

"I gotta go. Almost late already. Thanks for stopping by." Reggie stepped back, then wiped his eyes as he left the kitchen.

Bree turned to Carson with a look that said she needed to be held. He took over for her dad, enfolding her in his arms and holding tight while her brothers resumed wolfing down their breakfast.

Outside, Reggie's truck roared to life on the third try. Carson felt undeniable relief as it drove away, backfiring its way down the street. The visit had gone well—a whole lot better than he'd dared hope. Other than the scuffle with Blane, there hadn't been any violence. No shotguns removed from the wall.

Bree sniffed loudly, then pulled back from Carson, her shoulders squared. "Let's go."

He nodded and followed her lead, helping to gather up the dishes after they'd placed the leftover food on one of her father's plates. *When will she want to come back again? Will she want to return at all?*

He supposed visiting her family was a necessary part of their marriage, one he ought to get used to. It felt depressing just being here, though, and for a second he felt a pang of loss for the in-laws Anna's parents would have been.

It was easy to imagine holidays and birthday parties at their spacious, pleasant home, the way they would have doted on their grandchildren. There would have been cousins for the kids to play with, and he and Anna would have had a good time with her siblings and their spouses. Their grand house would have accommodated all. Carson still remembered the scent of Mrs. Lawrence's pecan bars baking in the oven. He could imagine the smooth feel of their hardwood floor beneath his bare feet. He'd never been inside a more welcoming house, and that included his own. It seemed impossible not to feel happy once you stepped on their porch.

But none of that would have mattered. It wouldn't have been nearly enough to make up for marrying the wrong woman. He believed that he and Anna could have been happy together, but it wouldn't have been the same as what he and Bree had now and were working toward. It wouldn't have been right, the way things were meant to be. Bree was the way things were meant to be, the one he was meant to be with.

What she came from, who her family was or wasn't didn't really figure into it at all.

Carson watched her now, hurrying about the kitchen she knew so well, stepping carefully over the holes in the linoleum, jiggling the drawer that stuck, just so, to get it to open. She'd had so little for so long. It was no wonder the condition of the Baker place didn't bother her.

Over the years, he'd both ignored and avoided the shabbiness, the poverty, the emptiness of this house. But this morning it felt as if it were just a shell, waiting to harbor a real family inside. Before, he had noticed only Bree when he'd visited. Everything else had faded into the background. The times he'd been at her house had grown less and less frequent over the years. Usually when he was home and he did see her, they met at Anna's or at his house. Bree's home had ceased being their hangout of choice years ago, with her mother's passing and her father's downward spiral.

Today had been a good step toward the positive. He wasn't certain, but Carson guessed that display of affection from her father was the most Bree'd had from him in a long time. She'd been so alone here, so lonely.

He didn't ever want her to feel that way again.

They said a quick goodbye to her brothers, then Carson took the empty dishes from her and followed her out of the house. With his free hand he opened her door, then handed her the pan to hold on her lap for the ride back to his dad's.

"Thank you," Bree said, when he'd come around the other side and was settled in his seat. "It was good to see him."

Him. Singular. Not so good to see her brothers, maybe. Carson wasn't sure if that would ever change. He and Charlie had their differences, but there was still love between them. Carson wasn't sure if Evan, and particularly Blane, were even capable of that emotion.

"How often do you think you'd like to visit?" *What are you thinking about living in Holiday now?* He didn't dare ask the question. It was the last thing he wanted to coax or push her into.

Bree pursed her lips in thought. "It depends, I guess. On how they're doing and where we are." She looked over at Carson, the unspoken question hovering in the air between them.

"About the house," she began.

"Yes?" Carson put the car in drive and started down the street.

She gave him a weak smile. "I think we should buy it."

Twenty-three

Fourth of July

"WELCOME HOME—OF sorts—Mrs. Armstrong." Carson took Bree's hand and pulled her from the car. They stood a moment surveying surroundings that Bree hoped soon would feel familiar. Her eyes swept the yard, ignoring the weeds and lawn long gone to seed and instead letting the magnificent trees capture her attention and bring a smile to her face.

Along with the requisite magnolias to go with the so-named river backing the property, their newly acquired land boasted sweet gum, pine, ash, maple, oak, and even a pecan tree. Bree hoped the latter wouldn't remind Carson too much of Anna and her family.

"And now, I shall carry you across our threshold—and hope it holds both our weight at once."

Bree shrieked as Carson swept her off her feet into his arms and marched toward the house. *Our house.* Or some of it would be at least. After two weeks of inspections and reports, she had reluctantly agreed with Carson that the most prudent thing would be to tear it down. But first, beginning today, they were going to salvage what they could.

"What are you doing?" Bree kicked her legs back and

forth playfully, trying to keep the atmosphere light. It didn't take much lately—being in the same room was enough—for things between them to quickly become charged.

"The custom of carrying one's wife across the threshold is said to keep evil spirits away." Carson mounted the steps with ease, as if he weren't carrying her at all. "Given the house we purchased, I thought it worth following any superstition that might keep away ghosts."

"And here I thought you were being romantic." Bree wrapped her arms behind his neck as Carson moved one of his hands to quickly open the door.

"Just you wait," he promised, stepping over the threshold. He set her down gently, but Bree didn't release her hold on him.

She'd been waiting, the past two weeks since Father's Day, for the sparks between them to erupt in full-blown flame. It seemed she'd conveyed well her desire to be kissed. Carson willingly obliged every day, several times a day.

Along with kissing, they cuddled on the couch and in bed, sleeping curled up beside each other every night. At first that had been enough. She felt comfortable, safe, and then gradually ready for the next steps in their progression as husband and wife. When they didn't come, she started to wonder if something wasn't wrong after all—with her. Carson had to want more, didn't he? If she was feeling this way, shouldn't her husband be even more so?

She hoped he meant to wait until they'd bought the house, to have their first intimacy as husband and wife be at this place that would be their home and special to them. She didn't care if it was in a tent or a trailer on their property—both ideas that had been bantered around as they decided what course of action to take with the house.

Right now, being this close to him, she didn't think she

much cared if it was in the foyer with a blanket thrown over the dusty floor.

"We're all alone. No one around for a few miles at least." Bree reached up on tiptoes, closed her eyes, and kissed him.

"So we are." Carson circled his hands around her waist and pulled her to him, deepening their kiss. After a long, breathless minute, he pulled back. A slow, somewhat devilish grin curved his mouth, and a mischievous twinkle shone in his eyes. "Which is why I know you won't mind wearing something for me, with no one else around to see."

Bree looked at him askance "Wh—at do you want me to wear?" Had he actually bought her something? After they'd agreed to buying nothing that wasn't absolutely necessary for the next several months?

Purchasing the property *and* building a new house on it meant their finances were stretched. She'd committed her $12,000 savings for the demolition, while Carson had emptied his bank account, all except the amount for a year of Charlie's tuition, for the down payment. A construction loan would see them through to the finished project, but they were going to have to live frugally in the meantime. Which meant no extra purchases. Like . . . *Lingerie? He wouldn't, would he?*

Bree felt her face heat, and her mind raced, *worrying* over what he might have possibly purchased for her.

"Close your eyes," Carson whispered, his breath tickling her ear.

She swallowed and complied. She felt him step away, heard him walk back outside, heard the trunk of the car pop open and then close. Her heartbeat quickened with each step of his return.

"No peeking," Carson said. Then, "I want you to feel like a woman in this—strong, empowered, like you can do anything. And I really hope this is your color. But even if it's not your favorite, I hope you know you look stunning in anything."

Bree scrunched her eyes closed and crossed her arms in front of her, feeling undressed already. Would he hand it to her and expect her to go change somewhere? Or would he help her get into whatever he'd bought?

"Ready?" Carson was right in front of her.

Was she? *Yes—maybe.* Bree gave a slow nod.

A weight lowered onto her head.

My—head? She opened her eyes as Carson fastened a strap below her chin. He knocked on the top of the solid hat.

"Hard hat. Have to keep my wife safe if she's going to be working in these dangerous conditions. And look. I've got one to match." Carson reached into the bag at his side and withdrew a second hard plastic, yellow construction hat.

Speechless, Bree watched him put it on.

"What?" he asked a minute later when she still hadn't spoken but continued staring at him. "Yellow not my color?"

"Not particularly," she said. "I can't believe this—" Her eyes lifted toward the hat perched on her head. "That it's—"

"What I bought you to wear?" A corner of Carson's mouth lifted. He was clearly pleased with himself and his joke. "Were you expecting something else, dear wife?" He leaned close to whisper in her ear again, their helmets clanking. "This is payback for the day you brought me here the first time, leading me on the whole way, then surprising me with thirty years' worth of yard work."

"I did not lead you on all day." Bree's hands went to her hips.

"No?" Carson's brows rose. "What do you call whispering seductively, placing your hand on my leg, leaning over me to unbuckle the seat belt?"

"Normal things. That's what I call them," Bree said,

feeling slightly disgruntled yet inordinately pleased that he felt she'd been leading him on that day. Maybe she wasn't as hopeless at the whole flirting thing as she'd believed.

"Darn right those are normal things." Carson snatched her around the waist and pulled her into his arms again, kissing her soundly. "That and a whole lot more is going to be normal from now on." He let her go with a ragged sigh and a look that said he didn't really want to let her go at all. He reached into his bag again and pulled out a handful of pry bars and chisels of different lengths and widths.

Bree held her hand out, and he placed the smallest in it, along with a screwdriver.

"And for the record, the hat isn't the only thing I bought you to wear. But work before play."

Bree paused to wipe another bead of sweat from her brow before it could trickle into her eyes like the last three. The July sun beating through the large, curtainless windows felt relentless, and they didn't have so much as a fan available to keep the place cool.

She knelt on the floor once more, wedging the pry bar beneath the next piece of oak flooring. The good news—the floor was quality. Solid, sturdy, and would one day be beautiful again. The bad news—the floor was solid and sturdy, and there was a lot of it. *A lot of savings*, Bree reminded herself. A wood floor like this could cost thousands. Today's labor meant tomorrow's savings and a beautiful wood floor in their new home.

At nine o'clock sharp a car pulled into the drive. Bree paused her work again, feeling exhausted and overheated, though they'd been at this barely two hours. She walked to the open front door to greet Carson's brother, who she knew was coming to help, and instead found her own brothers walking up the steps.

"Morning, sis." Evan had a smile for her. He'd always been the more cheerful of the two.

"Hi," Breanna said, startled to see them here. "What's up? Everything okay with Dad?" By now the entire town would know that she and Carson had bought this place, so she supposed it wasn't too surprising that her brothers had shown up to have a look around. But nine in the morning on a holiday did seem a bit early for them—unless something had happened.

"Dad's fine. He's working overtime today," Evan said. "A lot of that lately." He elbowed Blane, and they exchanged a knowing look.

"What am I missing?" Bree asked.

"If you were still at home, you might know. Aren't you going to invite us in?" Blane looked around with obvious boredom.

Bree dropped the subject of their dad for the moment and stepped back from the doorway. "Enter at your own risk."

"Nice hat." Blane made to smack the top of it as he walked past, but she ducked out of the way in time.

"I've got one for you, too," Carson called from the top of the stairs. He jiggled the railing a second, as if testing it for strength, then hopped on and rode it down. He was nearly to the bottom when the lower section gave way with a loud crack. Carson jumped off as the railing bent the opposite direction and crashed to the foyer in a cloud of dust.

"Meant to do that." Carson wiped his hands on a rag hanging from his belt loop and walked over to examine the damage.

"You're such a guy," Bree grumbled. "It would serve you right if you got hurt."

"Actually, I think you'd have to serve me." Carson looked over his shoulder at her. "You know, tenderly care for your husband who was severely wounded in the pursuit of salvaging treasure for his beloved wife."

Bree rolled her eyes. "I wouldn't test that theory."

Carson laughed. "Don't plan to." He squatted near the fallen railing. "Oh good. I didn't actually break the rail. It looks like it was built in two sections originally."

"Consider yourself lucky." Bree folded her arms and gave him a pointed look.

"Every day." Carson stood, placed a quick kiss on the bridge of her nose, then turned to her brothers. "I'm glad you decided to come."

"This place is a wreck," Blane muttered.

"And we're only making it worse." Carson grinned. Considering the amount of work before them, he seemed particularly cheerful. "You guys up for the task?"

"Yup." Evan nodded.

"Pay is ten an hour?" Blane asked.

He'd *hired* her brothers? Bree looked at Carson, unsure whether to feel grateful or worried. Heaven knows they needed the work. But last she'd checked, they also needed to learn *how* to work, particularly Blane.

"Ten an hour if you're doing ten dollars' worth of work," Carson said. "If I find you sitting on your butt, your wage goes down exponentially."

"Same deal for him? Or is he getting more?" Blane inclined his head toward the doorway and Charlie, who'd just entered.

"He doesn't get paid anything at all." Carson flashed Charlie a smile that was, surprisingly, returned. "But he gets to go to school this fall." Carson tossed a hard hat at Charlie, then handed one each to Blane and Evan. "Enough talk of wages. There is work to be done, and lots of it if I hope to have a roof over my wife's head by Christmas. Follow me."

He led them into the dining room. "Bree and I have been working on pulling up the hardwood floor in the library. You three can start in here. We'll be reusing the planks in the new house, so they need to be intact and banged up as little as possible. I'll show you the best method we've found."

Bree handed Carson her chisel and watched the demonstration with their brothers. Carson worked fast wedging the chisel in place, then placing the pry bar and lifting the plank far quicker than she was able.

Those strong arms. She suppressed a sigh, wanting them around her again. *Work before play.*

Carson finished his demonstration and stood, meeting her gaze, almost as if he knew the direction of her thoughts.

"Hungry?" he asked her as they left their brothers and returned to the library.

"Starved."

Carson gave her a quick peck on the cheek. "Me too. Glad to know it's mutual."

Twenty-four

BY FIVE O'CLOCK it was just the two of them again, hungry, sweaty, and exhausted. Charlie, Evan, and Blane had left an hour earlier so they could go home to shower before the Fourth of July festivities at the one park in town. Bree and Carson had declined to join them. They'd purchased a house within the city limits, but that didn't mean she was ready to become a full-fledged Holiday citizen again yet. They'd start with church on Sunday and see how that went first.

"A good day's work." Carson stood in the foyer surveying the mess they'd made. The library bookcases had been removed, the salvageable doors and knobs taken out, both banisters were down, with one stubborn newel post remaining until he acquired or borrowed some better tools. A good portion of the wood flooring had been pulled up too.

"That floor is a beast," Bree said, swiping her own hand across her forehead beneath the hat. "Can we take these off now?" She tugged at the chin strap.

"Only when we're outside. Ready to call it a day?"

She nodded. "That floor will still be here tomorrow—unfortunately."

"So will the crew to take out the window." Carson stared up at the stained glass on the second floor.

"I'm nervous about that," Bree said. "Do you think they'll really be able to keep it intact?"

"That's what they said." Carson shrugged. "It's worth a try, at any rate."

They left the house, closing the door behind them to keep critters out but not bothering to lock up. They brought the last of the tools to the pod that had been delivered earlier to hold the salvaged items from the house. Bree tossed their hats inside on top of everything else, and Carson secured the padlock, then turned and headed for the back of the house.

"Where are you going?" Bree asked. "Isn't your dad expecting us?" They'd moved their few belongings into Reverend Armstrong's garage last weekend and were now homeless, excepting the building before them, which was in no way livable, especially now. Staying in Carson's old room wasn't her first choice of housing and not the best she could think of for their developing marriage. But it was free, and if they were to build the house they wanted, free rent for the next six months would be helpful.

"It's hot. I was thinking about recreating the swim we took on our first visit."

Work before play, he'd said this morning. Did he mean for them to "play" out on the back lawn or at the river where any old fisherman like Sonny might be watching them?

Bree shook her head. She was hot—and tired and close to grumpy. A shower and a good meal might change that, and then maybe she and Carson could spend time together while they had the house to themselves and his dad and brother were at the park watching the fireworks.

"No swim for me, but I'll push you in if you want." She followed him past two ash trees to the magnolias that overhung the river. Near the broken deck, Bree stopped short, staring at a sizable houseboat moored near their dock, or what was left of it. "Whose boat is that?

"I'm not sure. I'll go see." Carson stripped off his shirt, then bent to remove his shoes.

"You can't just go on someone's boat," Bree called as he waded out into the river.

"Why not? It's parked near our property, isn't it?" Carson flashed her a grin before he dove under the water. He surfaced a second later, then with sure strokes propelled himself over to the houseboat. He grabbed the ladder near the back and hauled himself on board.

"Come on over," he called, waving. "It's nice. Look, there's a barbecue. He opened the lid of a grill on the back deck. "Even a freezer stashed with popsicles." He flipped open a chest freezer and pulled out one of the two-stick fruit variety. "Half for you," he called.

Hands on hips, Bree shook her head. She stood at the edge of the water and leaned forward. "What are you up to?" He really wouldn't walk around on someone's boat like that, would he?

"Just checking out your honeymoon suite," he called, ducking inside.

"Honeymoon—Carson!"

He either didn't hear or was ignoring her. It was tempting to get in the river and follow him, but it wasn't as simple a prospect for her as it had been for him to remove the top half of her clothing. No telling who might be in the nearby woods. They hadn't noticed Sonny the first time they'd come. And no telling what might be lurking in the depths of the river.

Carson reappeared mid-boat. He started some kind of motor, and a two-foot-wide metal plank emerged from the side and began making its way toward the shore. Bree waited until it hovered over the bank and was lowered successfully. The motor stopped as she stepped onto the ramp and hurried toward Carson.

"Whose boat is this?" she asked again. "What is it doing here?"

Carson reached for her hand and pulled her on board. "Welcome to your temporary home, Mrs. Armstrong."

"What's the catch?" Bree asked warily as Carson's fingers entwined with hers. That a houseboat had magically appeared at their dock seemed too easy, too convenient. *Not to mention exciting and romantic.*

"No catch." Carson offered her what was left of the popsicle. "Since you are so enamored with our little Magnolia River, I had the idea to take you on the mighty Mississippi, on a river cruise as a belated honeymoon this fall when the leaves were turning. I talked to Connor about it because he's been on at least one of those cruises. That's when I found out it would cost about two thousand dollars and realized we couldn't afford to do a cruise right now, not with building a house—and helping Charlie attend college."

"That's okay." Bree touched his arm. "I told you I don't need a honeymoon. Besides, you know us—we do things backward. Buy property and build a house first, honeymoon later."

"We do seem to go about things rather unconventionally, don't we?" Carson pulled her into his arms, his hands still damp from the river and cool against her back. Bree traced her fingers along his bare chest as her eyes slowly lifted to his.

"So you rented this boat for us instead. We *aren't* going to be staying with your dad and brother tonight?"

Carson shook his head slowly. "Not unless you'd rather stay in town. I thought this might be more private, that you might not mind sleeping on a boat for the next, oh, five or six months."

"That long? Really?" She raised up on her toes, thrilled at the possibility that they would have their own place now, here.

"I love it. It's charming, romantic... You're sure there's not a catch?"

"Just you." Carson grinned mischievously. "All to myself with no one to bother us. We can even pull the ramp in at night as an extra precaution."

"But where did you get the boat?" Bree pressed. "This had to cost more than a cruise."

"Connor was so grateful that we'd decided to stay in the same state as corporate that he offered the use of his boat for a few months. The only thing I had to do was pay to get it moved here and moved back when we're done using it. He said he won't be needing it again until next summer. And our house had better be finished by then."

"I can't believe this," Bree said. "That's so generous of him—" Their conversation at the Saint Patrick's Day party came back to her suddenly. "It's because he believes I'm Anna and decided to stay instead of taking the job on the West Coast." It shouldn't have mattered to her but somehow did. A lot.

"He doesn't think you're Anna." Carson held Bree at arm's length. "He suspected something wasn't quite right at the dinner in March, when you corrected your name for him. Then, when you lost the baby and I missed so much work, I told him everything. He knows the entire story, and he's happy for *us*, Bree. Connor says my work has never been so good and I've never seemed happier to him, since we've been married. All of that is true. And it's because of you."

Bree didn't know what to say. That Carson's employer had heard the whole sordid tale and still liked her made her feel like crying. *Happy tears.* At least one person, outside of their families, did not appear to judge them too harshly.

"Don't cry," Carson said. "Remember what I've been telling you all along. Things will work out. If we keep trying to make it right, things will all end up okay."

Bree laid her head against his shoulder and breathed in deeply. "We're so much better than okay."

Humming to himself, Carson flipped the steaks on the barbecue. Inside the houseboat, Bree had just finished her shower and should be getting dressed for the evening—in what he'd really bought her. He couldn't wait to see her in it or to share this meal with her. He was starving in more ways than one, and the next few hours promised to be a feast in every way.

When the steaks were done, Carson carried them on a plate to the front of the boat, where he'd set a table for two with a tablecloth from the buffet at his father's house, his mother's china, and two taper candles. At seven thirty it wasn't exactly dark yet, but the light still finding its way through the trees overhanging the river was more mellow than bright, casting golden shadows this way and that along the shore.

Carson placed the steaks on the china, then added the salad and corn he'd prepared earlier. He had a cheesecake in the refrigerator and roses in the vase in the bedroom. Everything was perfect.

Including Bree. She stood on the step leading down to the front of the boat, her long hair falling behind her in the gentle breeze and the dress he'd bought billowing about her ankles. It had taken him months to find this dress—a cross between a simple wedding gown and the gauzy, white fabric a woman might wear to the beach. He wasn't any kind of fashion expert but thought the sheer sleeves, lace bodice, and flowing skirt were perfect. He couldn't imagine any fancier gown could make Bree any more beautiful than she looked at this moment.

"I love it," she said, following Carson's gaze to the dress. "It's the prettiest thing I've ever worn."

"I wanted you to have a long white dress. I'm only sorry that you didn't get to stand up in the front of the church like this, for everyone else to see how beautiful you are."

"I stood up with you. That's what matters." Bree stepped down and crossed the small deck. "Others may not understand or accept that yet, but your father has helped me believe that God does. That he acknowledges this marriage and that we are doing our best to make amends, to make things right."

"Everything with you is right, Bree. Everything with us." He kissed her gently, only once, fearing their meal would be forgotten and go to waste if he risked more than that.

He held Bree's seat for her, then took the one opposite. They held hands while he prayed, bringing the custom he'd grown up with into their own home, their own table. Somehow this felt like home, far more than their apartment in Birmingham had. They were in Holiday, they were buying this land, they were husband and wife.

"This is delicious." Bree closed her eyes, a look of bliss on her face after her first bite of steak.

"You did say you were hungry enough to eat a horse," Carson teased.

Bree's eyes flew open, and she gave him a horrified stare.

"Just kidding," he hastily assured her. "The package is in the trash if you don't believe me. Grade A beef, straight from Texas or thereabouts."

"You can't joke about things like that." Bree pointed her steak knife at him. "Remember, I grew up in a house of the mighty hunters. You wouldn't believe some of the things that have been served at our table."

"Right. Forgot about that. Sorry." *Bree, the survivor*, he

could call her. He wondered how much of the hunting had been done for sport and how much for necessity. It was no secret her family had lived on little income the past several years.

"My brothers told me that my dad has been working a lot of overtime," Bree said, as if her thoughts had followed Carson's. "I wonder why this sudden change."

"I'm sure life has been more difficult without you there. It was time, though, Bree. Far past time for your dad and brothers to step up and—"

"I know. And don't worry." She smiled at him. "I have no intention of going back. They are three grown men who can fend for themselves."

"Agreed." Carson wasn't sure he could fend for himself anymore. He'd grown used to watching her asleep beside him before she awoke at the start of each day, to their easy banter and laughter, to their kisses . . .

"Save room for dessert," Carson admonished as Bree served herself a second helping of salad.

"More popsicles?" Bree asked as she drizzled dressing over her lettuce.

"Cheesecake." *And you.*

"The last time I ate cheesecake with you . . ." Her smile grew wistful.

"Junior prom." Carson remembered too. "If I have leftover cherry topping on my chin, will you wipe it away for me again?"

"Of course." Bree's smile turned seductive. "Or I could kiss it away."

"In that case, I predict I may be somewhat of a sloppy cheesecake eater tonight."

Bree laughed, and Carson felt a surge of joy and contentment. Could life be any better than this—eating dinner, flirting with his wife, in one of the most beautiful settings he could imagine.

"You make me so happy," he said, feeling oddly emotional and sentimental in spite of their laughter a moment ago.

Bree set her fork aside and leaned across the table toward him, taking his hand again. "I've only just begun."

Twenty-five

ANOTHER SET OF fireworks from the Fourth of July celebration burst overhead. "I'm surprised we can see them here, but this is a pretty great view." Bree lay on her back beside Carson on the top deck of the gently swaying boat. It was moored securely in several places, but the pull of the river could still be felt.

"The prettiest I've ever seen." Carson lay on his side, facing his wife, admiring her profile instead of the fireworks. There had been plenty of those earlier, in the bedroom below, both a sweet and sizzling celebration of their nearly five months of marriage. At last they had a new memory, one to hopefully wipe away the old from that night last November. He could never feel entirely sorry for it, as it had led them here. But he would always wish he would have done things differently. Better. The right way.

Being back in Holiday was both a good and a painful reminder of the wrong he'd done to so many that night. As happy as he and Bree were at this very minute—and he couldn't recall ever feeling happier—he didn't want to ever forget that they still had wrongs to right, people to mend fences with. Somehow. Someday.

But just now . . . Carson ran his fingers along Bree's arm,

feeling pleased as goose bumps rose along her skin, in spite of the warm night. As he'd learned recently, Bree was not immune to his touch.

"Yes? Was there something you wanted?" She pulled her attention from the display lighting the sky, rolling on her side to face Carson.

"You." He touched her chin, then leaned over her so he could kiss her soundly, the fireworks overhead nothing compared to those exploding inside of him.

"I love you, Breanna."

She attempted to return the sentiment, but his lips would not allow hers to fully form the words. And that was okay.

He preferred being shown to being told.

Twenty-six

"I CAN DO this," Bree said, summoning every ounce of courage she possessed as Carson parked their car in front of the building that had, at times, felt more like home to her than the house she'd grown up in. Church had always been a friendly place, full of warmth and good feelings, the words Carson's father spoke from the pulpit intended to uplift and inspire instead of instill the fear of God as some sermons did.

But today she worried all of that was about to change.

Carson got out of the car and came around to open her side. Bree accepted his hand and with her other smoothed the ruffles on her floral skirt, the same one she'd been wearing at least one Sunday a month for the last five years. She doubted the familiar fabric would do much in the way of having people treat her as familiar, or the way they used to, but wearing it felt fortifying all the same.

I'm the same nice girl I always was. Just married now, to the same nice boy who happens to be the reverend's son. We made a mistake. Forgive us. Please be kind.

Carson kept her hand tucked into his arm as they made their way up the steps with the last of the churchgoers. As planned, they'd arrived only a couple of minutes before the service started.

Once inside, Bree breathed an almost audible sigh of relief at seeing several spaces free on the back left bench. Carson had seen them, too, and steered her toward it, only to be stopped as she started to slide into the pew.

"These seats are saved," Mrs. Hendricks said, pushing her daughters to slide down the row and fill in the space. "Got cousins coming today. Guess they're running late."

"Of course." Bree retreated hastily and allowed Carson to lead her to the next available bench, two more up and on the right. Not as good as being all the way at the back would have been, but certainly better than up front, where everyone might stare at the back of their heads, thinking ill thoughts about them throughout the sermon.

This time Carson started to sit first, only to be told again that the seat was saved.

He gave a cordial nod and withdrew, muttering to Bree beneath his breath. "Since when has seat saving become so popular in Holiday?"

Since we wanted those seats. Bree felt her face heating with shame and wished they hadn't come, wished she could be anywhere but here.

Apparently giving up on the main benches facing forward, Carson led her up the aisle, in full view of every eye in the room, including Anna's parents sitting on their customary pew, third from the front on the left. Keeping her face straight ahead and her expression blank, she hoped, Bree followed Carson to the side benches, those usually used only by parents dealing with unruly children or who came in extra late. These straight-backed benches were part of the original church and not nearly as comfortable as those facing front, but Bree didn't care. She was simply relieved to have a seat. They settled on the pew closest to the front, and Bree crossed her legs and told her pounding heart to stop it.

The organ prelude continued, nearly loud enough to shake the windows as it was every week. It hadn't ceased at all during their search, yet to Bree it had felt like it—and time—had, with all eyes on her. Some were still on her and Carson now, and she hadn't missed the whispered snatches of conversation about the two of them as they'd made their way to their seats.

"Some nerve, showing up in Holiday again."

"Holding hands in plain sight, after what they did to poor Anna."

"Lost the baby, too, yet still she claims him hers."

This one hurt the most, and so closely echoed Bree's own thoughts in the weeks after her miscarriage that she could hardly breathe for the sob that had risen in her throat.

The Marshall family came in just as the last note hit. With their many children—six all under the age of ten—they were always the last to arrive. Bree found comfort in the familiarity of it all.

She mustered a smile for Savannah, one of the little girls who had been in the Sunday school class Bree had helped with sometimes. Mrs. Marshall caught sight of Bree, jerked Savannah to a sudden stop, then turned to whisper something in her husband's ear. Together they herded their brood back toward the center of the chapel and then to a bench on the other side. It was far too small a space for their large family, and Mr. Marshall ended up with two children on his lap just so they could all squeeze in.

Bree's eyes watered as she watched all of this. Carson squeezed her hand but didn't say anything. She moved her lips during the opening song, but her throat felt too constricted to sing. She closed her eyes during the prayer and wished that when she opened them she would be somewhere else. At last his father stood up, and the service began.

She was hoping for a sermon of forgiveness or perhaps a reminder of what the Savior had told others when they had wished to stone the woman caught in sin. *He who is without sin* ... Perhaps many here were. Or thought they were. Holiday had never felt so unfriendly. She'd known this might happen, had expected it, even, but living it was entirely different. Bree couldn't wait to leave, to go home to their little boat and weep in Carson's arms. Had they made a terrible mistake, buying property here?

Reverend Armstrong stood at the pulpit, his pleasant Mr. Rogers smile on his face—or so Carson described it. "Today I would like to speak with you on the subject of 'one nation under God.'"

Bree angled her body to face the front of the church, to better see Reverend Armstrong and to notice others less.

"The phrase 'under God' was not originally part of our nation's Pledge of Allegiance. It was added in 1954, after a sermon on the subject by Reverend George Docherty, a great supporter of equal rights for both those of other religions and races.

"He believed God must be involved if a nation or a body of people are to be indivisible. Why? For the precise reason that we are all different, and—" Reverend Armstrong paused, his eyes moving slowly over the congregation. "We are all imperfect. Every single one of us in this room. What we have in common is our ability to sin and our Savior, who died for all of us. He made no exclusions."

Bree felt her heart catch and her love for Carson's father swell. Perhaps this sermon would aid their cause after all.

"To make clear this point," he continued, "I would like to spend some time in history today, during the period when our nation had yet to be born, when a Revolutionary War that won our country its freedom was yet on the horizon."

Bree soon found herself lost in the stories of the early colonists, those on both sides of the war. The tale and words of loyalist Thomas Hutchinson, who had his home attacked and his family threatened, all because of rumor that put him on the wrong side of the Stamp Act, particularly touched her.

"'I pray God give us better hearts,' Hutchinson said publicly the day after his home was destroyed and his life and that of his family endangered. Of the many things Hutchinson might have said or done—demands for justice, retaliation, revenge—he instead called for love, for all to have better hearts. I extend that same invitation to you today." Reverend Armstrong launched into another story, this one about a young woman shunned for her brave actions at the start of the war.

By the end of Reverend Armstrong's sermon, the lump in Bree's throat had dissolved. She and Carson might not have many on their side here, but Carson's father, and even her father, it seemed, were a good start.

The final *amen* had barely been uttered when Carson pulled her to her feet and hurried out the side door. Bree almost had to run in her heels to keep up.

"I'm so sorry," he began, apologizing as soon as they were in the parking lot.

"It isn't your fault. We knew it might be like this. Small town, big sin."

"We are not a sin," Carson said vehemently. He opened her door for her, and Bree slid into the passenger seat.

"I didn't mean that we were," Bree said when he was seated. "What we did hurt a lot of people, though."

"Most of the people in there were not directly involved or affected. So why can't they leave well enough alone?"

Bree didn't answer. She and Carson had yet to quarrel, and she didn't want to start now.

"Maybe building a house here is a mistake," Carson said, echoing her earlier thoughts. "I won't have people looking at you like that." He drove faster than necessary down the street, away from the church. His father had invited them for lunch, but Carson drove past his house, heading for their property instead.

"They won't do it forever," Bree said, sounding far more confident than she felt. Carson seemed even more upset than she was, and on her behalf. She reached across the console to touch his hand.

"You're right," he said. "If we're not here, they won't do it at all."

"Carson..." She frowned at him. "Running away isn't the answer."

"Neither is subjecting you to such unkindness." He returned her frown with a deeper one.

"It's one hour, once a week. We can do this." She'd needed this pep talk herself an hour ago. Then, she'd wanted to leave, to go far away and never come back. Except that would mean crushing the last of Carson's dreams. He wouldn't father any biological children now. He wasn't going to live on the street or in the house he'd wanted. The least she could do was to tough it out here so he could be near his father and brother and live in the town he'd grown up in.

"And what about grocery shopping? How long will it be before you can shop at the Mulberry?"

"I don't know. Maybe I just need to go, to face Anna's parents and get it over with."

"Not without me," Carson said. "I don't want you going anywhere in town without me. If church was that brutal, I can only imagine what the diner or the market might be like."

Bree sighed. She didn't want to think about that either. But neither was she ready to give up. "We need something big and exciting to happen in Holiday to take everyone's minds off of us."

Carson looked over at her, his mouth forming a half smile. "We need a miracle."

Twenty-seven

Founder's Day

"How are you doing up there?" Bree called, hand held to her face, shielding her eyes from the sun as she stared up at Carson, kneeling on what would be the roof of their new home.

"There's a reason they call this sweat equity," he called down to her as he wiped his sleeve across his forehead. "Going well, though." He had the weekend to get the tar paper on the roof. Then the roofers and he and Charlie would start on the shingles Monday morning.

Six weeks into their project, and all was mostly on schedule. He and Charlie had helped with the framing and now the roof on the new house, while Bree and her brothers worked on cleanup from the old. After ten days of salvaging what they could, the wrecker had arrived and torn it down in a matter of hours. Unfortunately it was probably going to be a matter of weeks before all the debris had been transported by wheelbarrow to the dumpster.

But that hadn't hindered progress on their new home. The new house had a different footprint and location on the property—they'd added a garage, and the house would sit a little farther from the river as an extra precaution against flooding. Starting construction had not been contingent upon cleanup of the old building.

"Looking good," Bree called as she pushed her wheelbarrow full of wood and plaster.

"I am, aren't I?" Carson flexed his muscles and flashed her a grin, which earned him a shake of her head—and hips.

"You mean *she's* looking good," Charlie said. "I don't know how you got so lucky, bro, but if going to college is the place to start, I'm there."

"Sobriety is the place to start," Carson said. "How did you do yesterday—at the party last night?"

Charlie held up his hand, fingers and thumb forming a zero. "I enjoyed Sprite, though I got ribbed plenty for it."

"Excellent," Carson said. "I mean about the Sprite. Not the guys giving you a bad time." As far as he was concerned, Charlie couldn't leave for college soon enough. His old friends here were not the kind to encourage his change of habit.

"Thirty-four days without a beer—or anything else." Charlie spoke with a clear-eyed smile. "Every time I think about taking a drink, I do what you suggested and look at Mom's picture. I don't want to let her down again."

"You aren't," Carson said. "I'm proud of you, and so is she." He swung the hammer, feeling cautiously hopeful about Charlie's progress. If nothing else, being back in Holiday had been good for their relationship and good for Charlie.

Carson looked down at Bree, struggling with her load, never complaining about having to do so much of the work themselves, always cheerful. He knew they were here because of his dream to live in a grand old house in Holiday. She might have chosen the river view, but he was the one who'd wanted this town. Now all he wanted was for Holiday, the people here, to be good for and to her. But, his father's sermons aside, so far it seemed that was not so easily accomplished.

One bag of ice. Cold drinks for the workers. Such a simple request.

It had been Charlie's, called down from the roof fifteen minutes ago. Bree had been happy to comply—until she'd realized they had used all the ice from the chest freezer on the boat.

That left two choices—the one gas station in town or Mulberry Market, the store Anna's parents owned. Neither was particularly appealing, but the gas station was the obvious choice, though it was about a mile farther.

Put on your big-girl pants, she told herself as she drove Charlie's car off the sanctuary that was their property. Carson had gone over to his dad's house this afternoon, to use the Wi-Fi for a Skype appointment with a client. She missed him being right here with her, but didn't mind his absence too much, so long as she was at their house, sheltered and safe from the town that used to be hers. Here no one came to call, except construction workers who didn't know them personally or family members who did and who, for the most part, had found it in their hearts to move on.

The speed limit sign flashed as she neared the center of town, warning her she was going too fast. Bree put her foot on the brake. The last thing she needed was a speeding ticket. But going thirty miles per hour down Main Street was painful. It was lunchtime, so the diner was full, with people on the sidewalks outside the antique store on one side and the single movie theater and the post office on the other. Bree kept her gaze straight ahead and her hands locked on the wheel. When the one light in town turned yellow as she approached, she almost wished she'd risked the market.

She slowed the car to a stop, then looked down, fiddling with the radio, pretending interest in tuning it to a specific station. What felt like a minute passed, and she glanced up to see if the light was green yet.

Robbie Marsh was crossing the street and seemed as surprised to see her as she felt at seeing him. Her hand lifted automatically to wave, and she smiled. They'd remained friends, even after their senior year when she'd told him she didn't want to date anymore. Robbie had moved away shortly thereafter, and Bree had seldom thought of him since. But a friendly face was a welcome thing these days.

If it was truly friendly, which Robbie's, suddenly, was not. He'd started to return her smile, or at least she thought he had, but then he frowned instead and shook his head at her before turning away.

Inside the car, Bree lowered her hand, tucking it beneath her leg. *Why should Robbie treat me so unkindly?* Likely his mother had told him the entire story, followed by a lecture about how fortunate it was that Bree hadn't continued to date him.

She blinked away tears and drove on when the light was at last green. Before getting out of the car at the gas station, she made sure she had the exact change for the ice. Pasting a smile on her face and walking with confidence she didn't feel, Bree entered the tiny convenience store. Ernie Jensen, who'd been working the counter for as long as she could remember, had his back to her, stocking candy on the shelves.

"Hello, Ernie. May I have one bag of ice, please?"

He glanced over his shoulder at her, then turned to retrieve the bills she'd already placed on the counter. Countless times over the years, Bree had been in this same spot, making this same purchase. Her family had never owned a fridge with an ice maker, so once a month during the summer, she would buy a bag here to supplement the ice cubes churned out from their plastic trays at home.

Over the nearly twenty years she'd been coming here, Ernie had grown rounder and his hair whiter, which worked out well for his side gig playing Santa at the community center each December.

Bree smiled to herself, remembering the year he'd forgotten to change out of his red suit before coming back to the station to lock up for the night. The Daisy Scout troop had been out caroling and happened to pass by on their hay wagon as "Santa," clearly visible through the large glass window, counted out the till.

"Santa's robbing the gas station!" Molly Anderson had squealed, and soon the entire hay wagon was in an uproar, with little girls squealing and screaming. It had taken some fancy talking and a whopper of a story to get that mess all straightened out—without revealing Santa's true identity to eight six-year-olds.

Ernie slid the bills into the register and used his girth to slam the drawer.

"Thanks," Bree said and headed toward the door, relieved to have that confrontation over with. Now if she could just not run into anyone else on her way out.

"Crying shame what happened to Miss Annabelle," Ernie called. Bree didn't turn around.

"Never met a sweeter girl. Shame on those responsible. If I was really Santa..."

Bree grabbed the door handle and pushed. She stepped out into the blistering heat and swell of humidity with gratitude, the temperature far easier to bear than others' judgments.

Even Santa. Of course she didn't deserve any presents after what she'd done. But she hadn't been asking for any, had she? Just a bag of ice—nearly forgotten in her haste to escape.

Bree veered left, grabbed a bag from the cooler outside the store, then hurried across the parking lot to the car, tossing the bag in before her. Her fingers stung with cold, but it was nothing compared to the bite of frost she'd felt inside the store.

Twenty-eight

"August in Alabama has got to be one of the most miserable climates on the planet," Carson muttered. "Just the walk from the air-conditioned houseboat to the car has me sweating."

"Kind of amazing someone founded this place in August," Bree said, sliding into the driver's seat. She was driving these days because Carson had two handfuls of painful blisters from swinging a hammer. She'd been working, too, but she'd worn gloves.

"Seriously," Carson agreed. "Had it been me who'd wandered here, I think I would have kept on going."

Bree laughed. "No you wouldn't. Not when you spied the river and these beautiful trees—all this green."

"You're right," he agreed, with a smile her direction. "I'm a sucker for beautiful."

Bree held on to their happiness as she backed up and drove toward the main road. Already there was a significant difference in their property. The lawn had been mowed and fertilized so that the grass was starting to compete with the weeds. Their new home would have a roof and door and windows soon, and the brick had been ordered.

She could imagine how perfect it was all going to be and kept that thought to get her through another Sunday. She'd never minded going to church as a child or a teenager. As an adult, however, it had become the most difficult hour of her week.

She left their private drive and turned onto the main road into town. She hadn't gone far when a loud pop made her jump as the car listed sharply. Bree cranked the wheel over to the side of the road. "What was that? Did I hit something?"

"Bad tire." Carson opened his door and peered outside. "Probably a nail—or worse. I'm surprised this hasn't happened sooner with all the activity our driveway has seen in the past month." He began rolling up his sleeves.

"You're going to change it—now?"

"It won't change itself," Carson answered. "I'll try to be careful not to ruin my clothes."

"Do you want to go back to the boat and get others? I'll walk back and get them for you."

He shook his head and gave her a wry smile. "A little dirt on me at church won't make people think worse of us than they already do."

Bree frowned. Sunday had become Carson's least favorite day as well—sadly, and notwithstanding the enjoyable time they spent at his father's house after services.

Since that first awful Sunday back in Holiday when they'd had to search for a place to sit, they'd changed tactics, arriving early to ensure they got a bench in back, saving them the embarrassment of having to find one and being turned away.

A few people always felt the need to give them disapproving looks as they entered, but most simply ignored them. And at least during the sermon Bree didn't worry about anyone staring at them. Sitting in the back always made for a quick escape after services as well.

But with a flat to change, they were bound to be late.

"Maybe we shouldn't go this week," Bree suggested as Carson got out of the car. She popped the trunk so they could get to the spare, then followed him around to the back.

He grabbed the tire iron, squatted near the rear right tire, and began working on the lug nuts. "That would be the easy thing to do."

Like walking away from me last February would have been the easy thing. Or getting our marriage annulled when the baby died. Or buying an already-built house elsewhere. Carson did not take the easy way out. Ever. And she loved him for it.

Bree went to get the spare from the trunk.

They were only two minutes late.

"If we go straight to a side pew, we won't have the problem we had that first week," Bree, sweaty and thirsty and with a tire smudge on her skirt, suggested as they ran up the steps.

"Agreed." Carson squeezed her hand, then pushed the heavy doors open. They stepped inside to the sounds of the opening hymn and to discover the side benches full.

"Founder's Day crowd," Carson muttered beneath his breath as the doors closed behind them.

The third Sunday in August, the church always sponsored a Founder's Day potluck right after services. The normal crowd of 250 always seemed to swell to far closer to Holiday's 700-plus population as grown children and their families returned to Holiday for this annual homecoming. The same thing happened every Christmas.

"We didn't bring anything to share," Bree whispered.

Carson shot her a look. *Did you really want to stay?*

Part of her did—the part that still remembered the way

she used to feel when coming here on Sundays. But now . . . It didn't look like they would even get a seat for services.

There were only a few benches with space for one, and she wasn't about to be parted from Carson or ask if they could sit in any of them. Bree took a step backward, tugging Carson with her. He resisted for a second, his eyes scanning the room. Finally he looked his father's direction and shrugged, then stepped back toward the doors, following Bree's lead.

They were almost there, almost free, when Carson stopped abruptly.

"Come sit with us," a familiar voice whispered. "We have room."

Bree's heart skipped, and she raised her eyes to meet Anna's mother's. She was standing in the aisle, her hand outstretched, touching Carson's arm.

She can't mean it.

"Please," Mrs. Lawrence said.

Carson paused, as if not quite in belief of the offer himself, then nodded and switched directions, towing Bree with him toward the front. It felt like forever before they reached the third pew always occupied by Anna's family.

Mrs. Lawrence scooted in, nudging her husband to do the same. He, in turn, nudged Anna's older sister, who squished closer to her husband and children, as did her brother, his wife, and child—it appeared that everyone in the family but Anna was present and accounted for.

And they really *didn't* have room for two more. Perhaps that was the point Mrs. Lawrence was trying to make, that there wasn't room for Bree and Carson in Holiday anymore, not after what they had done.

Bree cast a longing glance toward the doors at the back and had her suspicions confirmed that pretty much every single person in the chapel was staring at them. She stood awkwardly in the aisle while the domino effect continued and until both of Anna's parents held a grandchild on their laps and there was barely enough room for two more on the pew.

Carson held his hand out, indicating Bree should slide in first. In this case, she wasn't certain that ladies first was the gentlemanly thing for him to do. The idea of being so close to Anna's mom frightened her.

Feeling all those eyes on them, Bree took her seat but felt her face burning. Cherry red, no doubt. Of all the people to make a place for them. *Of all the people . . .* Her embarrassment quickly gave way to guilt. The Lawrences were the ones in the congregation who *did* have the right to be angry at her and Carson. They had every right to shun them, to never speak with them again.

Instead they were sharing their bench.

By the end of the hymn Bree's eyes were stinging. By the end of the prayer silent tears slid down her face. They were silent but didn't go unnoticed, not by Carson, but by Anna's mom, who put a comforting arm around Bree. The simple gesture released a floodgate of tender memories and emotion, contained only by the tissue Mrs. Lawrence pressed into Bree's hand.

The sermon was lost on Bree for the live one taking place at her side. How many times over the years had Anna's mother hugged her and treated Bree as her own? How generous had she been with her love, her means, her pecan bars, and her daughter? *And how did I repay her?*

Bree couldn't seem to stop her tears. Carson noticed at last and looked over in alarm, taking her hand in his. Bree sat squished between them: the mother of her best friend, whom she had betrayed terribly, and the man she'd loved enough to do it. The tears of remorse kept rolling. How could she ever make this better? It was impossible, and she must have known that when she'd chosen a side months ago. She and Carson were the couple now, with Anna the third wheel, when for so long it had been the other way around.

How must Anna and her mother feel? *How can Mrs. Lawrence stand to be in the same room with me, let alone sit beside me? And if Anna were here?*

Anna, whose heart they'd broken so badly that she had yet to return home, even to spend this special weekend with her family. Maybe she never would, and it would be Bree's fault that the dear woman at her side did not get to be close to her youngest daughter.

The service ended at last. Bree couldn't have said at all what Reverend Armstrong had spoken about. Carson leaned over Bree, met Mrs. Lawrence's eye, and said, "Thank you." Still holding Bree's hand, he rose.

"Are you staying for the potluck?" Anna's mother asked.

Carson shook his head. "I think it's better if we don't."

"Thank you for sharing your bench," Bree murmured, not quite able to look Mrs. Lawrence in the eye. Anna's father was still staring straight ahead, though the sermon had ended. Perhaps he hadn't agreed with his wife's decision.

Bree followed Carson out of the church, taking longer than usual to exit since they'd sat near the front. She was jostled a bit in the exiting crowd, but the only talk she heard today was happy chatter about the picnic about to take place.

They'd parked on the street in front of the church since they were late, and hurried there now. Bree felt eyes on her again as she stepped into the car and a minute later when they drove away.

"Will people think us rude or unfriendly because we didn't stay?" It was something she should have thought of before now.

"Have they been friendly to us?" Carson asked, his usual after-church grumpiness making its appearance.

"Yes," Bree whispered. "Today."

"Yeah," Carson said, his tone softening. "That was— awkward."

Nice. It had been, sort of, once they'd finally sat down. "I don't know what to think of it," Bree admitted, and felt teary all over again, remembering the feeling of Mrs. Lawrence's arm around her.

"Me neither," Carson said. "But for now I'm going to think Anna's mom was simply being kind."

"She was," Bree agreed, and felt another dose of hope in her heart. "She's always been one of the kindest people I know. I want to believe that our actions didn't change that."

Twenty-nine

"IT'S A REAL house," Carson said. "We have a door." He pushed the still-knobless wood inward.

"And part of a roof," Bree added, following Carson into their shell of a house. It was almost dried in now, and just in time. Rain was predicted in the coming week. "Do you think they'll get the windows in and the rest of the shingles on before it storms?"

"With a little luck," Carson said. "If only Charlie and I didn't have real jobs we have to spend time at."

"If only we didn't need a paycheck, you mean?" She smiled over her shoulder at him, then wandered into what would eventually be their kitchen. "I won't be able to help much after this week either." She'd been assigned a second grade class in a school district thirty miles away. Between commuting, lesson plans, and actual hours teaching at the school, she'd be lucky to get home before dark most days.

She was going to miss these not-so-lazy days of summer and all the time she and Carson had spent together the past couple of months. They'd needed this time, still needed it. Bree watched as he exited the house using the new back door, then walked toward the ladder propped against the back of the house.

Probably going to check the roof. Because it may look different than it did a couple of hours ago. She grinned. Carson was loving this house already. And she loved him. More and more each day—it was frightening sometimes how much she felt for him.

A quiet knock came from the front.

"Come in," Bree called, wondering if it was Carson playing a joke. Maybe he hadn't gone up to look at the roof again. Or possibly it was his father. He'd said he would stop by today, and he seemed the sort to politely knock, even when the front door wasn't locked and didn't even yet have a knob.

Steps too light to be a man's crossed the threshold as Bree left the kitchen and entered the front room to find Anna's mother standing there, a plate of her famous pecan bars held in her hands. Bree stopped short.

"Mrs. Lawrence."

"Breanna." Mrs. Lawrence's mouth turned up, and her eyes crinkled at the edges, not in anger or even a forced attempt at a smile but . . . *relief?*

"Hello," Bree said, softer.

Anna's mother came closer, picking her way over the tools in the entryway.

Bree forced her feet to move as well, crossing the distance between them until they stood only a foot or so apart.

"I heard you and Carson bought this property." Mrs. Lawrence looked around, her eyes stopping at the top of the stairs and the empty space where the stained glass window would go. "It's been years and years since I've been out here."

Bree clasped her hands in front of her nervously. "There weren't a lot of choices in Holiday, and Carson really wanted to live here."

"What about you? Did you want to live in Holiday too?" Mrs. Lawrence asked, sincerity and kindness in her tone.

"I did," Bree admitted. "Though, I'm starting to think it maybe wasn't the best idea."

Anna's mother nodded.

Agreeing with me? Did she come to tell us to leave? Bree couldn't blame her. She realized this might be her only opportunity to talk to Mrs. Lawrence, to give the apology that had been in her heart and on her mind for so long. She didn't feel especially prepared for it right now, but there were words that needed to be said—and hopefully heard. *Accepted, perhaps, in time.*

"Mrs. Lawrence, I need to tell you how sorry I am. I've never apologized for what I did, except in the letter we left for Anna, and that—"

"—was not found until several hours after she was to have been married." Mrs. Lawrence's lips pressed into a thin line.

Bree's mouth opened in surprise. "But we left it on the porch. Carson said he put it mostly beneath the mat—enough to be seen but not so much as to blow away."

"It didn't blow away but somehow slid entirely beneath the mat. We didn't see it. We went to the church. And waited. Anna was frantic. She just knew something terrible had to have happened to Carson. He's never late, and his phone kept going straight to voice mail. His father and brother hadn't arrived either. What was she to think except that some sort of tragedy had struck? She was wearing her wedding gown, pacing at the back of the chapel, when I called Carson's house and reached his dad. He told us that the two of you had eloped. We found out right there in front of a church full of people."

Bree closed her eyes and tried to swallow, to breathe, as she imagined Anna standing in the chapel in her beautiful gown, the train trailing halfway down the aisle. Her own humiliation of late, standing in that same aisle, seemed paltry in comparison.

She forced her eyes to meet Anna's mother's. "That wasn't our intent. I'm so sorry. I never wanted to hurt Anna. She was my best friend."

Mrs. Lawrence's tight-lipped look continued.

Bree stumbled on, knowing that whatever she might say was never going to be enough, but she had to say it anyway. "Carson and I didn't plan what happened. It just—did. And once done, we couldn't go back and fix it. We should have told Anna. Should have done a million things differently. Shouldn't have done it in the first place."

The part of Bree that had made peace with their decisions that night warred with her words. She was sorry, but she wasn't sorry she and Carson were married.

"Do you love Carson?" Mrs. Lawrence asked.

Bree nodded, tears filling her eyes. "Very much."

"And does he love you?"

"I do."

Bree's head whipped around to see Carson standing in the doorway. He entered the house, then stopped short, as Bree had.

"Mrs. Lawrence."

"I'm glad to see neither of you have forgotten my name," she said dryly. "I did wonder—when you didn't come by the market. Tell me you're not driving all the way to the Piggly Wiggly for groceries."

Bree and Carson exchanged a guilty look.

Carson moved quickly across the room to stand at her side, placing an arm around her and bestowing a tender, appraising look on Bree, as if to make certain she was all right.

Grateful for the support, she leaned into his embrace.

"I do love Bree," Carson said, turning his attention to Anna's mother. "My mistakes began long before last year. I should have recognized much sooner that what Anna and I had, the things our relationship were built upon, weren't the building blocks for a marriage. I cared for your daughter greatly, and I always will, but as a friend. What Bree and I did was wrong, and we will always wish we had gone about things differently, but it is right that we are together. We both love Anna and your family and deeply regret the hurt we've caused."

Mrs. Lawrence nodded, her expression still tight-lipped, but perhaps less so.

"Whatever your complaints are—" Carson began "—and I understand they may be many and justified—please don't take them out on my wife. Bree isn't the one at fault. I'm the one who went to her house that night. I'm the one responsible."

"Yes, you are." Mrs. Lawrence stooped to set the plate of pecan bars on top of a cooler. She straightened and faced them both again. "But I didn't come here with complaints or accusations. I didn't even come soliciting apologies, though I appreciate yours, Breanna."

"You have mine as well," Carson said, his tone slightly less defensive. "I am sorry for all the pain and inconvenience and expense and embarrassment and suffering my actions caused Anna and your family."

"Thank you for that," Mrs. Lawrence said. "And for your check. It covered the cost of the caterer and some of the other things we were, obviously, unable to get a refund for."

Carson nodded. "The least I could do. If there are other outstanding expenses—"

Mrs. Lawrence shook her head. "None that can be counted in monetary terms."

"I wish there was some way to make it up to Anna, and you. To heal her hurt." Bree didn't know what this might be, but it was her daily prayer that Anna might be this happy too. "Is there something—"

"Wishing won't change anything—not that I don't spend my fair share of time doing it too. Now is the time for prayers, and patience." Mrs. Lawrence's gaze flitted back and forth between the two of them. "And love."

"You've been talking to my father," Carson said.

"Many times these past few months," Anna's mother confirmed. "His words have helped me and many others. I only wish—" Her expression turned sorrowful. "There I go again. I hope and pray that Anna finds someone in Seattle who can help her the way your father has helped me. That she can hear words to help her heal."

Tears slid down Bree's face. Anna was in *Seattle*. So very far away. "I know wishing won't change anything." Every time she started down that path, thinking about the baby she'd lost, it only led to more pain. "But I am so sorry. I love Anna and your family."

"We love you, too, dear girl." Mrs. Lawrence sounded teary herself, a fact confirmed when she took both of Bree's hands in her soft ones and met her gaze, her own eyes moist. "I was so sad when I heard about your baby."

"It still hurts," Bree admitted. "Sometimes I'm just so sad." *Like Anna is still hurting and sad.* Maybe they both always would be, deprived of what they had hoped for, nearly had, and lost forever.

"It will for a long time." Mrs. Lawrence stepped closer and gathered Bree close. Carson's arm fell away as Bree returned her hug enthusiastically, clinging to her, inhaling her sweet, motherly scent, a mixture of home-baked goods and fresh flowers peculiar to Anna's mom.

"I'm sorry," Bree said again, her tears falling faster. "I don't know if Anna will ever be able to forgive me. I don't blame her if she doesn't."

"She's hurting too. These things take time."

Bree tried to answer but found she could only cry harder. It was so good to see Anna's mom. Being held by her felt so good. But she felt so bad about everything all over again.

As if she'd read her mind, Mrs. Lawrence said, "I'm not here to blame anyone." She released Bree, held her at arm's length, and looked her directly in the eyes. "I'm not angry with either of you. Still worried about Anna, yes, but I've decided I cannot allow that to get in the way of our friendship." Anna's mother turned toward Carson and extended one arm, pulling him into their embrace.

"I came today to see how you two are faring, to check on you. I figure someone has to." She looked at each of them and smiled. "*I'm* sorry it has taken me so long to allow God to give me a better heart. But the way I see it now—I'm all the mom either of you has left, and I wouldn't want to disappoint *your* mothers by not taking care of you both."

Bree blinked away more tears and looked up at Carson, watching as his expression turned from dumbfounded to incredulous.

"It's more than we deserve," he said.

Bree nodded her agreement. How could Anna's mother possibly care about her still, after what had happened and the way they had broken Anna's heart?

"We all get more than we deserve at times," Mrs. Lawrence said. "And many times less. Did either of you deserve to lose your mothers? Did your fathers deserve to have their wives die young? Of course not. Life is hard sometimes. A lot of times." She released them both and stepped back with a weary sigh. "But it can also be good if we choose to make it so. I am trying to choose the good."

"You are goodness itself." Bree reached out for Mrs. Lawrence's hand and held it tight. "Thank you."

"You're welcome, Breanna."

"Does this mean those pecan bars aren't poisoned?" Carson asked, reaching for the plate.

Mrs. Lawrence swatted his hand away. "Just for that, they're all Breanna's. Poisoned," she huffed, then rolled her eyes, turned, and started picking her way toward the front door. "I'll give you two this: you're ambitious with this project."

Bree followed her. "It is going to take a lot of work, but it will be worth it to be in Holiday, to be home."

Mrs. Lawrence paused at the door, her smile wistful. "I hope that someday Anna will feel the same, that she will want to return home."

"I hope so too," Bree said.

Thirty

Labor Day

"I THOUGHT LABOR Day was supposed to be a day to *rest* from our labors." Bree propped herself up on her elbow to watch Carson packing an overnight bag.

"Next year." He leaned over and kissed her swiftly, but with a promise that said more to come later.

Unfortunately it wasn't going to be later today.

"If my job wasn't flexible ninety percent of the time, I might argue for having today off—so I could labor here," he added with a wry grin. "But Connor has been more than generous allowing me to work mostly from home and allowing so many days off this year."

"Not to mention sharing his boat." Bree rolled onto her back and looked up at the low ceiling. She loved their little home on the river. As much as she was excited for their actual home to be finished, she was also going to miss the charm of living on the houseboat.

"That too." Carson zipped his bag and shouldered it. "I'll be back tomorrow. I'll pick you up from school, and we'll come home and snuggle beneath the stars—if you'd like."

"I'd like." One of their favorite pastimes had become

lying on a blanket on the top deck, sharing their memories and dreams, and kisses. More than a night or two they'd ended up sleeping up there all night.

"Me too. Until then, enjoy your day of rest." He gave Bree another kiss, this one lingering, then, with a reluctant look back, left their room. She lay back on the pillows, feeling the sway of the boat as he walked from the deck to the ramp.

Day of rest. Ha! Carson believed that nothing would be accomplished in his absence. The contractors had the day off, Charlie had left for school, and Bree had given the excuse that she had lesson plans to prepare. Technically she did, but that didn't mean she couldn't work on the house today as well. She'd even convinced Evan and Blane to come out and help her.

As soon as she heard Carson's car start and drive away, she threw back the covers and jumped out of bed. Within five minutes she'd thrown on a pair of old overalls, put her hair in a messy bun, and grabbed a granola bar. Bree ran down the ramp to the grass, remembering on her way that she'd hadn't checked the mail for a few days. She'd been getting home so late, it was easy to forget. She detoured briefly, crossing the lawn to the new mailbox posted where their new dock would eventually be.

She opened the white metal door and reached inside, pulling out a stack of envelopes, all plain except for one that was pale pink with hearts doodled all over it.

Carson. Bree felt like she was floating on a cloud of happiness as she tore open the envelope and unfolded the paper inside. Carson's signature stick drawing of the two of them kissing graced the top, followed by his familiar handwriting below.

Bree, my love, I hope your day is as beautiful as you are. Those second graders don't know how good they've got it, seeing your pretty smile and hearing your voice for six hours a day. I would gladly do math drills and diagram sentences every hour for the rest of my life if I had you as my teacher. Lucky for me, you choose to teach me other things. My education in our bedroom has been most illuminating as of late.

Looking forward to more lessons this weekend.
Your loving husband and pupil, Carson

Bree clasped the letter to her heart and sighed. Carson had obviously meant for her to get this last Friday, but she was glad she hadn't found it until today. He had taken to mailing her little presents and cards, these hand-drawn letters—reminiscent of their grade school days, though the content was a bit spicier. In return she enjoyed slipping surprises into his laptop case, from notes to the chocolate chip cookies he so loved her to bake, to items intended to remind him of her throughout the day.

With a mischievous smile, she wondered what he'd think of the card and lacy panties she'd slipped in there last night. Hopefully he wouldn't open the envelope in front of his coworkers.

She laughed out loud at the thought, knowing that even if he did, Carson wouldn't be mad at her. Tucking the letter into the front pocket of her overalls, Bree skipped off toward the house. Half of the front still needed the brick wainscoting, and today she and her brothers were going to complete it. If Carson could labor on Labor Day, she could too.

Blane and Evan never showed up, and neither answered their phones. By noon, Bree had given up calling them and had two rows of brick across the bottom completed by herself.

She wasn't sure why she was surprised that they hadn't come. Carson seemed to inspire some ambition in them, but she'd never been able to and shouldn't expect anything different now.

At least Carson's brother seemed to be doing better, doing something with his life. Charlie was loving school already. Carson would be staying with him tonight—convenient for Carson's work and for checking up on Charlie, now that he was at school and faced all the temptations of readily available alcohol there. Bree hoped the project Carson was working on went well. But even more than that, she hoped Charlie continued to do well. When Carson had been a little short on cash for Charlie's books, Bree had felt an immense amount of satisfaction and genuine happiness gifting Charlie $500 from the money she'd saved for her own college expenses.

After all, Connor Sheehan's generous loan of his boat had made it so Bree didn't need to spend the money she'd planned to on living expenses while student teaching. *So many good people in this world.* Bree allowed that happy thought to crowd out the negative ones she'd been thinking about her brothers.

By five o'clock she was starving, exhausted, and had three rows left to complete. It was tempting to call it a night. She needed to go over her lesson plans for tomorrow. But she really, really wanted to surprise Carson with one less task on his endless to-do list. Bree stood and stretched, then reached behind to rub her sore shoulders as she studied the red brick they'd chosen. A classic look that would go well with the front porch and pillars that would come later.

Just three more rows. At about an hour a row, now that she had a good rhythm going. *I can do this.* She'd just have to get out the lights they'd purchased for working after dark.

She grabbed the wheelbarrow and headed toward the hose and the bags of mortar mix piled there. Her hands were probably never going to be the same, and her poor nails . . . Bree glanced back over her shoulder at the house, examining her work from farther away. The brick looked good. Level rows, staggered pattern, even mortar. She and Carson had learned quickly, after just one afternoon working with the mason. It was how they'd accomplished much of the labor on the house. Their budget allowed for hiring framers, an electrician, a plumber, HVAC technicians, and other specialists. It just didn't allow for keeping them long enough to do all that needed to be done. But she didn't really mind. When this house was done, she and Carson would be able to claim they'd built much of it themselves.

At 8:45 Bree placed the last brick, and not a moment too soon, as the light drizzle that had been falling for over an hour had turned to a steady and significant rain. Too tired to care, she fell back on the ground, letting the water pelt her face. She was too exhausted to even start cleaning up for a few minutes.

Covering the newly placed brick with tarps took a lot longer than she'd planned, and she could only pray that would be enough to allow the mortar to dry. They'd struggled with the problem of keeping the unfinished house dry for the past month, which had brought more storms than the South had seen for years, including more tropical storms and hurricanes, which—thankfully—had all chosen to make landfall elsewhere.

Bree talked to Carson when he called to tell her good night. From the shelter of the pod—so he wouldn't realize she was outside—they spoke about his day and hers, vaguely. She wanted to ask him if there was anything else she should do to protect the freshly lain brick but managed not to spoil the surprise, alluding, instead, to the lesson plans she would be working on tonight and that she needed to get to bed soon for a good night's sleep.

It took her until 9:50 to wash out the wheelbarrow and tools and return everything to the pod. She unplugged the lights last, using only her phone light to set the lock and walk back to the boat. The trees she loved so much during the day turned a little creepy by night, and Bree hurried, anxious to be safely on board with the door locked and the ramp pulled in. Carson would be upset when he learned she'd spent the night out here by herself, but there was no help for it now. Neither her brothers or dad had come to pick her up—they were probably off on some last-minute hunt—and with Carson gone she didn't have a car but relied upon their families for transportation. His dad was going to drive her to school tomorrow morning—she'd need to call him before he left to let him know she'd stayed out here instead of in town—and Carson would pick her up on his way home tomorrow afternoon.

Once the ramp was in and she'd checked all the lines to make sure they were secure, Bree showered and made dinner for herself. It was 10:30 when she finally sat down on the bed with tomorrow's lesson plans spread out before her.

At 12:01 she pushed her papers aside, crawled beneath the covers, and fell into a sound sleep almost at once, her phone on the bed beside her, forgotten.

Thirty-one

CARSON STEPPED OUT of the shower at Charlie's apartment to the sound of his brother shouting and banging on the bathroom door. *Just like old times.* Carson rubbed a towel across his face and torso. They'd shared a bathroom the entire time they were growing up, and it seemed Charlie had ever been impatient for his turn. *Still, this is* his *apartment.* One sixth of it, anyway. Maybe having five roommates would teach him some patience.

Carson threw the towel around his waist and opened the door. "I didn't take that long. There's hot water left, I promise."

"It's not that. Bree—" Charlie stopped, his breathing heavy as if he'd just finished a sprint.

"Is she on the phone now, or did I miss her call?" Carson wished he'd waited to get in the shower. He should have known Bree was likely to call before her school day began. He should have thought to call her. She'd seemed preoccupied when they'd spoken last night, a sign she was probably stressed about teaching today.

"She might be in trouble," Charlie blurted.

"What?" Carson's brow furrowed. "What are you talking about? Was she in an accident?" He glanced at Charlie's watch. Dad should have just dropped her off at school. "Was she with Dad? Are they okay?" Or had something happened *at* the school? Or with her brothers? Or—

"Not with Dad," Charlie said, shaking his head. "Hurricane Tanya changed course in the middle of the night. It missed New Orleans and headed east instead. It hit Dauphin Island around three this morning, then skimmed the bay and made a beeline straight for Magnolia Springs and Holiday."

"Bree spent the night at her dad's—house." Carson clapped a hand to his forehead. Her dad's *old, falling apart* house. His mind conjured an image of it in pieces.

"Is she okay? At the hospital?" He grabbed Charlie's shoulder.

"I don't know." Charlie looked like he had the night their mother died, like he might cry.

"What do you mean you don't know?"

"The power is out in Holiday. She's not at her house. No one is. Dad went there this morning. When he didn't find anyone home and Bree didn't answer her phone, he drove out to your place. Your new house was a wreck. Shingles all over the place and—"

"I don't care about the house." Carson shook Charlie. "Where's Bree?"

"She's missing." Charlie shrugged out of Carson's grasp. "Dad's worried she spent the night at your place alone and—"

"She wouldn't have." Carson pushed past Charlie, heading for the bedroom to grab his clothes. "Maybe her family went somewhere else when the storm hit."

Charlie followed. "Where would they have gone?"

"Anywhere would be better than in that house, probably." *Where* would *they go? Grandma Fay's, maybe?* Carson grabbed his duffel off the bedroom floor and tossed it on the bed. His meetings today were going to have to wait. "Did Dad try calling Reggie? Or Bree's brothers?"

"I doubt he has their numbers, but he did call Reggie. He didn't answer, either, and his truck wasn't at the house."

"See." Carson dug through his bag. "They did go somewhere." He wanted to believe that, but something in his gut nagged. If plans changed, Bree would have called him or his dad. "The Wagners' house was still standing?"

Charlie nodded. "Mostly. Less damaged than yours, in any case."

Carson tried not to think of their last couple of months of work wiped out. That's what insurance was for, right? And who cared about the house, so long as Bree was safe. He stepped into his jeans, then tugged a T-shirt over his head.

"Isn't that a little casual for work?" Charlie asked.

"Work just got canceled. I've got to make sure Bree's okay." Carson grabbed his phone and wallet off the dresser, and headed for the door. "Connor will understand. He's Irish, and a family man. Their whole history is about facing one disaster after another."

"I'm coming too." Charlie grabbed his shoes from the pile by the door.

"You shouldn't. You've got classes." Carson slipped his own shoes on, picked up his laptop bag, including the card and surprise Bree had tucked in there, and stepped into the hall.

Charlie followed. "I've also got a brother. I'm coming."

"What do you mean Bree never came over last night?" Carson stood in the Wagners' depressing front room, lit only by the meager light coming through the front window, wishing with all his heart it was any other time or occasion for this visit. He'd even take reliving that awful night last February, because it would mean Bree was here with him, safe.

"The boys and I left Sunday afternoon." Reggie sounded defensive but appeared distressed, running a hand through hair Bree had recently cut for him. "We hunted until it got too wet to see last night. I dropped them off at their grandma's around eight, then spent the night in Foley so I wouldn't be late for work this morning."

The pit growing in Carson's stomach deepened. "Bree was supposed to sleep *here* last night. It was all arranged. I talked to both Evan and Blane about it a few days ago."

Reggie shook his head. "You can't count on those boys for anything. My fault, I know. They've had a poor example. If it doesn't fit their plans or isn't important to them, they don't often remember or follow through."

"Their sister isn't important?" Carson shouted, then stormed out the door, with Charlie on his heels.

"I'll help you look for her," Reggie called.

Carson didn't bother responding. Reggie probably wouldn't have heard him anyway, over the sound of the pouring rain. It had continued all day, an aftermath of the Category 3 storm that had ripped through Holiday.

Charlie reached the car a second before Carson and hopped into the driver's seat.

"Move," Carson ordered, holding the door so it wouldn't close.

"You're in no condition to drive," Charlie said. "Being emotionally out of control can make you as reckless as a couple of beers." He jerked the door closed and hit the lock.

Carson scowled but ran around to the other side. He could pummel his brother and especially Bree's later. Right now he just needed to find her.

"My place," he ordered as Charlie backed out of the driveway.

"On it."

While Charlie drove, Carson called the county sheriff and the volunteer fire department and reported Bree missing.

"We'll find her," Charlie said when Carson had finished both calls.

Carson gave a tight-lipped nod.

"Bree's not Anna," Charlie said.

Carson glared at him. "What's that supposed to mean?"

"She's not a fragile flower," Charlie said. "Not pampered. Look at what she came from. She's a lot tougher than she appears. She's a survivor. If she got caught in the storm, she'll figure out how to take care of herself until you get to her."

"Yeah." Carson somewhat agreed, except he'd learned that she *was* fragile. He'd never forget Bree collapsing in his arms the day they married, or being put in the back of that ambulance, or lying in a hospital bed with the alarm on her monitor suddenly blaring. He bowed his head.

Please, God. This time he wouldn't wait to pray.

Thirty-two

"We need more searchers," Carson's dad said quietly, an observation instead of an urgent, rushed command, like those being barked by everyone else around them.

"I know." Carson stopped at the edge of their—his and Breanna's—property, where the lawn met the river, and leaned over, hands braced on his knees as he caught his breath. Rain dripped from his hair to his forehead as he stared at the shredded rope floating listlessly on top of the water. It was the only one remaining of the four that had held Connor's houseboat in place. *His missing houseboat.* Presumably blown away by the storm last night. *With Bree on it?*

Twenty feet away another boat trolled the river, its spotlight shining down into the murky depths, searching.

Carson turned away, unable to bear the sight or the thought of what they might find. Pieces of the houseboat had been recovered already, and items that had been on it—the barbecue and freezer from the back deck, the table from the front.

"You know the most respected family in town," Dad continued in his gentle voice. "The one who could rouse people to search quicker than anyone else. You've done what you can on your own, son. You've already walked the bank a mile in both directions."

With nothing but a sore throat and wet feet to show for it. He'd shouted Bree's name for over two hours straight as he scrambled along the muddy shore.

"Don't you think it's time to call in reinforcements?" Dad asked. "The Lord helps those who help themselves."

"You're right." Carson turned from his father and the river and resumed running—away this time, across the grass Bree had been so carefully tending, past what was left of their home, including the brick she had to have placed herself yesterday. *By herself. She must have been exhausted last night. Tired enough to sleep through a storm.*

He didn't want to believe it, but they were out of other options. She hadn't been to her father's house or Grandma Fay's in Summerdale. *And without a way out of here, except on foot...*

Carson cursed himself for not leaving her with a car as he stepped in theirs and sped down the drive toward town and the Mulberry Market.

Eleven minutes later he stood on the threshold of what used to be one of the happiest places in the world to him. The feeling like he was stepping back in time had as much to do with personal memories as it did the Mulberry's old-timey atmosphere. When he was a child, the market had meant ice cream at the soda fountain or a watermelon sucker or lemon drops from the glass candy jars on the counter. It had meant playing hide-and-seek with Bree and Anna among the barrels of beans and oats and wheat while their mothers visited. They had been the original three best friends. It had been only natural that he and Anna and Bree followed suit.

Through his teenage and adult years, the market had been like a second home, a place to drop in with Anna after a date or even as part of one, where everything and everyone was as familiar and welcoming as the bottles of cold soda they pulled from the cooler near the door or the mugs of hot cocoa served at the counter in winter.

God willing it would be so welcoming now. Carson pushed open the bright-red door, and the bell jingled overhead, announcing his presence. He needn't have worried about a reaction, about shoppers and shopkeeper alike stopping to give an unwelcome stare. Instead, he was barely noticed, the store was so full. Only the few closest to the door nodded and continued with their business, filling gunnysacks and tin buckets of supplies to be handed out to townsfolk waiting out the storm.

He should have known.

As the only grocer in town and for miles, the Mulberry made a tidy profit, but the generations-old Lawrence family business had always been about more than money. They were the first to lend a hand, or a candle or a flashlight, or a week's supply of groceries when need arose. As it inevitably did from time to time in a small town so often afflicted by weather. Holiday would be the last place to have power restored. Sometimes it took a full week, as the other, larger communities took priority.

No matter. The lights were on at the Mulberry, the coolers cooling, even the attached floral shop—Mrs. Lawrence's pride and joy, aside from her family—was provided for, thanks to the hum of the generators out back.

Carson wove his way through the organized chaos to the long front counter, behind which stood Anna's father, his back to Carson as he retrieved a string of onions hanging from a high rafter.

Carson cleared his throat. "Mr. Lawrence."

The gray-haired man stiffened, then descended the stepladder, turning around slowly. He met Carson's gaze, his own level. Not cold exactly, but neither was it brimming with warmth. Mrs. Lawrence had said her husband needed more time and was still grappling with how to forgive the injustice done to his daughter. Carson knew all this, yet he had come. He would ask.

"Yes?" Mr. Lawrence said, his attention entirely focused on Carson despite the commotion and noise around them.

"I've come to ask for your help. Breanna is missing," Carson said. "She's not been seen since yesterday morning, and the boat we had anchored near our property—" Carson stopped, his throat swollen, head and heart pounding. "It's—gone. Swept away in the storm, we think. I've searched a mile in either direction, and the county sheriff and fire are there. But—" He gripped the edge of the worn counter, the rest of his unspoken plea evident in his face, he hoped.

Mr. Lawrence stared at him, and Carson could only guess what was going through Anna's father's mind. Why should he help? The two people who'd so grossly wronged his daughter and broken her heart? Perhaps he would gloat at this turn of events, thinking it justice at work.

After what had to have been a full minute, Mr. Lawrence gave a curt nod, reached behind him, and grabbed his hat from the hook near the back door. He picked up a cowbell on the counter and rang it loudly.

"Everyone!" he shouted as the hive of activity ground to a halt. "Our help is needed elsewhere. Get your cars, round up your able-bodied family and friends, and meet at the old Baker place. Bring your raincoats and flashlights." He glanced at Carson. "And your prayers. One of our own, Breanna Armstrong, is missing."

"There must be over two hundred people here," Charlie said, mouth gaping slightly at the townsfolk heading out to comb the woods. A dozen boats had joined the search on the river in the past hour and a half, and more people were arriving by the minute.

"About a hundred and fifty," Carson corrected. "But more are searching elsewhere in and around town. Everyone but the very old and the children have come."

"The children are here too." His dad nodded toward a van that had just pulled up and from which a dozen Cub and Daisy Scouts were spilling out.

"What do they think they'll be able to do?" Charlie asked.

"They're going to help Anna's mother at the tables, passing out pictures and maps, drinks and snacks," Dad said. "That will free the rest of us up to continue searching."

"Where to next?" Charlie asked, rubbing his hands, poking out beneath the sleeves of a cheap rain poncho.

Carson looked up from the map he'd been staring at, one of many copies provided by Anna's father, thanks to the printer at their store. "This area." Carson pointed to a blank space at the edge of the map. "The current flows downstream to Magnolia Springs. We haven't searched that far yet, but it's entirely possible the boat—or pieces of it, with Bree on board—made it that distance."

"But the storm was blowing the other direction," Charlie argued. "Everything we've found was east of where it started."

"Every*thing*," Carson agreed. "But no one. Bree wouldn't have been an inanimate object to be tossed up on some bank." He refused to let himself think of that possibility. "It's more likely she would have bobbed along with the river to a point she could get out."

"Let's go, then," Charlie said.

"Call me if there's an update, Dad." Carson ran with Charlie to their car, parked with several others along the drive. He climbed in the driver seat and shut the door against the relentless rain. The thought of Bree out there, alone in the storm, was unbearable. He started the car, threw it into reverse, looked over his shoulder, and backed up, careful not to hit the truck parked close behind. "We have to find her."

He started down the muddy drive, moving slowly, as cars lined either side.

"So many people," Charlie said, nodding to more walking toward the house.

"We'll find her," Carson said as they neared the street. "We have to."

"We may have already." Charlie placed a hand on his arm. "Stop the car."

Carson put his foot on the brake and followed Charlie's gaze. Through the rain-spattered rear window, he saw his father running toward them, waving his arms wildly overhead.

Carson jumped out of the car. "What?" he cried. "Have they found her?"

His dad shook his head. "Not Bree, but the boat. It's upstream and underwater. Not too far from the Lewises' place. Searchers are being redirected there."

"Is there a boat I can use?" The Lewises lived out in the county, even farther from town than he and Bree. Other than the river, there wasn't a quick way to access their land.

"I'll find one." Charlie ran ahead.

Dad put an arm around Carson. "Come on, son. We're one step closer."

To what? Hope fulfilled or ended?

He left the car where it was, and they walked quickly, passing people huddled in groups, whispering among themselves, casting furtive glances Carson's direction. Little Savannah Marshall came up to him with a napkin with a piece of corn bread on it held in her hand. "Mama says you need to eat, to keep your strength up."

"Thank you, Savannah." Carson forced a smile as he accepted her offering. It was warm in his hand and smelled good, but he couldn't eat now, not while Bree was out there somewhere—cold and wet and—"

Someone tapped him on the shoulder. Carson turned to find Savannah's mother looking at him.

"I just want to tell you that we're praying for you—for Miss Breanna—Mrs. Breanna now." Judith Marshall twisted her hands in the apron she wore beneath her unzipped jacket. "She was always nothing but kind to us, helping me with my youngsters and teaching them. It was wrong of me to do what I done, to shun her at church like that. I'm sorry."

"Thank you," Carson said. "Hopefully soon, you can tell her yourself." He turned away, his eyes scanning over the crowd to the river for a boat he could use. He needed to be searching again. This was no time for corn bread and socializing.

"Reverend's right," Judith continued. "So is Mrs. Lawrence. We all need better hearts. Like your Mrs. has."

"Like you have as well." Carson's dad left his side to divert Mrs. Marshall. "Your prayers are appreciated, Judith. As is your bread. May I have a piece?"

"Of course, Reverend. It's at the table over there."

Their voices faded into the background as Carson wove his way through the throng of people matting Bree's carefully tended grass. He reached the remnant of their dock, and when he didn't see Charlie, began waving his arms overhead, shouting to get the attention of those on the river. After a few minutes, Ted Hansen's boat swung his direction. It seemed the least likely craft for search and rescue, old and beat up as it was, kind of like Ted, but Carson wasn't about to be picky.

"Can you take me upstream, near the Lewis place?" Carson shouted.

"Sure." Ted pulled in close, killing the motor and drifting

sideways near the shore. Carson sloshed down the bank—the same he and Bree had trudged up after their unexpected swim last June. He threw a leg over the side of the small boat and used his hands to pull himself aboard, smashing Mrs. Marshall's offering in the process. Carson brushed the crumbs from his hand, letting them fall into the river for some fortunate fish.

"Give her a tug," Ted shouted. "Before we run amok on the wreckage." He nodded to the wood pier and loose boards remaining from the Bakers' dock.

Carson faced the back of the boat and pulled the string on what looked to be an ancient outboard motor. Surprisingly, it started right up. Ted cranked the wheel, narrowly avoiding the decaying pier. The boat picked up a little speed as Ted guided her away from the bend and out into the main flow of the river.

Carson sat on a drenched seat and noted his feet were sitting in three inches of water. Overhead the rain continued, relentless. Carson shifted so he was facing the south side of the river, the side the Lewis property was on. Since the storm had carried the houseboat that far, it seemed likely it had dropped other things along the way. Maybe Bree had been able to get off before it sank. *Maybe she was never there to begin with.* His secret hope was that she'd been caught in the storm while trying to walk to her dad's house and had already been found and taken to a shelter or hospital somewhere.

But why wouldn't I have heard from her by now? He would have. Bree would have wanted him to know she was safe.

Carson's eyes strained to see the opposite bank, tears mixing with the rain washing down his face. For being such a small place, Holiday had never felt so immense.

Thirty-three

"THEY SAY IF you don't find a missing person in the first forty-eight hours, you probably won't." Evan Wagner picked up a rock and skipped it across the river. "How long have we been at this now?"

"Fifty-two." *Hours and*—Carson glanced at his watch—*thirty-three minutes.* Carson stood on the bank, staring down into the depths, waiting. His feet and hands and nose were numb with cold, his heart not far behind. *It's just a matter of time now.*

The two volunteer divers from Mobile had gone down to the submerged houseboat again five minutes ago. Their last trip up they'd brought something that had chilled him straight through. Bree's phone, now in a Ziploc bag in police custody for further investigation.

"Don't be an idiot." Reggie grabbed Evan's hand before he could release another rock. "There are men down there searching. You want to hit one of them?"

Evan mumbled something unintelligible and dropped the rock.

"We should just go home," Blane said. "What's the point of waiting here?"

"We're waiting because we're her family," Reggie ground

out. "And should be here when they bring her up. It's called respect." He smacked the back of Blane's head but looked like he wanted to do substantially more damage elsewhere. Carson could relate. The part of him that hadn't gone numb yet felt volatile and angry at the world. How could Bree have been spared last spring, only to die now? In this senseless and horrific way.

"Maybe they won't find her body," Blane said. "Maybe a gator got her."

"Maybe a gator'll get you!" Carson grabbed Blane's jacket and shoved him toward the river, afraid that if he kept hold of him for more than a second, he really would strangle Bree's brother.

"You boys get out of here," Reggie barked. "You're not doing any good to anyone. Just making things worse."

Have they ever done good to anyone? Carson had tried to be patient with them, tried to teach them how to work and to give them some skills they might use elsewhere. Countless times over the summer he'd come close to losing his cool with their mistakes and laziness. Today was the end of his patience.

Blane glared at Carson as he trudged out of the water, his pants wet to the knees.

Carson stepped in front of him, blocking his way. "It's *your* fault Bree is missing, *your* fault if she's dead. You were supposed to pick her up, supposed to bring her to your house to stay the night so she wouldn't be all alone. We talked about this, about personal responsibility, remember? You gave me your word."

When Blane didn't answer, Carson grabbed his jacket front and hauled him closer, shaking him. "Bree has spent her entire life the past twelve years looking after you two." He threw a disparaging look at Evan. "She's cooked for you and washed your clothes, cleaned up your messes—she even got up at three a.m. to work, to earn enough money so your power wouldn't be shut off and you'd have gas in the car for your precious hunting trips. But enough is enough."

"That's *enough*, Carson," his dad said, placing a hand on his arm.

"No. I don't think it is." Carson shrugged his father's arm away while still holding Blane, who looked pale and frightened, tight in his grasp.

"If you'd done what I asked you to, what you *promised* to do, Bree would not be missing right now. So you'd better fix this. You'd better find her. Both of you! Right now!" Carson shoved Blane toward Evan, who barely caught him from falling. Together they raced off through the brush, away from the river.

"Anger never helps anything, son," Dad said.

Carson held up a hand. "Not now." His voice broke. "*Not now.*" He was furious with everyone, especially himself. Hadn't he made a promise not to leave Bree again? A vow, after finding her on the bathroom floor five months ago, that he'd work from home so he could always be nearby? *I never should have left her alone.*

Reggie looked around, a helpless expression on his face. "I let her down so many times. I let them all down." He buried his face in his hands, sobbing.

From the corner of his eye, Carson watched as his dad offered Reggie comfort. *Just like when Mom died,* he thought bitterly. *Who will be there to offer me comfort this time?* He'd gone to Bree then. This time he would be all alone.

The search and rescue crew chief walked toward Carson, regret in his expression. "We're going to call it a night. Everyone's tired, and if we start making mistakes, more lives are in danger."

"I understand." Carson shook his hand. "When can I expect you tomorrow? Do you want to start here again, or . . ." He didn't know what to suggest. Four different dives to the boat hadn't given them any other clues, or Bree's body—thankfully. Every time they'd come up empty-handed, he'd thanked God vocally. There was still hope. Though Blane's careless words rang through his mind. There were gators in the river, and snakes—endless dangers, aside from just the river itself.

The crew chief hesitated. "I'm not sure. I'll get back to you in the morning. With the hurricane we have a lot of situations right now that need our attention. We may need to cut back here. But you've got a great community. I've never seen so many people come out to search so quickly. Your wife must be a pretty special lady, and Holiday is a pretty amazing place."

He was rambling now, trying to soften the blow. Carson could read his discomfort. "Thank you for everything," he said, feeling weary and numb more than anything. He hadn't slept in over two days, hadn't eaten much, either, and didn't think he could. His anger had been spent earlier, and to what purpose? Blane and Evan were probably at home playing a video game or watching television. Dad was right. Arguing with people and losing his temper wasn't going to bring Bree back. Maybe nothing was.

"Carson! Carson, we found her!"

"Blane?" Carson and the crew chief both looked in the direction of the voice but saw only the wild, wooded bank.

"Bree's alive!" Blane's voice and the sound of a body crashing through brush preceded him by a few seconds. He burst from the wood, running full speed straight toward Carson. "She's with Sonny. At his cabin. Hurt bad, but alive. Evan's with her."

"Where's this cabin?" The chief pulled out his walkie-talkie. "We need an ambulance. Address to follow."

"She's okay? You saw her?" Carson couldn't trust the news, especially from Blane.

But he nodded. "I swear it. On my mother's grave."

Carson reached for him, pulled him close in a fierce hug. "Thank you, Blane. Thank you."

"Later." Blane started in the direction he'd just come. "Follow me."

"Wait," the chief called. "I need directions or an address."

"Have the ambulance go to the Lewises' place," Carson shouted over his shoulder, already starting to run. "Their old corncrib isn't really a cabin, and it's not accessible by a main road, but Jeremy Lewis can get you there."

"How is she?" Carson asked as he caught up with Blane.

"Bad," Blane said, with a wary look in Carson's direction. "But breathing when I left."

Thirty-four

"WE NEED TO quit meeting like this." Carson leaned over the hospital bed and pressed a kiss to Bree's forehead. "What is this, three hospitalizations in the past six months?"

"Seven months, but who's counting?" Bree managed a weak smile, which promptly turned to a frown when she attempted to reach for him.

"Not that arm," he scolded. "I hear you're lucky to still have it, so let's not test fate. Let it rest for, say—six weeks or so."

Bree glanced at the cast running from her hand to her elbow. "What happened?"

Carson arched his brow. "You tell me. All I know is that for the past three and a half hours you've been having some pretty tricky surgery to put your wrist and hand back together. Before that, you'd apparently decided to leave me for another man, though your taste in gentlemen definitely gives me pause."

Bree's forehead wrinkled. "Leave you?"

"Staying with Sonny, at his place? Really, Bree. I'd have thought—" Carson broke off abruptly, his attempt at lighthearted teasing failing. He'd thought she might be dead, had feared finding her body at the bottom of the river or, perhaps worse, never finding her at all.

Ever in tune with him, she must have sensed his distress. Her own appeared from her compressed lips to her overbright eyes. "I'm sorry." She held his gaze, and Carson wasn't sure he could ever break it, could ever stop looking at her, touching her, staying at her side.

"I remember . . ." Bree's forehead scrunched again. "I woke up, and water was pouring into the boat. The wind was so loud. I was trying to get out, get off the boat. It was moving. The freezer slammed into me and pinned my hand. I called for help. Sonny came. Then everything just hurt so much. My arm . . ." She looked down at the cast again, grimacing.

Carson nodded and swallowed. "The storm moved the boat upriver." And once released from the worst of the wind, the boat had sunk pretty fast. Or so all evidence indicated. Carson felt bad about this, but Connor had assured him there was no need to worry. It was insured, and he'd been thinking about getting a newer houseboat anyway.

The mystery of why Sonny had heard Bree, had been lingering so near on more than one occasion, had been solved as well—a great deal had in the past twenty-four hours, but that could wait for another time. Carson didn't want to overwhelm her. "You got caught in Hurricane Tanya. She decided she liked Alabama better than Louisiana and headed our way instead."

"Ah." Bree gave a slight nod. "Guess I should have watched the news."

"But you were too busy laying brick," Carson said, a note of scolding in his voice. Half of him wanted to shake her, half wanted to kiss her. All of him wanted to gather her in his arms and never, ever let go again.

She smiled. "Do you like it?"

He didn't have the heart to tell her about the house. Not yet. "You did good." Carson touched her cheek. "It was a nice surprise. But you shouldn't have stayed out there by yourself. Never again."

"My brothers didn't come. They were supposed to help, and then I was going to go home with them."

"I know." Carson frowned. "I was seriously contemplating bodily harm to them both, but they're the ones who found you at Sonny's. So I guess I'll have to forgive them—for now."

She shook her head. "You have to forgive them forever. No grudges. We know what that feels like, remember?"

"I do." Carson brushed the hair back from her eyes. "You're beautiful, Bree. Even with a face full of bruises and hair that looks like it hasn't seen a brush in a week."

She grimaced, then gave him a lopsided smile. "Thanks—I think."

He pulled up a chair and sat beside her, determined to stay, in spite of what the nurse had told him. Bree could rest. He wouldn't bother her. He just wanted to be nearby, to keep her in his sight.

"I love you, Carson," she said, her eyes closing as she drifted off to sleep again.

"I love you, Bree," he said. "And I think, from now on, we're both going to love living in Holiday too."

Thirty-five

Halloween

"Hang that sheet over there," Bree instructed. "Beneath those cobwebs near the door."

"Why?" Blane asked. "Why put up a fake ghost when you've practically got the real thing? Just set Sonny in the rocker by the door. He's closer to dead than he is alive, anyway."

Bree frowned. "Be nice. Ninety-six years old and he pulled me from the river up to the bank, then somehow got me back to his place. That seems pretty alive to me."

"He probably thought he was back in the war again," Evan said. "And you were his comrade he was carrying from the trenches to safety."

"Maybe," Bree agreed. She'd considered that herself. How else could Sonny have done such a feat?

"Too bad Old Man Baker wasn't around to see it." Evan shook his head. "Imagine, his boy's been here since the eighties, living in Holiday, poking around this place..."

"Because, somewhere, in the recesses of his mind, he remembered it had once been home." Bree felt sad when she thought about Sonny, alone in his dilapidated shack all these years. He'd come as a drifter, doing odd jobs here and there but mostly keeping to himself. After a while he'd moved into an old corncrib on the edge of the Lewises' land, leaving occasional gifts—fish he caught or wildflowers he picked—on their front porch.

He hadn't bothered them, so they'd decided not to bother him and had allowed him to stay. "Every town needs a hermit" had been the joke for years. Sonny had filled that requirement for Holiday, rarely being seen. He kept to himself, fended for himself, and talked to himself, as anyone who ever happened upon him had witnessed.

Everyone had long thought him crazy but harmless. Only Bree's stay in his corncrib had produced the truth about his identity, discovered in his few belongings stacked in a neat pile on the floor inside, among which was an old, black-and-white family photograph, taken in front of the original Baker place, and newspaper clippings about the prisoner of war camp he'd been interned at from 1942 until the end of the war.

"Sonny has a home again now." Carson stopped to give Bree a kiss on the cheek before heading inside, an armload of pipe fittings in his hand.

"What are those for?" Blane asked.

"The bathrooms," Carson said. "If we're going to invite the entire town out here for a haunted house, we'd better have at least a couple of working toilets."

"You can practically move in once those are installed," Evan teased.

"Practically." Bree rolled her eyes. They were barely back to where they'd been nearly two months ago, before the hurricane had destroyed much of their hard work. Her brick wainscoting had survived the storm, but much else on the house had not, nor had her floating honeymoon suite, now at the bottom of the river.

They were living with Carson's dad in Carson's old room, and Sonny was staying across the hall in Charlie's room while he was away at school. Sonny didn't much care for the arrangement. He'd rescued her, but that didn't mean he intended to start being social. So she and Carson had decided to add a small guesthouse to their plans, something slightly more functional than the corncrib, with a heater and some basic furniture. It seemed only right that Sonny should be able to end his years on the land he'd begun them on, free to fish from his favorite bend in the river anytime he wanted.

Bree continued working the spiderwebs across the front porch while Evan dug holes in the yard and planted various fake limbs coming out of them. What had started as a silly idea had turned into what Bree hoped was a way to thank the people of Holiday for coming out to search for her. She owed them gratitude for not only that but the cleanup effort that had taken place a few weeks after the storm, when much of the town had shown up with shovels and rakes, brooms and garbage bags in hand and had helped Carson clean up the place, mucking the mud and debris from the house and hauling off garbage so construction could resume.

"It's what we'd do for anyone," Ernie Jensen had told her, when Bree, handing out drinks from the front porch, her arm still in a cast and useless, had tried to thank him.

That much was true. The citizens of Holiday did often help one another. Carson had been assisting with the cleanup in other parts of town the past couple of weekends. Putting the town back together after a big storm was always a town-wide effort. But still, for everyone to come out here . . .

"You're a resident of Holiday, aren't you?" Ernie finished his lemonade and set his cup down on the rail.

"Yes." Bree nodded, teary eyed. "This town is my home."

Ernie glanced away as if uncomfortable, then cleared his

throat. "Well then, we take care of our own. And if at times we forget—both our manners and our compassion—well, we hope you'll forgive."

"Oh, Ernie." The tears spilled down her cheeks. "Of course. There's nothing to forgive."

"Ah." He held up a pudgy hand. "Don't be telling no lies now, missy." He hitched up his suspenders and grabbed his rake once more. "Santa knows when you do." He left her with a wink and a smile, and—notwithstanding the destruction and mess surrounding her—Bree had felt all was right in the world once more.

It was more than she would have ever imagined. More than she and Carson deserved. And it had all been spearheaded by Anna's parents.

Bree found herself whistling as she worked, transforming their shell of a house into a haunted mansion, her heart swollen with gratitude for the good people of Holiday. Carson was right. Slowly, little by little, everything was getting better.

"Candy apple, my deary," Bree said in her best wicked witch voice, handing a still-dripping caramel apple to a miniature princess.

"Will it make me sleepy?" the little girl asked, accepting the apple warily.

Bree laughed and shook her head. "Not at all. It *will* make your teeth sticky, though. Be sure to brush them tonight." She smiled as the little girl skipped off.

"That's not a very witchlike thing to say." Carson stepped up behind her and nudged her neck with his fake vampire teeth. "Shouldn't you want the little children's teeth to rot and fall out?"

"I'm afraid I'm not very wicked." Bree turned in his arms for a quick kiss.

"Perhaps we should work on that," he teased.

Bree shook her head and pushed him away. "Not now, Dracula." She handed an apple to eight-year-old Junior McLaughlin, though she was fairly certain he'd had one already.

"Is Madam Witch doing a brisk business this evening?" Carson drew his cape close and peered over her cauldron of caramel.

"Very brisk," Bree said. "I'm on my third bushel of apples. And I'm pretty sure I'm going to be sticky for a month. I feel like I have this stuff everywhere."

"Sounds fun," Carson said in his best Transylvanian voice as he raised his eyebrows up and down.

Bree rolled her eyes. "I'll be sure to save a little for you." She glanced around the yard at the cornhole games, apple bobbing, cupcake walk, and pumpkin carving. "Do you think everyone else is having fun?" Her gaze drifted to the house, temporarily *haunted* by Charlie, her brothers, and a handful of their friends. The inside was lit only with battery-operated candles, and the torn spiderweb curtains hanging in the glassless windows looked truly creepy.

"I think they're having a *great* time. This may rival the Founder's Day picnic for crowd size. We may have started a tradition."

"That's fine," Bree said. "But next year I want us, instead of the ghosts, to be living in the house."

"Deal." Carson pulled back his cape to fist bump her. "It won't be done by Christmas this year like I'd promised, but next Halloween I think I can manage. Good things come to those who wait."

"I know." Bree handed apples to the Ellis twins standing near her cauldron. "I waited a very long time for you, and look how good it's turned out."

"How good indeed, Madam Witch, since I have fallen under your spell." He stole another kiss.

"Really, Carson. My face is painted green, and I have a wart." She turned away from him to find Anna's parents watching them from across the yard. Anna's father gave a tight-lipped nod, but Anna's mother smiled, her expression both kind and wistful.

Good things come to those who wait. Bree was still waiting for the day she could be a friend to Anna once more and help her find as much happiness as she and Carson had.

Thirty-six

Thanksgiving

"Eating outdoors will make this feel more like the *first* Thanksgiving." Bree moved along the makeshift table in the yard, setting places for Carson's dad and brother and her own family—plus a few more, as her father had requested. "I wonder who he's bringing," she mused for at least the twentieth time since his phone call a few days earlier.

"Someone female, is my guess. Maybe that, or *she*, is the reason he's been so committed to being at work on time these past months." Carson placed the bench he'd finished last night alongside the table.

Bree paused to admire his work. "That looks great."

"Yes, you do." Carson grabbed her hand before she could get away, then pulled her close. "That apron becomes you, Mrs. Armstrong. Perhaps you'd consider wearing it with less clothing beneath sometime."

Bree laughed and swatted his hand away before he could untie the strings. "What's on the menu today is turkey, and both Tom and I will be well dressed."

"Dessert?" Carson asked hopefully.

"All the pie you can eat," she promised, then extracted

herself from his arms. "Later. We still have things to do. Entertaining, especially when we don't exactly have a finished house, is a lot of work." She hummed cheerfully as she continued setting the table with Carson's mother's china, gifted to them by his father. It looked both out of place and charming on the rustic table—old doors from the Baker house, balanced over sawhorses. Long pieces of burlap—bags she'd sewn together and trimmed with old denim—ran down the middle and were topped with leaves and fresh cuttings from the yard. Bree thought the effect quite lovely and wondered if the pilgrim women had felt the same about their feast so long ago.

At three o'clock their families started arriving. Carson's father and Charlie were first, and Carson promptly took them in the house to show off the stained glass window they'd just had installed. Had the storm in September hit a week later, the window probably would have been damaged. But at the time, the glass had been safe in the storage pod and had remained unharmed.

Bree was setting out baskets of rolls when her father pulled up. Blane and Evan were in the back of the pickup, while two female passengers sat in their places in the cab. Bree wiped her hands on her apron and walked down the drive to greet them.

By the time she reached the truck, her dad had jumped out and run around to the other side, where he held the door open for the ladies. Bree felt her mouth open in a silent gasp of surprise. The last time she'd seen her father hold a door... *Was when Mother was alive.*

"Breanna, I'd like you to meet Madelyne Kinsey and her daughter Candace."

"Hello." Bree offered her hand and a smile to each. Madelyne looked to be about her father's age and was a pretty woman, tall and willowy with short, blonde hair. She returned Bree's smile as Dad took her hand. Bree arched a questioning brow at him, and his sheepish, though delighted smile told the whole story.

Dad is in love. Bree wasn't entirely sure how to feel about this and wanted nothing more than to find Carson and share the news with him, but that would have to wait. For the moment she decided that Madelyne Kinsey was a good influence on Dad, and for that reason alone, Bree should be happy about their relationship.

Madelyne's daughter did not appear to be happy about anything. The downturn of her lips only increased as she looked around the yard.

"We're eating outside?" Her voice was filled with disdain.

Bree nodded. "The house isn't finished yet, and the yard is so lovely, we thought—"

"—that everyone ought to experience being outside in Holiday in November." Carson stepped up beside Bree, his hand at her back in a show of support. "November is the month here that makes up for August. You just can't get better weather and scenery than this anywhere."

"Agreed," Bree's dad said.

Candace did not appear to agree at all but continued scowling at everything and everyone as introductions were made.

Bree guessed the girl to be around seventeen. Like her mother, she was on the tall side, but her hair was darker. She was a pretty girl, or would have been if she'd tried to be a little more pleasant. When it came time for seating arrangements, Bree placed Candace and Blane across from each other, knowing it would either be a disaster, or they might find they had misery and grumpiness in common.

At 3:20, Carson pulled the turkey out of the smoker. Evan

had brought both over two days before, and Carson had been surprised to find the bird still had its feathers attached.

"That's what you call *fresh* turkey," Bree had teased, grateful she wouldn't be the only one facing the distasteful task this year.

After being plucked, cleaned, stuffed, and smoked, it tasted wonderful, as did everything else she and Carson had prepared. They'd had to do most of the cooking at his dad's, but she'd wanted to have Thanksgiving here, at what would soon be their home.

Leaving everyone still visiting at the table or down at the river, Bree snuck inside after dinner, closing the door behind her and relishing a moment of quiet. The afternoon light shone through the stained glass on the landing, spilling a kaleidoscope of dancing color down the stairs.

Bree leaned against the door, her heart brimming with gratitude for the past year, the times her life had been spared and how beautiful and precious it was.

A minute passed, then two. The colors shifted with the setting sun. Bree wanted to linger but instead hurried to the kitchen, to the ice chest where she was keeping the pies. Another hour and it would be too dark to eat. But there would be many more days she could stand inside their foyer and stare up at the beautiful window.

Behind her, the front door creaked open.

"Want to help me bring these outside?" Bree called to whoever it was—most likely Carson or his dad. Her dad and brothers had yet to come to the realization that they could and should be of help in the kitchen.

"Sure."

Bree turned toward the soft, feminine voice. Candace walked across the bare floor, her earlier expression of disdain replaced by a look of uncertainty.

"If you're looking for the bathroom, it's over there." Bree nodded to the opposite side of the house. "Flushing toilet, running water and everything."

"Thanks." Candace didn't change directions. "I'll use it in a second, but first, could I talk to you? Your dad said you might."

"Of course." Bree closed the cooler and straightened, wondering what Candace could possibly want. She'd been silent and sullen all through dinner, surpassing even Blane's grumpiness. It was almost impressive.

"I was wondering if you might tell me about the past year." Candace stopped a few feet away. "When you got pregnant."

"Oh." Bree sucked in a breath, then let it out slowly. "O—kay." What did her dad mean by suggesting this, by sharing her story with someone she didn't even know? Was she supposed to give some pep talk to keep other girls out of trouble? *Or this one at least?*

Bree lowered herself onto the cooler and pointed to the one that had held the mashed potatoes and vegetables. "Have a seat."

Candace complied while Bree's mind scrambled for how to begin such a conversation. This wasn't something she wanted to talk about, but maybe doing so would somehow help Candace. She supposed she ought to at least try and finally settled on a question to start. "What has my father told you?"

"That you got pregnant and eloped, only then you lost the baby."

"That's all true. Carson and I—well, we made a mistake, going about things that way. Then we had to get married, and it wasn't the kind of wedding girls dream about." Bree grimaced, remembering her trip in the ambulance that day.

"A couple of months later I miscarried the baby and nearly died." She twisted a dish towel in her hands. "I'll never be able to have more children. All of that could have been avoided if I hadn't gotten pregnant." She paused, waiting for Candace to say something. When several seconds passed and she didn't, Bree tried another question.

"Do you have a boyfriend?"

Candace shrugged. "Sort of."

"Do you love him?" Bree asked.

"Sort of." Candace shrugged again. "Not like you love your husband, I think. The way you two feel about each other is obvious to anyone. Kind of like my mom and your dad."

"Yeah . . ." Bree would have liked to talk about that, to see what Candace knew that she didn't, but first things first. *Why did Dad want her to talk to me?*

"I'm not sorry I married Carson. He's wonderful, and we love each other very much. But we both wish we'd done things differently, the right way. We might have had a different outcome. We wouldn't have hurt a lot of people. I might not have been alone when I miscarried; I might have received quicker medical attention and maybe avoided surgery." Those were a lot of maybes for a small town like Holiday. Anna still would have been hurt, though not as publicly. And Bree realized that chances were she might have come out worse, with the hospital being so far away. But none of that would be helpful for Candace to hear.

"So you wish you'd never gotten pregnant?" Candace asked.

Bree sighed. That answer was complicated, and this was such a difficult thing to talk about, especially with someone she'd just met today. *But maybe it will do her some good.* "I definitely should not have gotten pregnant. We should have considered what we were doing."

"But since you did get pregnant, do you wish you'd had an abortion? Then maybe you'd still be able to have other kids someday."

"*No.* I don't ever wish I'd had an abortion," Bree said, taken aback. There was no need to think about that answer. Even if she'd known what the cost would be, she couldn't have ended her baby's life. "I never could have done that." She pressed a hand to her stomach, remembering the miraculous feel of the child she and Carson had created moving inside her. "No matter how small, that baby was alive. To abort it would have been to end that life."

She leaned forward, elbows braced on her knees. "Before Carson asked me to marry him, before he knew about the baby, I had made plans to go away to a home in Mississippi where I would have medical care and be taken care of until the baby was born. The family paying my expenses was then going to adopt that baby when he or she was born." Bree paused, noting the change in Candace's demeanor.

Her lip was trembling, her eyes watery, as she looked past Bree, as if lost in some memory.

"Are *you* pregnant?" Bree asked softly.

Candace nodded. "And the father won't want to marry me. I don't know what to do."

Bree remembered those feelings, the terror and fear of being completely alone. She stood, scooted her cooler forward, then sat again, her hands reaching for Candace's. When Candace accepted her gesture and didn't turn away, Bree took that as a good sign.

"Did you want to talk to me today because you're trying to decide what to do?"

"I thought I knew what to do. I have an appointment next week to get it taken care of. I just want it over." Candace tugged her hands away from Bree and held her head in them. "I want to forget."

"Do you think you'll be able to?" Bree asked.

Candace didn't respond.

Answer enough.

"I can get you the information for the home in Mississippi," Bree said. "You could continue your schooling while you're there. No one at home would have to know. There are a lot of good people out there who can't have children and would love yours."

"Like you?" Candace looked up, her expression serious.

Bree froze, her heart nearly stopping, or so it seemed.

Someday, Carson had said. She'd believed that would be years from now. *But what if...*

Bree swallowed, held Candace's gaze, and answered.

"Yes. Like us."

Thirty-seven

Christmas Eve, one year later

"It was a beautiful wedding and reception." Bree wandered through the great room picking up cups and tossing them into the garbage bag she was holding. "Thank you, Carson."

"Our first real party here, a grand Holiday affair—I was glad to do it." Mostly he was glad it was over and glad Reggie was married and now had a wife to care for him and his boys. Bree had been doing her best to manage everything at home—both theirs and her father's—far too long. *No more.* Or at least not nearly as much. Though Reggie and his new family would still be an important part of their life. They were tied together in more ways than one now.

"Grandma Fay told me you thanked her today." Bree brushed crumbs off a folding chair and into the bag.

"Every time I see her," Carson said. "I'm not sure if she really forgets that I already have, several times, or if she just wants to remind me what a great catch I made with you."

"Or if she's just gloating that she was right." Bree grinned at him.

"She can gloat all she wants, and I will always be grateful to her." Carson picked a plate with cake still on it off the floor.

"Call me selfish"—He stole up behind Bree and plucked the trash bag from her hand—"but I'm pretty excited to have you all to myself, now that your dad is married."

Bree started to turn in his arms, then froze as a wail came from upstairs. "Almost to yourself, you mean?"

"She can wait." Carson wrapped his arms around Bree, then proceeded to kiss her soundly as the cries from upstairs increased in volume. "I'll go," he said at last, reluctantly. He didn't usually begrudge time with his daughter, that tiny imp who'd entered their lives so abruptly last spring, a full month earlier than expected. She was a blessing they'd both never dreamed of having—this soon at least. But tonight he was hoping for some time with the other woman in his life, the one who'd spent nearly every waking minute for the last month helping her new stepmother plan this party.

"I'll be up in a few minutes," Bree called, resuming cleanup.

"I'll come back to help if you're not." Carson took the stairs two at a time, noting there were even plates and cups stacked on some of the lower steps. It seemed most of Holiday had turned out for Reggie and Madelyne's wedding at the church, Christmas Eve morning, followed by the reception he and Bree had hosted here.

Their home was good sized, but it had been standing room only for much of the afternoon, the rooms packed with the very young to the very old—seven-month-old Anna to ninety-seven-year-old Sonny—people they'd known and loved their whole lives. Santa had even taken a break from last-minute flight preparations, making an appearance in his red suit. For a good two hours he'd made himself comfortable in one of the few pieces of furniture they owned, the old wingback chair Bree had recently recovered, as Holiday's children lined up to see him.

At one point during the afternoon Bree had taken Anna over and placed her on Santa's lap. Carson had watched from the sidelines as the two spoke and Santa gave Bree a hug.

Fences mended. Hearts healed. Most of them, anyway. There was one that still weighed heavily on both their consciences.

Naming their daughter after their former best friend had seemed so logical to them both, though it had baffled others in town. Bree had explained it best, and rather eloquently, Carson thought.

"Anna Lawrence is everything I could want my daughter to be—kind, generous, intelligent, ambitious, a lovely person and a wonderful friend—" Bree's voice had caught on the last. "Why wouldn't I name my daughter after my best friend and hope she will grow up to be just as wonderful and dear to so many?"

Carson had come to understand that, as close as he and Bree were, as happy as their marriage was, there were still some roles he couldn't fill in her life. She missed her best friend. It would take a miracle, but they were determined that someday . . . *all* the fences they'd torn down might be mended. All the hearts healed.

Carson pushed little Anna's bedroom door open and crept inside. The baby's eyes were wide, and she smiled and stretched her arms out to him. Carson obliged, scooping her from the crib.

"Feeling left out, are we?" He bounced her in his arms and walked her out to the hall. Her mood improved at once, the tears drying on her face as she giggled.

Their Anna was already dear, to them and everyone in town. After her arrival and adoption—and with Sonny's improved health, now that he had a real roof over his head and ate more than the fish he caught from the river—the town council and Ladies Aid had decided to join forces and funds to update the population sign. Holiday, Alabama, was a solid 767 these days. They still counted Anna Lawrence a citizen, though she hadn't been back for nearly two years.

This weighed on Carson and Bree as well. They'd broken more than Anna's heart—they'd broken up her family. Somehow Mr. and Mrs. Lawrence had found it in their hearts to forgive and move forward. These days Bree frequented the Mulberry Market, lingering to ask Mrs. Lawrence and the other women's advice on this or that regarding all things baby and homemaking.

Mr. Lawrence had thawed, too, understandably not quite as warm as he once was toward Carson but cordial enough that their interactions were no longer uncomfortable.

Looking at the baby girl in his arms, Carson understood this a little better. How would he treat a boy who broke her heart?

"All done." Bree swept the plates and cups from the stairs into the trash bag and tied it. She looked up at him and Anna. "Everything okay?"

"I think so," Carson said. "She just wanted to play."

"It's naptime," Bree said, only partially scolding. "She knew her dad was home and that he's a softy."

"Yep." No arguing with that as far as his girls were concerned. Carson headed down the stairs with his charge. Maybe she would be content watching the lights on the Christmas tree while he and Bree watched each other for a while.

Bree waited for them at the bottom. "Look." She nodded to the stained glass window. "Magic hour is starting."

They'd named the early evening hour such because the light shining through the colored pieces of glass and dancing on the stairs did seem magical. *As is my life.*

Carson stopped beside Bree and turned around so he and Anna could enjoy the light show as well. He wrapped his free hand around Bree and pulled her close. She leaned her head against his shoulder with a contented sigh.

"Merry Christmas, family," she said.

"The merriest," Carson agreed.

Michele Paige Holmes spent her childhood and youth in Arizona and northern California, often curled up with a good book instead of out enjoying the sunshine. She graduated from Brigham Young University with a degree in elementary education and found it an excellent major with which to indulge her love of children's literature.

Her first novel, *Counting Stars*, won the 2007 Whitney Award for Best Romance. Its companion novel, a romantic suspense titled *All the Stars in Heaven*, was a Whitney Award finalist, as was her first historical romance, *Captive Heart*. *My Lucky Stars* completed the Stars series.

In 2014 Michele launched the Hearthfire Historical Romance line, with the debut title, *Saving Grace*. *Loving Helen* is the companion novel, with a third, *Marrying Christopher*, followed by the companion novella *Twelve Days in December*. The Hearthfire Scottish Historical Romances include *Yesterday's Promise*, *A Promise for Tomorrow*, and *The Promise of Home*.

When not reading or writing romance, Michele is busy

with her full-time job as a wife and mother. She and her husband live in Utah with their five high-maintenance children, and a Shitzu that resembles a teddy bear, in a house with a wonderful view of the mountains.

You can find Michele on the web:
MichelePaigeHolmes.com
Facebook: Michele Holmes
Twitter: @MichelePHolmes

www.ingramcontent.com/pod-product-compliance
Lightning Source LLC
LaVergne TN
LVHW010155070526
838199LV00062B/4373